Ride

LISA GLASS

Quercus

QUERCUS CHILDREN'S BOOKS

This book was written while the author was in receipt of a grant from
the Arts Council England, whose help is gratefully acknowledged.

First published in Great Britain in 2016 by Hodder and Stoughton

1 3 5 7 9 10 8 6 4 2

Text copyright © Lisa Glass, 2016

The moral right of the author has been asserted.

A CIP catalogue record for this book is available from the British Library.

ISBN 978 1 84866 344 2

Pr...ted and bo...d in ...at ...t...by...s plc

London EC4Y 0DZ

An Hachette UK Company
www.hachette.co.uk

www.hachettechildrens.co.uk

For Amelie, Alyssa, Laura and Eve

'There's quiet in the deep:
Above let tides and tempests rave'

John G. C. Brainard, 1795–1828

sunday 26 april

new smyrna

The Florida wind in my face, I paddle into shark park, acutely aware of several long-lens cameras trained on me. I've made the decision to stop wearing bikinis when I compete, even in warm water. Instead, I'll dress in either a one-piece swimsuit with men's boardshorts and my contest jersey or, if I can surf without getting cooked by neoprene, a spring wetsuit. I've learnt – the embarrassing way – that coverage of girls' surf contests is too often exploitative: lingering shots of boobs, bums and thighs; endless jokes over tight bottom turns. I'm no longer going to play that game.

The blazing sun of the past week has disappeared and it's a cool, grey day. Good. I can do without the glare on the water burning my retinas and the sun aggravating my heat rash.

A decent swell has arrived, after days of nothing, and the waves have potential.

I can win here.

1

Beth is ahead of me and she's a fighter: bicepped and six-packed, but that's the least of her strength. Mentally, she's Kevlar. No amount of pressure can break her.

But I've become stronger too, and I've surfed this Florida contest with cold determination. I've beaten my way through round after round, leaving everything on the line because I couldn't bear to face what was happening on shore, and I've made it all the way to the final.

Behind me, the beach is buzzing with activity. Billabong sails are planted in the sand, and logo-covered tents have sprung up everywhere. Two towers have been erected for the judges and commentators, and a huge clock and scoreboard has been hung from them.

The crowd on the beach is tense. They've seen me scrap it out in my heats, just as they've seen Beth demolish the competition in hers, and they're expecting fireworks. Somewhere in that crowd of strangers, Zeke and my sister Lily are standing together, hearts racing, willing me to win.

Beth and I reach the line-up and elect to surf different peaks, keeping our distance, not talking to each other. When our eyes meet, there is no friendship. I want to knock her out of the contest and not just that: I want to humiliate her. I want to get a huge score on the board. Leave her combo'd so she'll have to get not just one, but two high-scoring waves to have even a chance of beating me.

There's an onshore crumble on the wave and I pull

back on it. Wave selection is everything and I won't take off unless I'm sure I have a good one. New Smyrna Beach, also known as the Shark Attack Capital of the World, is a tricky sandbar to read, unpredictable. I've seen how the end section of a wave can stamp out and send a surfer flying for a sand facial and a belly full of brine. I can't let that happen. I won't. I have to focus.

Beth may be more experienced than me, her surfing more explosive, but she's not as motivated. On this day, in this heat, I can beat her. I will beat her.

three days later

chapter one

One of the names locals use for my home town, Newquay, is Never Never Land, because our most devoted surfers don't grow up. Newquay is home to people who've been riding waves for fifty years; surfers who've never had families or nine-to-five jobs, because surfing is all they need. They stay in a watery playground their whole life and even when their long hair silvers, they still ache to paddle out.

If I hadn't met Zeke, I would have become one of the Never Never Land kids. I wouldn't have gone to uni. I'd have stayed working in the surf shop for as long as they wanted me, and when I was too old to fit with their young-in-the-sun corporate image, I'd have served in the cafe next door. Eventually I'd have worked my way around to bin duty – driving the tractor that collected the beach rubbish – and I'd have been fine with it, because morning, noon and night I'd have been free to surf.

When I'd found out who Zeke was, I'd assumed he was

just like all the others. He was not the first pro-surfer to breeze through Newquay and everyone knows those guys live their lives untethered, bouncing from country to country, beach to beach, girl to girl.

'Zeke,' I'd said a few weeks into our relationship. 'Can I ask you a question?'

'Shoot,' he said, hopping, one leg inside his wetsuit, one out.

'Why Newquay? You could be literally anywhere in the world.'

'How'd you figure?' He got into his suit and pulled it up over his waist, nothing but bare skin underneath.

'You've got serious cash in the bank and a valid passport. Why aren't you in Hawaii surfing Pipeline?'

He turned to face me, all high cheekbones, sun-bleached hair and intense blue eyes.

'I've surfed Pipe my whole life. Now I'm here with you.'

'But you could be on the north shore of Oahu.'

'I'll surf it again when you do.'

I laughed and shook my head at the ludicrousness of that statement. 'Zeke, get real. I'm never going to surf there.'

'You wanna bet?'

Within a few months, I was riding the waves of Hawaii.

Now I'm back in England, Zeke thousands of miles behind me. Lily and I are making our way through

Heathrow, and I'm waiting for her to say something reassuring, tell me I haven't made the biggest mistake of my life.

'We timed that well,' she says, looking at the *BBC News* feed on her phone. 'Apparently there's a hurricane building in the mid-Atlantic. Could have been bumpy if we'd gone later in the week.'

'Lily, maybe I should . . .' I start to say, but she's busy searching for her passport in the many zipped compartments of her bag. She puts up her hand and says, 'Let's just get through this hideous airport, shall we? We can talk when there aren't a million tourists coughing all over us.'

Almost everyone around us seems to be ill. This year I dodged the grim British winter for the first time in my life and escaped its ugly chesty coughs and throat infections.

I see a tiny white-haired lady splutter into a handkerchief and I think of Zeke's late grandmother, Nanna, who never got to see another winter. Without thinking, I search for Zeke in the mass of strangers, scanning unfamiliar faces for him, even though I know he's on a plane travelling to the other side of the world.

'Come on, little sis, cheer up,' Lily says. 'It'll all come good in the end.'

'If you say so.'

We have some time to kill before our bus transfer so we sit in the airport Costa, fortifying the table with our

7

baggage. Lily gets up to stretch her long legs while we're waiting for our lattes to arrive. She walks past a girl who is wearing the exact same boho dress I'd worn on a night out in West Hollywood a month ago, a few days before our contest in Santa Cruz. In the blistering heat of a full-capacity nightclub, I'd danced opposite Zeke. His T-shirt was damp, clinging to his chest, which was toughened from years of daily surfing. His hair was falling in his face. I could feel beads of sweat running off the end of my nose and dripping onto the floor, but I couldn't remember when I'd been happier. Skrillex was mixing beats in the DJ booth and apparently somewhere in the VIP lounge were Kim and Kanye. We were there to talk to a man about a sponsorship contract for Zeke. We'd had the meeting earlier in the evening, which lasted fifteen minutes before the Cristal started flowing. I felt like the coolest possible version of myself. I was no longer just an unremarkable surfer girl from a small town in the arse-end of Cornwall. I was competing in a specialist surf competition, travelling the world and surfing its best breaks with my boyfriend, who was without question the best person I'd ever met.

I check my phone, but there's nothing except a bunch of favourites on Twitter and a few new likes on Instagram. He hasn't tried to contact me. Maybe he never will.

Finally, when we've drunk our coffee and made it out into the icy London air, Lily turns to me. 'You did the right thing, Iris. Don't overthink it. He'll be fine. People like

Zeke are always fine. And more importantly, *you'll* be fine. That's what this was about, right? Choosing the right thing for you? It is allowed, you know. It doesn't always have to be about them.'

Her tone is cold and her words feel like a drink thrown in my face.

'Did I say different?'

'You seem like you're already having second thoughts.'

'Well, I'm not. Thanks for the sympathy, though.'

'Tough love is still love,' she says.

We catch a shuttle that smells of BO, urine and diesel to Victoria, and wait on a metal bench for our coach to arrive. The urge to phone Zeke moves past pressing, through strong, to desperate, and my thumb twitches against my iPhone in my pocket.

I make my excuses and go to the loo. Standing with my bum against a cold sink, I scroll down my recent contacts list, and see him.

Zeke from Hawaii.

That was how I'd first put him in my phone, only last year.

I press call and it goes straight to voicemail. He must still be in the air. We'd gone our separate ways at Miami International Airport, our two planes taking off in different directions, mine to Newquay, his to Oahu.

'Zeke, it's Iris,' I say, even though this will be clear from the moment he claps eyes on the display screen of his phone. 'I'm in London. Call me when you land. If you want to. OK . . . bye then.'

I go back out to Lily, and I can feel my body filling with stress hormones, because even though it's only been two minutes since I called him, I'm already waiting for him to call me back.

Lily puts in headphones and loads up her *I Am Stressed* playlist of chill-out tunes. She closes her eyes, despite the fact that she's slept during most of the plane journey from Miami.

After a few minutes, I crack and nudge her. She takes out her headphones and looks at me with resignation.

'You saw his face, Lil. It was like I'd picked up a screwdriver and stabbed him in the heart.'

'Stop thinking about it, Iris. You'll just make yourself miserable. You're going home like you wanted. Be at peace with that. He's not the first guy who got dumped and he certainly won't be the last.'

'I didn't *dump* him. I just said I couldn't carry on like we were, because we were messing each other up, and I wanted to go home.'

'And he got on one plane and you got on another, and you've no plans to see each other again . . .'

'Yes, but—'

'There you are, then. Dumped.'

'Jesus, Lil. It sounds so horrible when you say it like that.'

'Well, do you want to be with him, or not? Because if you do, then maybe you shouldn't have given him the flick.'

At this moment our coach rolls up and the other passengers scramble to form a neat queue.

With people in front and behind us, I shut up. I don't want them to hear my feelings. I don't even want Lily to hear them. I can tell she's deeply bored of the situation and it's only been half a day.

Eventually, Lily steps forwards in the queue, waiting for the coach driver to grab our luggage and sling it in the hold. As he takes hold of my board bag – which contains four surfboards, bound tightly in bubble-wrap, with half my clothes tied around the tail and nose – I slip a leftover ten dollars into his hand and say, 'There's three grand of surfboards in there, so can you do me a solid and find a spot where they won't get wrecked?' Then I turn back to Lily and say, 'Good talk. Thanks.'

'Look, it sucks to break up. It just does, and it hurts like hell at first. But you get over it with time. You already know that from your break-up with Daniel.'

I follow her up the steps and right to the back of the coach.

My relationship with Daniel wasn't anything like my relationship with Zeke. It was kids' stuff. We hadn't explored the world together. We hadn't even spent one night together. The highlight of our week had been playing pool in the youth club and sharing the occasional 500ml can of Excelsior from Lidl.

I stow my bag and make Lily move over so I can sit in the window seat, look at the grey view and stew in my misery.

As mortifying as it is to admit, I'd mostly got over Daniel by falling in love with Zeke. I'd been in self-absorbed emo mode for months, hate-watching *America's Next Top Model* and living on dry cereal, when Zeke arrived in Newquay on a tropical breeze and pushed away the clouds.

'Oh, Iris, don't get upset,' Lily says, touching my cheek. 'Ignore me. What do I know, eh? My longest romantic relationship lasted three and a half weeks. And that's only because for two weeks of it she was working at a summer camp in Massachusetts. I'm hopeless at this stuff. I give in to the urge to run as soon as I start finding them irritating, which is generally by the end of Week One.'

'I didn't give in to the urge to run.'

'Well, no, but you were clever enough to know it'd come to a natural end. So yay for you.'

I look through the window at loved-up couples embracing like they'll never see each other again. I watch a mother say goodbye to her teenage daughter, kissing her on both cheeks and her forehead, taking ages to let go of her hands.

My mum would have probably driven up to meet us at the airport if she knew we were coming, but I'd made Lily swear not to call her.

Suddenly, there's a pain in my chest and I get to my feet, bowing down so I don't crack my head on the overhead luggage lockers.

'I'm getting off,' I say, climbing over her and hyperventilating. I reach up for my bag.

'Whoa, slow down, Iris, you've just paid a fortune for your ticket!'

'I'll get a refund.'

I don't know where I'm going. Back to the airport and on a plane somewhere. I've made a couple of friends during my time away. One of them will let me sleep on their couch until I've sorted my head out. I can't go home now. I can't face it: all the wondering, the assumptions, the cheerful advice about how to get over this and move on.

I rush down the aisle, jump down the steps and accost the driver, who's taking the final drags of a cigarette before the long journey to Cornwall.

'Sorry. I need my bags. You can keep the ten bucks,' I say as he exhales a plume of smoke in my face and murmurs something uncomplimentary about hippies and timewasters.

'Mine, too,' I hear a voice say behind me.

'Lil, you don't have to come with me.' I'd assumed she'd go on to Newquay, irrespective of my plans.

'If you're not returning to the motherland, then neither am I,' she says. 'Ooh, let's have a city break! Oslo is lovely

13

at this time of year. No, scrap that, let's go to Reykjavik and buy a nine quid pint of lager! What do you say?'

I can see her excitement, and immediately stamp it out.

'Are you deliberately choosing whaling nations?'

Zeke is mad into animal rights and I've spent a lot of time with him and his friends, discussing the plight of cetaceans. It's apparently had an effect.

'You've just been in America, Iris. They kill whales there too.'

'Not commercially,' I say moodily. 'It's subsistence whaling carried out by indigenous people.'

'Which is arguably crueller, as it takes longer for the animals to die. Anyway, OK, fine. Somewhere you won't need to think about whaling. Or surfing. You deserve a proper break after New Smyrna. How about Munich?'

'There's river surfing in Munich . . .' I begin to say, but then stop. In the distance I hear shouting.

14

chapter two

'WHAT UP, FOXES!'

I spin round and spot my best friend Kelly. Our bodies collide and we hold each other tight.

She pushes me back to arm's length and grins. 'Well, look at you. All grown up and at least half an inch taller.' She says this seriously, as if she's my Great Auntie Phyllis.

'At last,' Lily says. 'I thought you'd changed your mind.'

'Sorry.' Kelly embraces me again and talks into my hair. 'Phone died and my cab got stuck in traffic.'

'I didn't even know you were in London,' I say to her, completely amazed and delighted that she's here.

'Looked at a uni. Saw the sights. Caught up with a friend.'

She looks so uncomfortable as she says this, that I ask, 'Not a bloke?'

'No, not a bloke,' she says, which is a relief since she already has one on the go – my ex's brother, Garrett.

'Where's Zeke?' Kelly says, looking around.

I open my mouth to answer, but Lily gets in there first.

'Busy elsewhere,' she says.

'Ditched you and gone on a surfari? Lemme guess: Mentawais. Nope, Gold Coast. Final answer: J Bay.'

I shake my head. 'He's gone back to Hawaii for a bit,' I say, in my rehearsed speech. 'His mum's selling the house – you know, the geodesic dome place I told you about – and he wants to say goodbye to it properly before the new owners move in.'

'Lighting candles and wafting incense, is he? I bet he has a chant lined up already, and he'll be omming.'

'Something like that.'

I hate lying to her, but it's not the right time or place to explain what's happening. She's going to be so upset when she finds out.

'I reckon Garrett'll end up flying over to do the same thing. What is it about that place? They all go on about it, Wes too. Those boys are so bloody sentimental. Ah well, it just means more us-time – hurray! Right, I suppose we'd better get on this coach. As if I haven't spent enough time today sniffing diesel.'

I look at her and try to take in her newness. Her hair is longer, ombred so harsh it's almost white on the ends, and her clothes are different. She generally rocks cleavage and bare legs, but she's dressed in surf-wear: a Roxy checked shirt, loose jeans and Havianas. The sort of stuff

16

I wear. In the selfies she posted over the past six months she was glammed up for big nights out, and I'm unprepared for the make-under.

'You look great,' I say. 'Chilled.'

It's true. She's even standing in a more relaxed way. Her shoulders look stronger and instead of standing with a hand in front of her stomach, which she did sometimes without even realizing it, she's standing with her elbows out and her hands in her back pockets. My mum used to tell me off for this exact thing. Tomboy posturing, she called it.

'Consider me a card carrying member of the Surfiety. Paddle out most days now,' she says, proud of herself, and rightly so. 'You never know, in another year or two I might be after your crown.'

'I don't have a crown.'

'You will!' She hugs me again.

'I can't believe you're here,' I say, my eyes welling up despite my best efforts to stay cool.

'Neither can I, really. I received a mysterious text message last night informing me that you were coming home early and imploring me to meet you here if I possibly could. Oh, and to keep it secret, on pain of social media death.'

'Seemed like a good idea at the time,' Lily says, picking at her nail cuticles.

I'm stunned that Lily has been so thoughtful. I'm not

even irritated that she ignored my instructions to keep my return quiet. Of course I wanted my best friend to be there, I just didn't want to put her to any trouble.

Lily gets out her phone and shows the driver an e-ticket she purchased on the sly for Kelly and he looks at us like we've completely lost the plot as we file back onto the coach again and he stows our luggage for the second time.

'I want to hear *everything*,' Kelly says to me, as we take our seats. 'The filthier the better.'

Lily puts her headphones back in.

The coach pulls out and Kelly grins at me. 'So, now you've been going out with him for ages, you can tell me.'

'Tell you what?'

'What he's like in bed.'

My head begins to thud. Of all the chats to have, she chooses this one, the day after I've split up with him.

'Pretty deep sleeper.'

'You know what I'm saying, Iris.'

'You serious?'

'Um, hello? Quite frankly I think it's a major lapse of your best friend duties that you haven't told me already.'

'No way am I telling you that. Why are you even asking? You're dating his brother. It's just . . . weird.'

'You'll crack eventually, so you might as well spill now. I know *some* of it anyway.'

'Er, you'd better not know any of it.'

'Yeah, not like that, but Garrett told me about some

18

random chick who dated Zeke. Apparently, they were hanging out at some desert ice rink in Palm Springs and she told him stuff.'

I know I'll regret this, but I ask her anyway, 'What stuff?'

Kelly grins and says, 'That Zeke goes down like a champ.'

'I can't believe you actually went there. Jesus, Kel, objectification hurts men too.' I'd got that line off my sister, who only ever used it ironically, when she'd said something deeply pervy about a bloke.

'So,' she's looking at me expectantly, 'care to elaborate . . . ?'

'Mind your own business.'

'Hahahaha! That's a yes!'

'Shut up.'

'OK, tell me the most annoying thing about Zeke. I bet he snores. His nasal passages are probably wrecked from the half-ton of cocaine he blitzed.'

'Hey, that's in the past,' I say, my voice tense. 'Zeke doesn't do drugs any more.' *Except when he fancies making an exception to that rule*, I think, like for the street antidepressants I've just discovered he's been using to self-medicate post-traumatic stress disorder. A condition he developed and kept secret from me after his near drowning at the Cribbar reef – the UK's gnarliest big-wave spot, which just so happens to break in my home town.

19

'I'm only teasing.'

'He snores when he's drunk.'

'Gassy? He eats a lot of lentils.'

'Only when they're combined with kidney beans or jalapenos. Otherwise, no, not really.'

'Jealousy issues?'

'Sometimes, but I'm not exactly in a position to criticize.'

'Hmm. Stinky feet?'

'Mate, he's in the ocean most of the day. He smells of saltwater.'

'Bites his toenails?'

'He does, but I actually think that's quite cool.'

'Well, I know he's hotter than a thousand suns but there's gotta be something about him that you find gross, because if there isn't, you're not paying attention.'

'OK, there is one thing . . .' I say, starting to get into this game. It's mortifying on one level because it's part of a horrible pretence, but it's also a relief to talk about Zeke as if everything's fine and he's still my boyfriend.

'Spill.'

'He has sort of weird flavoured nipples.'

Kelly lights up at this, as if I've said something truly delightful. Then she gets serious. 'Like weird how? Salty from being in the sea so much, or *something else*?'

'Salty, definitely, but in a normal sweat way. Maybe it's not a flavour exactly, but when I go there, I get a weird sort of metallic aftertaste in my mouth and the end of my tongue tingles.'

Kelly's gazing at me in approval.

'We're still talking about his nipples, right?'

'Yes.'

'That is weird.'

I nod in agreement, feeling more embarrassed by the second.

'And you didn't get that sensation when you went . . . anywhere else?'

'No, Kelly. Also, this conversation must cease.'

'OK, OK, it's not like I was going to ask you details about . . . anywhere else.'

'Yes, you were.'

'Damn you, Iris, why do you never talk about the filthy stuff?'

'Because you're always talking about it?'

'True, true. So, do you want to hear about Garrett's stuff?'

'I really, *really* don't, thanks.'

'Here if you change your mind.'

She's quiet for a few moments, rolling around in the filth of her dirty mind, and I take the opportunity to say, 'I'm knackered. Haven't slept properly in days and I have the worst jet lag.'

'Get some kip. We have all the time in the world to catch up. You rest.'

I feel wired and can't drift off, so I lean back in the uncomfortable seat with my eyes closed, and breathe deeply so she'll think I'm asleep, which is pathetic, but the thought of having to lie to Kelly any more in my first face-to-face conversation with her is unbearable.

I fake sleep for half an hour, trying to get my mind on other things, but I can't stop thinking of Zeke, the two of us alone together in what felt like paradise. When the soporific motion of the coach sends me to sleep for real, my brain transports me across two oceans.

chapter three

Zeke was carrying me home on his shoulders through the Oahu evening, the sun beating against my face, my thighs pressing against the sides of his head and my fingers tangled in his hair.

'You think you can lean forward a little?' he'd asked, picking his way carefully along the path. 'I don't wanna drop you.'

I'd slipped out of my flip-flops on one of the trails, cutting open the ball of my left foot, and couldn't face hopping half a mile to his house.

No matter how exciting my home turf in Cornwall had once felt to me, Hawaii made it seem pale and small. The north shore of Oahu stretched on for miles, one incredible wave spot after another. Zeke was like a little kid, proudly showing me the best reef and point breaks, the places he'd been surfing his whole life. We rode mountain bikes along ragged trails, edged by deep gulches, and I tried to take it all in, but Oahu was almost too much to process, and I felt dazzled by the intensity of it all.

Earlier I'd left the beach and gone with some of the other female surfers and our film crew on a guided walk in the rainforest to see the sights. It was annoying to have cameras shadowing us, zooming in on everyone's efforts to climb the steep trails in inappropriate footwear, bikini tops and micro shorts. I suspected the end product was going to be a video that attracted a load of misogynists in the comments section, people who'd rank us in terms of shagability and boob-size.

No one wanted to wear the skimpy stuff, but the film crew thought the video would get more hits if the female surfers showed some skin. I just hoped my mum didn't see it.

The trail was breathtaking. The light was green, the spores of musky exotic plants spun around my lungs and diamonds of light filtered down to the ground at our feet. After a few hours, I stopped stressing about the camera crew and got totally immersed in the jungle vibe.

'Hey, hold up!'

I'd turned to see Zeke, fifty feet away, jogging towards us. He was wearing cargo shorts and no T-shirt and his chest glistened in the humidity.

He kissed me, not caring what the others in the group thought. I was secretly a bit self-conscious, not helped by the fact I knew it'd all be caught on camera. The cameramen were already zooming in, because just adding his name to the video header would attract hundreds of thousands more views.

'I thought you were surfing?' I said, when we finally came up for air.

'I missed you. Wanna see something amazing?'

'Not in public.'

'Haha, you'll see. Follow me.'

As I went after him I heard the sound of gushing water, then came upon a turquoise pool, disturbed by a waterfall.

'Used to come here with Garrett and Wes when we were little,' Zeke said. 'Man, I'm so stoked to be here with you.'

He reached for my hand and I looked into his face, where I could see so much stirred-up emotion.

'Garrett would climb up like twenty feet next to the falls and we'd watch as he dove right in.'

'Sounds like Garrett. Hope you didn't do that.'

'Wes was smart enough not to try such a dumbass stunt, but yeah, guilty . . . It was cool until one time I screwed up the take-off, hit the shallows and broke both wrists. Lucky I didn't break my head.'

'Seems quite unfortunate for a teenage boy to break both wrists,' I'd remarked, pursing my lips to hide a grin.

'For sure,' he said, wincing at a memory I'd not be enquiring about, 'and it didn't do my surfing a whole lotta good either. Still hurts sometimes when I paddle out.'

When they'd got all the footage they needed, the

camera crew and the other girls hiked back to the beach, and we told them we'd catch up later. A few of the girls sniggered and Beth, the Australian girl I'd later go head to head with in New Smyrna, made a comment involving wet anatomy.

Zeke and I kissed on the hot rocks by the pool. Stripped off. Kissed some more. Let go.

Afterwards, when we'd redressed and the light was failing, Zeke got quiet. I asked what he was thinking about and he replied, 'You ever wonder where we're headed?'

'Anders gives us a pretty detailed itinerary every Sunday, so not really . . .'

Zeke opened his mouth to say something, but held back.

'What?' I asked.

'Nothin'.'

He settled himself against the rocks; looked up into the tree canopy.

He was talking about the future of our relationship, but I didn't want to hear it, because it felt too much like constructing walls around it. I didn't want our relationship to reside within a box. I'd had enough of that with Daniel.

It was so hot and humid. I dived into the pool and swam away underwater, held my breath a fraction too long and, when I broke the surface, coughing up half a lung, I found myself in the fronds of a water fern, with Zeke right behind me, reaching for my ponytail. I kicked harder than I'd meant to and felt my toes connect with his nose.

'Sorry!'

'So kiss it better,' he said, climbing out of the water, feet and hands slipping on the wet rock.

'Nah.'

I swam across the pool and clambered up a rotten tree that had fallen and formed a natural slide. I turned and balanced there, arms out. A deep breath and I dived down again into that cool green swamp of weed and fish.

When I broke the surface of the water, he was gone, away to pee he said afterwards, but I wasn't scared to be alone, even in that tropical wilderness, because I knew Zeke would always come for me.

chapter four

I'm woken by an announcement for Exeter, and Lily clears her throat and says, 'Okie dokie. This is me.'

'Seriously, you're leaving?' I say, a massive yawn undercutting my aggro tone. 'You said you were coming back with me to Newquay!'

'You're practically home, Iris. Another ninety minutes and Mum will be force-feeding you three helpings of sausage casserole.'

Kelly is watching my argument with Lily play out as if it's the final episode of *Breaking Bad*.

'You could have mentioned it a bit earlier, Lil.'

'I've only just decided. I thought it might be nice to spend a night or two under the bright lights of the big city.'

'Exeter's not a big city,' I point out. 'There are three lights and they're all faint. And we've just been to bloody Miami!'

'Bye, Iris. Take care, Kelly.'

'Who are you staying with?'

'A friend.'

'Not Stan?'

Lily has been in a love-hate friendship with Stan since she was fourteen. They've never technically been girlfriend and boyfriend, but they've managed to make themselves miserable, even so. For a year Lily lived in Stan's London flat-share. Her bedroom was the flat's communal bathroom. She'd slept on a blow-up mattress next to the shower. At one point, Lily lived there with three of the girls in her punk band. When she slept with two of those girls, Stan got in a huff and chucked her out.

'I don't know. Quite possibly,' she says, smiling enigmatically.

'Great.' This is so typically Lily, who has built her life on last-minute acts of the completely annoying.

'Look, you've got Kelly with you, so there's no need to get all indignant about it. I'm just catching up with an old friend. Don't look at me like that. I'll be back in the TR7 by the weekend, I promise.'

Yeah, right, I think. *See you next year.*

After Lily's got off, we look out of the window and she turns to blow us a kiss, before blending into the crowd of passengers spilling across the bus station.

Kelly gives Lily a wave, but I blank her. I think of my mother, who I'll now be facing alone. I've totally proved my mum right and even if she doesn't actually say to me, 'I told you so, Iris,' she'll be thinking it.

29

Before I left Newquay, she asked me, 'Is this wise, love? You're leaving behind everything you know and care about.'

'Basically the opposite, since Zeke's going with me.' I'd said this without thinking of how much it could hurt her feelings. 'There's more to life than Newquay – there's a whole other world out there.'

'And Zeke's going to hand you the keys to this kingdom, is he?'

'What's that supposed to mean?'

'Oh, Iris, you really think one boy can change your world?'

Lily overheard this, and said, 'Course he can. Probably for the worse.'

'Lily,' my mum said, 'don't let in the green-eyed monster. For goodness sake, I thought the pair of you were past this sort of thing.'

'I'm not jealous. I've been to eighteen countries, Mother. I'm happy for Iris, but I'm also a realist.'

Then my mum turned her back on us and pulled a dozen fairy cakes out of the breadbin, which she'd made especially for my leaving tea, and that was the end of the conversation.

So much had happened since then. It was painful to remember just how clueless I'd been.

chapter five

By the time the coach rolls into Newquay, the sun has set. It's not raining, but the air is damp and cool. I feel a rush of emotion as we disembark and look around at familiar sights, but I rub away the pressure behind my eyes.

'Home at last,' Kelly says, 'and I'm keeping you. Really, I'm never letting you leave. You're here forever, mate.'

'You'll be sick of me by the end of the week. Anyway, I have that contest in Mexico next month.'

'That's what you think.'

Mexico is the only remaining contest before the Fistral final and is thankfully girls-only, so there'll be no chance of running into Zeke.

We embrace again and I say, 'Er, sorry about the BO.'

I've been travelling for the better part of two days and smell as fresh as a chip packet blown across a slurry pit.

'Yeah, I didn't like to say, but you are a bit rank. Shower, bed and I'll see you tomorrow.'

I tell Kelly to take the last cab, as she lives all the

way up the other side of the valley in Treloggan, and I start to walk, my rucksack on my back and the thick strap of my board bag over my shoulder. The streets are quiet and my shadow falls on old houses and grimy pavements lined with litter.

A dead seagull, a young one by the looks of its brown speckles, lies in the gutter just opposite the church. I remember an article I read online in the *Cornish Guardian*, about a gang of boys in Newquay throwing half-eaten burgers in front of cars so that seagulls would swoop and be killed, or so badly injured with broken wings that they'd be doomed to suffer a week of starvation and dehydration before nature took its course.

I think of Zeke; what he would say to the people who hurt animals like this. What he would do to stop it, and I turn a corner and find myself in my street. The awesome yellow camper van my dad bought me for my birthday is parked on the road. I walk up to it, run my finger down the wing. One day, when I pass my test, I will drive myself to every surf beach in Europe in this van.

Standing at my garden gate, my heart thudding, I can hardly believe that in one of the rooms inside the house my mum's watching telly or getting ready for bed, with no idea that I'm loitering outside.

My house looks drab and unloved. The winter was hard for Cornwall. Storm after storm coming in from the jet stream being pushed too far south, creating havoc all over our beautiful stretch of Atlantic coastline. The front door paint is peeling and green mould from the garden has risen up the cream walls. If I'd been home, I'd have borrowed a pressure washer from the neighbours and hosed it all down. My mum never has time for things like that; never seems to see that they need doing.

None of it's right, nothing's happening as I thought it would. But why? It's not as if I'd been hoping for a welcome committee. I insisted Lily not warn anyone we were coming. She'd gone against my wishes even telling Kelly.

It's 9.30 and the hall light isn't on. I place my rucksack on the garden bench and lean my board bag against the exterior wall of the kitchen. I try to get my head straight. Try to figure out where to start. I know I have to soon, but I can't deal with a major conversation, not tonight, so I'm going to have to lie through my teeth to my mum, just like I've lied to Kelly, except my mum is much more likely to rumble me as she's had way more experience of me deceiving her.

I search through the front of my rucksack for my keys, which I haven't used in half a year, and let myself into the house.

It's dark and quiet. There's no TV noise from the living room, so she's either down the pub or has decided to have an early night. I kick off my Toms and pad upstairs as quietly as I can.

The door to her bedroom is open a few inches and I decide to check if she's there, before turning in. I won't wake her up. She'll see my shoes in the morning and know I'm back. Better for her to find out that way than seeing my face looming over hers and going into cardiac arrest.

The room's completely dark, there's a smell of stale alcohol and the sound of heavy breathing. I walk closer and shine the light from my phone onto the bed. The duvet has ridden down around my mum's waist. She's wearing some fancy black silk nightie. Next to her, face down, arm slung over her waist, is a man.

He turns over and I see he is not just any man. He is Mick – the ice cream man.

I exhale, too loudly, or maybe my mum just senses there's someone in the room, because she opens her eyes, takes one look at me and screams blue murder.

Mick is on his feet in a flash, stark naked, pointing his finger in my direction and repeating, 'You there!'

'It's ME,' I say, turning away so that my peripheral vision doesn't catch any more of his swinging apparatus.

'IRIS! Good grief. I thought you were Hannibal bloody Lecter! What in the world are you doing here? *June*, you said,' my mum exclaims.

'I came home early. Sorry!'

'Oh, it's your girl. Nice to see you again, love,' Mick says, holding out his hand to me, which he's just been using to shield his junk. I think about the merits of politeness versus the merits of preventing biological transfer, and decline his offer.

'Mick, put on some trousers, please,' my mum says. 'Iris is blushing.'

'I'll leave you to it, ladies,' he says, putting on his boxers and chinos. 'I expect you'll have a lot to talk about.' He leaves, bare-chested and hairy, evidently not fussed about wearing his T-shirt, which I see has landed in a cat litter tray by the bay window.

I wait for the slam of the front door and say, 'Nice one, Mum. Hooking up with Mr Whippy.'

'Oh, he's just a friend.'

'You were in bed with him, Mum.'

'We're keeping it casual. Going about things in the modern way.'

'Please don't tell me you're on Tinder.'

'Don't be so ridiculous. Mick's a nice person, and he seems to like me. Lord knows why. Plenty of women would like him as a partner. He has his own business and is doing rather well for himself.'

'Yeah, the ice cream man's clearly a keeper.'

'There's no need to be so snooty about it. We can't all run away with a surf Adonis. Anyway, your father's probably had two new girlfriends in the past five minutes and nobody's criticizing him.'

'Nobody expects any better of him.'

'I'm being held to unreasonably high standards because

35

I'm your mother? I am entitled to a life, Iris.'

'I know you are,' I say, struggling with anger I can't rationalize, 'it's just I don't want to stumble in on your new life and see its testicles.'

A cat jumps down from a fluffy bed on the radiator and stretches in front of us.

'Fair enough,' my mum says, reaching for a black silk dressing gown that matches her nightdress. 'Let's go downstairs and I'll put the kettle on. I've just bought the most wonderful tea leaves from the Eden Project.'

The cat begins rubbing itself around my calf and I reach down to stroke it.

'I'll be needing some brandy in that tea,' I say, and my mum whips around to me, her eyes hawk-sharp.

'And you may have it. Next year, when you're eighteen.'

'Mum, get real. I've been drinking what I want for months.'

'Yes, I expect you have. Now you're home, where there are rules that you will respect.'

'You know what,' I say, frustration getting the better of me, 'I think I'm gonna stay over at Kelly's tonight, if that's cool with you.'

'Oh, Iris, don't be like that. I know you're upset, of course you are, but stay here and sleep in your old room. I've waited all this time to see you and I don't want you to leave.'

I walk downstairs, suddenly overcome with a strong urge to flee, and stand in the entranceway, my fingers on the front door handle. The cat follows me and waits expectantly.

'It's just one night at my best mate's house,' I say. 'No big deal. We'll see each other tomorrow. I'll make you lunch!'

'I'm your mother and I'm asking you to stay. I don't want you walking the streets at this hour. It's not safe.'

And I smile, because she has no idea. Absolutely no conception of the things I've done in my time away. I've hitchhiked with truckers. I've passed out drunk with Zeke on city beaches and woken up to drifters trying to steal my stuff. I've cut open my forehead volcano-boarding in Nicaragua. I've smoked and experimented and done whatever else I felt like, and she's worried about me walking around Newquay after the sun's set.

'It's just the other side of town, Mum.'

'There could be criminals about at this time of night. A girl was abducted from her doorstep and raped on the Barrowfields not two months ago. Why take the risk? Let me run you over there in the car.'

'Stop stressing!' I say, opening the door, the cat slipping past me. 'I'll be fine. I'm not a kid any more.'

'No, you're all of seventeen. Promise you'll text me as soon as you arrive at Kelly's house.'

'OK, I promise.'

I turn to her and see how anxious she is, how much love is etched across her worried face.

'Sorry I was grumpy,' I say. 'Long day.'

'You must be absolutely exhausted,' she says, before her expression changes to confusion. 'Wait – why Kelly? Why aren't you staying the night with Zeke at the apartment? Or is he at the house with Dave and Sephy?'

I'm not expecting her to ask this and it takes me a moment to realize she has. I'd thought I'd got away with it, that I'd be free of this conversation for at least another twelve hours. There's a second in which my senses feel completely overwhelmed; a buzzing in my ears and a temporary loss of vision. I swallow and try to make my voice sound normal.

'Zeke's not with me. He had stuff to do. Anyway, I want to spend some proper time with Kelly, especially as she's got school and work this week.'

'Zeke's not here? Where is he then?'

'Hawaii. I might not see him for a while.'

She looks at me askance, waiting for me to drop clues that she can follow to the truth.

'It's fine, Mum. See you tomorrow.'

'I love you, Iris. So much. And I'm so very glad you're home.'

'Love you too.'

38

chapter six

I swing up Treloggan Road, where several streetlights are blown, and text Kelly an SOS.

She replies instantly.

What ice cream man? Not the hot one from the Killacourt???

Mono-brow Mick. From the Gazzle.

Oh, he's nice!! Used to give us the manky old broken cones for free!

I've just seen his manky old broken cone.

TMI.

I put my phone in my back pocket. The night is eerily quiet and still, the roads free of cars. I'm half tempted to break into a jog; my mum's warning has worked its way into my head and I figure a moving target will be harder to ambush. I won't, though. That sort of preventative measure is, as my sister would so happily tell me, 'living life in fear', which is apparently no way to live at all.

The streets are empty, apart from an old dude with a springer spaniel who appears behind me from a lane cutting between houses. I'm two minutes away from Kelly's house and I walk briskly. Ahead of me is a parked-up van with its lights on and its engine running.

For a moment I'm spooked and wonder if there's a psychopath in the van, waiting to abduct defiant daughters. When I get closer I see a man talking on his mobile phone and hear him telling someone exactly why he can't leave Donna this week. Something to do with their son's half-birthday, apparently. He shoots me a guilty look as I stride past pretending to have heard nothing.

Finally, I rock up to number twelve and knock gently. A rectangle of light dazzles me as Kelly opens the door with a mug of hot chocolate and a plate of warm doughnuts fresh out of the microwave.

'Best friend ever, no question,' I say, and relieve her of a doughnut.

'I can't believe your mum has a bloke on the go. Good for her. Get it, gurrl.'

'You didn't have to see him in his birthday suit.'

'Bull balls?'

'I don't even know what that is.'

'You know – low hangers.'

'Please stop.'

Kelly chuckles and I follow her upstairs and into her room. It's been redecorated in shades of red. All of her bog-standard pine bedroom furniture has been replaced with antique rip-offs and there are tapestry throws strewn

40

about. It looks like an upmarket Parisian brothel.

I text my mum to say I've arrived without being murdered, while Kelly pushes about eighteen silk and velvet cushions from her king-size bed onto the floor.

'I see you upsized.'

'Yeah, Garrett's been staying over a bit.'

'He isn't gonna turn up tonight, is he?'

'He and Wes were here when I got back. They'd been caning Wes's new motorbike along the Watergate Bay road and stopped in for a cuppa on the way home. You should have seen them riding off together. Nuts to butts and not a care in the world.'

'Can we stop talking about genitals now? Do they know I'm in Newquay?'

'Yeah, course.'

'Where did you say Zeke was?'

'Gone to see the old house in Oahu, like you said. Why, something wrong?'

'No. Just thought they might be disappointed he's not here.' I try to make my voice sound carefree, and I fail.

'They were a bit gutted, but they're used to him being in a different country, what with all his epic globetrotting. I imagine he'll be here within a few weeks, right?'

I consider telling Kelly the truth, and I almost do, but bottle it.

I'm exhausted. I can't face doing any more feeling.

'Yeah, probably,' I say, before changing the subject:

'So Garrett's stays over loads and your mum's cool with that?'

'She doesn't care. Thinks he's well fit, and he's always flirting with her, which she loves. He's here probably five nights out of seven.'

'How clean are these sheets?' I say, having visions of stains that would glow under a black light.

'Fresh on before I left for London. Want to borrow a nightshirt?'

'Cheers. But let me get showered first. I'm proper reeking.'

I use her bathroom shower, coming back into the room to dry off. I get changed in full view of Kelly, who is blatantly watching me.

Kelly always looks. It's like she keeps tabs on my body, and is genuinely interested to see how it changes with time. She's always been like this.

'You do know you've got rippling muscles in your back?'

'They're not "rippling", Kel. I'm not the Hulk.'

'They were just then, when you pulled on the shirt. I saw actual rippling occurring.'

'Two thousand hours of paddling would probably give anyone bigger back muscles,' I remark, trying to get a quick glimpse of my back in the new gilt mirror hanging next to the bedroom door.

'Ooh, look at you, all vain about your amazing

ripply back. You've changed.'

'Shut up, you,' I say, throwing one of my balled-up socks at her. 'I'm exactly the same as always. Just . . . musclier.

'Well, maybe not exactly the same. Check it out.' I unclip my surf watch and hold up my wrist for her inspection.

Kelly looks at it and starts laughing. 'Seriously, Iris? Is that real?'

'Yep.'

On my wrist there is a small black tattoo. Three letters inked in a gothic font. The letters that so many of the local men have inked on their biceps and chests, surfers who have vowed to be 'Newquay forever'.

TR7

I'd never understood it before, that need to brand yourself, especially not with something as random as a postcode, until, suddenly, I did understand.

I'd only had it done on my last night in New Smyrna Beach and it was still a bit scabbed.

'Zeke have one of those too?' Kelly asks me.

'No, he wasn't with me when I got it. I was with a bunch of the Billabong girls. They were trying to get me to have a dolphin or a turtle, or some flowers to jazz it up a bit, but I only wanted this.' I shake my head as I say this and wait for it. The question. But it doesn't come.

'I bet the tattoo artist thought you were well weird.'

She looks as if she's about to say something else, and thinks better of it.

We spend an hour talking about nothing and as soon as the hall clock strikes midnight, Kelly rolls over and pulls the duvet up to her neck.

'I think I'm coming down with something,' I say, feeling sweaty and picking up on the start of a headache. 'Shall I sleep on the sofa downstairs? I don't want to give you a dose of plane lurgy.'

'I'll take my chances,' she says, reaching over to switch off a beaded lamp on her bedside cabinet.

Whatever else is going wrong in my life, the thought of spending time with her makes my heart sing.

'Night, Kel.'

'Night, superstar.'

'I'm not a superstar. Not even close.'

'At New Smyrna you were.'

For one moment, I'd felt like one. I'd felt euphoric with the crowd cheering as I drank from an enormous bottle of virgin champagne. I'd offered some to Beth, but she was having none of it. She wanted this victory more than anything and I'd stolen it from her. She was wiping away tears, trying to hold back sobs. I could see she was furious with herself for breaking down like this in front of the cameras, but all the stress and disappointment was flowing out of her and she couldn't dam it. It was the first time I'd seen her fall apart.

I'd locked eyes with Zeke, who looked drained and exhausted, despite the smile on his lips. The contest had been a distraction for me. Focused on that, I could put away my other emotions. But the contest had ended and it was time to face up to the fact that my relationship with Zeke was stamping out.

He came over to congratulate me. 'You were amazing. Real explosive, aggressive surfing. I've never seen you compete that way before.'

'I didn't want to lose. Thought I was gonna get disqualified at one point.'

'No way they'd DQ you. Third wave looked like the ride of your life.'

The ride of my life – how I'd once thought of my relationship with him.

'Hey, don't look so sad. You're a champion now,' he said.

I rested my head against his chest and felt his heart pounding.

'So . . . what do we do now?' I said.

'Fix this,' he replied.

And we did. For a whole two days we were golden.

chapter seven

Kelly's alarm goes off and she prods me in the back until I turn over and face her. The curtains are open but no light is streaming through. It's pitch black outside.

'Are you serious?' I say, squinting at the time on her alarm clock.

5.45.

'Deadly. Dawn patrol.'

'You're waking me up at piss o'clock to go surfing on my first day back? Really, Kel?'

'Best waves of the day. Anyway, I have school later.' The headache of the night before is still with me, and it worsens at the thought of getting out of bed.

'Aaargh. I need a couple paracetamol before we go.'

'Top drawer,' Kelly says, and I root through the tissues, contraceptive pills and condom packets until I find some cold and flu capsules. I take two of them with a sip of stale water from the glass on her desk.

'I don't have my gear with me.'

'Good job your best mate will let you borrow a board and a wettie then.'

'No one says wettie, Kel, and I don't have a swimsuit to put on underneath it.'

'Wear one of mine or go naked. Do you want the C-Skins or the Billabong suit?'

'C-Skins,' I answer immediately. The last thing I want reminding of is the competition.

I swish some toothpaste around my mouth, splash my face with water and then put on Kelly's wetsuit, without bothering to put on one of her swimsuits. Kelly's body type is really different to mine, and her wetsuit has been cut for a woman with proper curves and a hip-to-waist ratio of more than one. It juts out over my hips and is uncomfortably tight in the middle. I pull the sleeves over my arms and zip up the suit, still slightly weirded out that Kelly is now apparently a surf addict; until last year she'd always claimed she was happy enough just bodyboarding and kayaking.

When I meet her in the kitchen, she's made a stack of toast, and she hands me some instant black coffee, served in a tiny espresso cup as if it's the real thing.

'How are we getting to the beach?' I ask. 'I don't fancy walking barefoot from Treloggan.'

'We'll wear our trainers and leave them on the beach.'

'Not loving the idea of carrying boards up Trenance Hill. Ding the nose to shit, it's so steep.'

47

'We'll go to Tolcarne Beach. Fistral is gonna be gnarly today.'

Fistral is too exposed to the raw power of the Atlantic, facing due west and picking up any swell that's about, whereas Tolcarne is protected by the bay and usually OK, even when Fistral is unsurfable.

'OK, fine by me.'

The secret I'm keeping from her is walling up, growing higher with every hour, and I want to come clean about Zeke, but I also don't want to do that. Partly because of the fact that she's in a relationship with his brother, but mostly because she's going to give me hell. Not for the break-up – she'll be on my side, I know she will – but for not phoning her the minute it happened. Spending a seven-hour coach journey with her while pretending everything was fine – she will definitely not understand.

'Kel,' I say, wondering if there's a chance to work it into the conversation now in a way that won't cause her major offence.

But her phone begins to vibrate on the kitchen worktop. She swipes to read a text. 'Cool, Garrett's coming too. He's picking us up in Zeke's van.'

I try to take this news calmly. Zeke's brother will be here in a few minutes, with his comments and questions, and then we'll all go for a surf and pretend everything's normal.

I follow Kelly into the living room and she points to the

stairs. On the underside she has some hooks and bungees, and three surfboards suspended. One mini-mal, one fish and one egg.

'Check out my quiver. Which one do you want?'

I look at them. They're the boards of the novice-recently-turned-intermediate surfer.

'Does Garrett have any boards in the van?'

'Ooh, shots fired. What's wrong with my boards, eh?'

'Nothing. Sod it, I'll take the mini-mal. When's he getting here?'

'Fifteen minutes. He's just gotta do the three S's.'

'Huh?'

'Shit, shower, shave. Except he probably won't shower or shave. Sit down. We've got time for a cuppa.'

I suddenly worry that Kelly is going to interrogate me and I feel a bit panicky. Sensing weakness, she moves in for the kill.

'Have you heard from Zeke this morning?'

'Not yet.'

She wipes down the table and puts up her heels to fill in the crossword of the *Cornish Guardian*.

'How come?'

'He's busy with work stuff.'

She doesn't look up. 'Oh yeah? Like what?'

'Loads of things. Interviews. Meet and greets. Signings. Press always goes wild when he's home in Oahu.'

'And you don't have to do that stuff?'

49

'Not at the moment.'

Which is a huge relief. I hate video and print interviews. It seems as if I have to be a glossy brochure when secretly I feel like a tatty street flier someone printed off on their mum's Hewlett Packard.

'Three down: *Number of people in a theatre*, twelve letters. No bloody clue. So how long's he staying?'

'I don't know. It depends.'

'So, he's doing vital surf stuff in Hawaii.'

'Yeah.'

'OK, OK. I believe you.'

'What? I know you want to say something, so just say it.'

'Nothing. It's fine. Zeke is in Hawaii. But he'll be back for the wedding?'

'Sure thing.'

'*Sure thing.* What do you sound like!'

'Sorry. Picked it up on the road.'

'*On the road.* That one was on purpose, right?'

I nod, even though it totally wasn't on purpose.

Kelly goes on, 'You do have a bit of an American accent, mate.'

She grabs a can of Lilt from the fridge and holds it up as if she's displaying a prize on a game show. 'Tell me what this is.'

'A fizzy drink with a totally tropical taste?'

'Yes. Not a soda. So tell me one last time. Why didn't

Zeke come over with you?'

'He's in Oahu saying goodbye to his old house and doing work stuff. Wanna ask me another hundred times?'

I look at my watch and see that Garrett should be arriving at any moment. I feel hemmed in, trapped, and desperate for cool sea air.

'Let's wait outside,' I say, heading for the front door and feeling her eyes burn into my back.

She locks up and follows me out into the freezing morning. We clutch our boards and move around to stay warm, our breath steam-training the air around us. This could go either way, I think. She could let it lie for now, or challenge me to tell her the truth. She looks up and catches hold of my hand.

'We've been friends our whole lives, Iris Fox, and I can see there's more to this Hawaii thing than you're letting on, and for now I'm OK with that, because I know you have your reasons, but all I'm saying is they'd better be good ones.'

She's seen through me. Her bullshit detector is even more finely tuned than my mum's. I stare at her, and somewhere behind us, in Treloggan's only farm, a rooster crows.

'Kel . . .'

She takes my hands, pushes my palms together and covers them with her own. Like something a mum would do. Or a nan. Six months older than me and always trying to be my protector.

'I'm here if you need me. You can tell me anything and I won't judge.'

And she won't, because she never judges me.

'Kelly, it's no big deal,' I say, in my calm voice, 'but the thing is, Zeke's not exactly –' I stop here. Can't say it.

She gives me a meaningful look, and I muster the courage.

'– my boyfriend, any more.'

'WHAAAT?'

'I know. Don't say anything to Garrett. Please, Kel. There's more to it. Zeke wants to tell his family everything himself.'

'When the hell did this even happen?'

chapter eight

So I tell her everything. How things had been slowly going wrong; how they'd fallen apart in Miami. How hard it was to walk away, because this love of ours had its jaws clamped around my torso and I didn't know how I'd ever shake myself free of its fury.

How we'd stood at the airport and said our goodbyes.

'I don't want this any more,' I said. 'I want to go home.'

Zeke had exhaled, long and slow, trying to calm himself down. 'You don't want *this* any more? Or you don't want me?'

'No, it's not like that. I just don't know how to make this work. It feels like we're breaking each other.'

'That's some next level BS right there.'

'No, it isn't, Zeke.'

He looked away from me, staring angrily at a boozed-up bachelor party whooping and staggering in our direction. There were maybe thirty of them, all decked out in cowboy hats and blow-up alligators.

'Is this because of Daniel? Do you still have feelings for him? Is that who you're going home to?'

'Zeke, no. Daniel and I are ancient history. Look at me,' I said, touching his chin; turning his face towards mine. 'I need to be in Newquay.'

'Awesome. Solid plan. Follow your bliss. Go nuts.' He kicked at a discarded sweet wrapper lying crumpled on the marble floor. I'd seen a kid walk by earlier, leaving a trail of them in his wake. The wrapper was sticky and got caught on the end of Zeke's trainer. Despite his best attempts to shake it loose, he couldn't dislodge it. He had to kneel down to peel it off, then walk a hundred metres to deposit it in one of the airport trashcans.

When he returned, he looked even angrier.

'Will you be all right?' I asked, regretting these words as soon as they'd left my mouth.

He laughed, a bitter sound. 'Is that a real question?'

'Yeah, so how about you answer it?'

'How about you take a wild guess.'

I pursed my lips. Bristled. Heard my mother's voice when I spoke. 'I'm sorry. I know this is the right thing to do, however much it hurts now. We'll probably both be grateful in the long run.'

'Go to hell, Iris.'

I felt my temper rise. 'That's nice, Zeke. Really charming.'

'Let me tell my folks we're through, OK? If they're

gonna hear it, they're sure as hell gonna hear it from me. Guess they won't be too surprised, since I screwed up everything else in my life.'

I opened my mouth to say *whatever*, but hesitated.

'You have an issue with that?' he asked.

'I'll probably bump into them as soon as I get to Newquay. What am I supposed to say when they ask where you are?'

'Tell 'em the truth – that I wanna see our old place in Oahu one last time before it gets sold. Just give me a few days.'

'That's not the whole truth though, is it? Come to Newquay with me. Tell them face to face.'

'That town is the last place I wanna be.'

'You'll have to go back eventually.'

'Not today.'

He touched my wrist, the tips of his long fingers barely making contact, the temper fading out of his face as if it had never even been there. His mood could whip 180 degrees like the wind, and I could never keep up.

'Don't say we're done, Iris. We can't be through.'

I had no words. Nothing. But I held his gaze.

'It's a huge mistake. We do this, we regret it, like, forever.'

His words were halting, his throat choked with emotion. He was suffering. I was busting his brain, shredding his heart. If we stayed together, we wouldn't stop until we ruined each other and there was nothing left worth saving.

Yet I could feel myself starting to unravel, my resolve beginning to dissipate into the air.

'I've got to go,' I said, disconnecting myself from his fingers.

'Then go,' he'd said.

It hurt to leave, but I held myself together, made it to the ladies bathroom, where I locked myself in a cubicle and wept as silently as I could manage onto my knees.

When I came out, there were people everywhere and he was gone.

Lily was sitting on a wooden bench outside the airport bar. She sauntered over, unzipping her handbag, and handed me a miniature from Duty Free. 'You're going to need at least five swigs of this. Possibly six.'

'Did he say anything to you before he left?' I asked, taking a gulp of liquid that burned hotter than lighter fuel.

'Yes, but not much, which was understandable really. Goodness, his eyes looked so blue just then, all wet and shining, poor thing.'

'What did he say?'

'Are you sure you want to know? Have a bit more Wodka first. I did just say Wodka, yes. Loads cheaper than the other stuff.'

'Tell me, Lil.'

'Well . . . if you're absolutely sure.'

'Go on.'

'He said *Mahalo* and wished us good health and great happiness, which was decent of him, all things considered. Then he might have mentioned that he can't bear the thought of his life without you, and that he'll love you until he takes his last breath.'

'Oh, mate,' Kelly says. 'I'm so, so sorry.'

At that moment, we hear an engine and Zeke's old silver VW Camper comes cruising around the corner with his brother at the wheel.

'Don't say anything, Kel. Please.'

Saying it out loud to Kelly makes it suddenly feel so real. I've pulled the ripcord.

I'd been spinning towards the ground, and he was falling with me. Yeah, it was the ride of our lives, but we were headed for disaster. I chose breathing space, thinking time, stability, and even though he had all his pain to face without me – and I knew that better than anyone – I released my white parachute and left him to fall the rest of the way alone.

chapter nine

Garrett parks up, the wheels of the van skewwhiff, and leaps towards us.

'Queen of New Smyrna Beach,' he says. 'All hail.'

He's not suited up. Instead, he's wearing a faded pink T-shirt, brown leather jacket and knee-length cut-off jeans. His hair has grown longer and is surprisingly curly. He looks like some Eighties throwback, and yet somehow dead cool at the same time.

He has Zeke's wide shoulders. Zeke's cheekbones. Garrett's a bit shorter and a lot blonder, but the two of them are so much alike it hurts me to look at him. He wraps his arms around my shoulders and does the knuckles into the top of the head, big brother routine.

'Lady, it's so good to see you,' he says. I hear a wobble in his voice and wonder if he's spoken to Zeke already.

'Good to see you too,' I say. 'How's life treating you?'

'Still hustling. Thinking of buying a surf school, if you're interested? You and Zeke could come do star-rider events.'

He hasn't spoken to Zeke.

'Garrett, she's just arrived! Leave her alone.'

'Uh-huh,' he says, waving Kelly's protest aside. 'I was thinking we could charge people a bunch of money to hang out in the line-up with you guys. You give 'em a few tips, we make a killing and everyone goes home happy. What d'ya say?'

He holds out his left hand for me to shake as if to seal the deal. His left-handedness catches me out. He's the only Francis brother to surf goofy, right foot first instead of left, and I always manage to forget this. I shake, wrong-handed, and say, 'Um, maybe.'

The odds of Zeke agreeing to this plan are, I'm sure, zero.

He smiles at me again, kisses me on the cheek and Kelly whacks him on the shoulder.

'Hello there,' she says, reminding him of her existence.

He kisses her on the mouth and when she still looks miffed, he says, 'What? I see you every day. I haven't seen Iris in months. So how's my kid brother doing?'

'He's good,' I say, even though I'm pretty certain the truth is the exact opposite.

'I hardly heard from him this past two weeks,' Garrett continues. 'I guess he's been training a bunch.'

'Yeah, it's been heavy,' I say. 'Florida was insane.'

'You stoked to be home? Bet you're frothing to catch

some sweet Cornish A-frames, amirite?'

I nod, don't risk words. I was not expecting my heart to go out to Garrett like this. All my emotions tumble together. Garrett is part of Zeke's family, part of his identity. Garrett is also part of my surfer family. We've spent ages together in the water and I feel an intense bond with him.

I want to sit in silence with him. Lean against him and feel his warmth. Cry on his shoulder. But I can't show any of this, because he has to believe everything's fine.

I look at the camper van and try not to think of all the nights I spent in there with Zeke.

Garrett starts talking to Kelly about someone getting a picture of them the week before when they went naked rock-pooling late one evening and rescued a stranded dogfish. The pictures of their bare bums are there on Instagram for everyone to see, apparently.

Kelly looks sheepish but also sort of proud of this escapade and I'm sure I'll hear the whole story later. For now, I avoid glancing at Garrett and try to make myself feel OK about being so close to him.

'So, Fisty or the bay?' he asks us.

I'm not ready for Fistral, not in the right headspace. I'm already on the brink of tears.

'Tolcarne,' Kelly and I say in unison.

I slide Kelly's boards into the back of the van and when I turn around, Garrett and Kelly are engaged in some sort of silent conversation. They stop, like they've been rumbled, when I raise my eyebrows at them.

'Right,' Kelly says. 'Let's go get wet.'

chapter ten

Garrett parks behind the Bristol Hotel because the van's clutch is ropey and not up to the challenge of the steep lane leading to the beach. I absent-mindedly take one of Garrett's shortboards and we stroll across the empty main road, angling our boards so that they don't get jacked up on the narrow stone steps of Tolcarne.

Behind me there are rows of brightly coloured beach huts, painted in blue, red, yellow and green. It's ridiculously quaint, like a postcard.

Before I've even had a chance to look at the surf, to work out the rips and sandbanks, Kelly's running down to the waves, mad keen to get in there. I kick off my shoes and go to follow but Garrett says, 'You got a minute?'

'Sure,' I say, immediately edgy.

Garrett never bothers with a towel or Robie to get changed; he strips off and pulls on his wetsuit as if it's a nudist beach. I'm not bothered. I've seen him naked more times than I can count due to his naturist tendencies, but it does occur to me that it's less than a day since I arrived in Newquay and I've already seen two blokes starkers.

'How's it my little bro ain't here?' he says.

'He went back to Oahu to see the house one last time before it gets sold. Didn't Kelly tell you?'

'She told me. Why didn't you go with him? You said you weren't planning on coming back for another couple months.'

'I was homesick,' I say. 'Should've come back for my birthday last week.'

'So you haven't split or nothing?'

Zeke hasn't made the call yet and I'm trapped.

'It's not like that,' I say, and feel like the worst human who ever lived.

We both turn to watch Kelly battle it out in the impact zone. There are punchy set waves coming in and she's getting hammered. If she'd just waited another few minutes it would have been flat. She's not duck-diving, instead she's jumping with each wave. It's horrible to see her struggling to push her board over them, getting knocked backwards several metres each time. At this rate, she's going to get washed in, which is just about the most humiliating thing that can happen to a surfer trying to paddle out. Me and Garrett look at each other, both thinking the same thing, and walk to the water's edge.

Kelly finally makes it out of the zone and begins to paddle to the line-up, whereupon it immediately goes flat and still as the set passes by. Garrett and I paddle through the now glassy impact zone and meet Kelly out back.

'Should have waited, in hindsight,' she says, drily.

'Great work-out, though,' I point out, and Garrett whistles as he catches sight of the next set far out in the bay.

We let the first wave go by. I think about taking the second but Garrett and Kelly are both paddling for it. Kelly looks over her shoulder, sees Garrett closest to the peak of the wave and, instead of falling back, she drops in on him and totally cuts him off.

She's on her feet in a blink. There's no scrambling up via a knee: she's nailed her pop-up. The last time I surfed with Kelly she was on a foamy in the whitewater and now she's claimed her place in the line-up and is surfing like a boss.

Garrett's grinning, apparently used to Kelly's new super-hostile style of wave-riding.

She catches an edge, there's a little bit of rippable wall, and she rides the wave for a few seconds, before stepping off and paddling back out.

The last wave of the set is coming and I paddle for position. Kelly's also in the vicinity.

'I'm going,' I shout to her.

'So am I,' she says, laughing. I keep paddling for the wave, not sure if she's serious.

'Are you serious? I don't want a board to the face, mate,' I shout. 'Can you back off?'

'You back off!'

I go for it and at the last moment see Kelly slide off the back of the wave.

This one is steeper with a lot of triangular wall wedging up, thanks to the backwash coming off the cliff. It's the best wave of the set and I find a ramp section, attempt a tiny bunny-hop 270 that's all horizontal spin and no lift, and manage to land it for a few seconds. Still, I finish the manoeuvre and am buzzing that Garrett and Kelly have seen me stick an air.

But when I look back to the line-up, Kelly and Garrett are bobbing in the calm water, kissing, their boards knocking together.

'Good ride?' Kelly says, when I paddle over to the sandbank.

'Yeah,' I say, disappointed.

Garrett paddles to a different sandbank and Kelly and I surf alternate waves for another hour, but the paracetamol is wearing off and, even in the ice-cold water, I can feel a bit of a fever setting in. I wait for a wave and ride it, no-hander, straight to shore.

I leave my board on the beach and then wade into the baby waves where it's warmest, and lie back.

chapter eleven

We get changed on the beach and when we're done Garrett pulls out a tiny disposable barbecue from his backpack and gets it going. Tolcarne is a strictly no-barbecue beach, but it's still before eight o'clock and there's hardly anyone around, plus, we'll take the evidence with us. He goes to set it up by the rocks, where it's sheltered from the wind, and throws on an eight-pack of sausages.

Kelly and I take a minute to drink some water, as we're both gasping from saltwater and exertion. We look out to the waves and I feel Kelly take my hand.

'How are you doing?'

I think about this.

'I don't think it's hit me yet.'

'What happened?'

'We're just . . . bad for each other.'

'No, you're not. You've become a pro-surfer and started travelling the world since you've met him!'

'Yeah, and since meeting me he's been stabbed by my

ex-boyfriend and almost drowned in my home town.'

'See, so much excitement! What more could a boy desire?' Kelly says, with a grin. 'Are you totally sure it's over? Maybe you should give him a call.'

'Can we change the subject? I can feel myself getting upset.'

'Oh, babe,' Kelly says, hugging me tight. 'Course we can. Hey, it was so nice to surf with you again,' she says.

I take a breath, manage to stop myself crying.

'Thought you were gonna drop in on me out there!'

'Ha, I was just psyching you out. I only drop in on Garrett. He finds it hilarious. Thinks he's created a monster.'

'He has. Did he teach you to surf, or did you get proper lessons from one of the surf schools?'

'Bit of both. I've been going whenever I can. I'm never gonna be a pro, but I feel way happier if I've been in, you know?'

'Yeah, I know. You've caught the bug. That's it for you now. Hooked for life.'

We watch as a grey seal pops up his head a few metres from shore.

'Hey Garrett!' Kelly shouts. 'It's your mate.'

Garrett grimaces in the direction of the seal and gives Kelly the finger.

'What's his problem?'

'He's terrified of them. Grows up in Hawaii. Surfs all

67

over the world. Not bothered about giant sharks giving him the once-over, but paddles straight back to the beach if a seal turns up.'

I narrow my eyes. 'Are you having me on?'

'Nope. We were surfing Towan last year when some bloke got bitten on the thigh by one. Mating season makes 'em more aggressive. Almost had his knob off.'

'Oh, that'll be it, then,' I say, feeling strange that I've missed so much. 'Explains everything.'

'Yeah, he can cope with the thought of losing an arm or a leg to a shark attack, but the thought of losing his penis to a seal is too horrifying for words.'

Kelly and I walk over to the rocks. Garrett pulls a tacky-looking musical instrument out of his backpack and Kelly groans. It has a little keyboard running down the side and a mouthpiece. He lifts it to his lips and plays a song, which is surprisingly tuneful given it looks like a children's toy from a car boot sale.

'What is that?'

'Melodica,' Kelly says. 'He can't just have a harmonica or a guitar like a normal surf bum.'

Garrett finishes his tune, and then pulls sausages off the barbecue, stuffs them in unbuttered hotdog rolls and hands them out.

I'm starving and demolish two. Kelly gets through three and Garrett scarfs down the rest. My headache backs off a bit and out of my wetsuit I don't feel as hot.

'Garrett's mates with the chef in The Breaks. He'll be opening up in a bit. Come for a free coffee with us. Quick one, cos I've gotta get to school.'

'All right, just give me a minute and I'll see you up there.'

They go inside and I walk up and down the water's edge, trying to decide if it'd be a mistake to phone Zeke again.

I dial his number before I can stop myself, but it rings out and goes to voicemail.

'It's me again. I'm back in Newquay. I've just been surfing with Kelly and Garrett. When are you planning to tell your folks? Kelly knows we've split, but nothing else. OK, then, bye.'

A small dog runs onto the beach. It's on a long leash, and it does a few loops around its owner, almost tripping him up. I recognize the tanned skin and ponytail immediately. It's Zeke's stepdad. He comes over to me, a huge smile on his face.

'Hi Dave,' I say, kicking myself for not making my getaway sooner. He's one of my favourite people, but I'm nervous as I hug him because, like everyone else, he'll have questions. And then from somewhere between The Breaks and the snack bar, I hear another voice, loud and distinctly Hawaiian, telling Dave to wait up.

'What! First day! How lucky are we?' she says, when she claps eyes on me.

Zeke's mum, Sephy. Awesome Sephy, whose warmth

wraps round her family like fleece pyjamas on a winter's night. Sephy, who is the centre of it all.

She dashes in front of a group of surfers, evidently not able to wait an extra few seconds, and gets grumbled at.

'Chill out, kids,' she yells, although these men look at least twenty-five, before reaching us and hugging me for longer than my own mother did. 'How's life treating you, honey?'

'Good. You've just missed Kelly and Garrett. They're getting coffee.'

'Awesome, we'll go join them.'

Really *not* awesome, I think, because now I'm going to have to make small-talk with Zeke's folks, without telling them anything, while Kelly batters me with just-checking-you're-OK glances.

The puppy starts barking, tiny little yelps, and Sephy picks it up and hands it to me.

'Who's this?' I ask.

'Meet Maverick. He's overcompensating.'

'For what?' I ask, laughing.

'Wash your mind out. Compensation for his tiny little legs. But he's only four months old, so he has plenty of growing to do yet.'

'So . . . Maverick?'

'We Skyped Colton and let him choose a name and of course he went for a monster surf break. Cara picked his second name.'

'Which is?'

'Swishy.'

I smile. I can't wait to catch up with my little cousin. I've missed her so much.

'I bet she's changed loads since I was last here.'

'Full of her own lovely ideas and opinions,' Dave says. 'Starting to look like her big cousin, the surf champ.'

I smile. 'Really?'

'Totally. So it sucks that Zeke's not back. He sounded so bummed out not to be here, and I bet it's gonna be a real long six weeks for you, Iris.'

So he *has* already rung them and apparently made concrete plans to come to Newquay. They don't, however, seem to know anything else.

'He's planning on arriving early Thursday morning so he'll be on British time and all good for our rehearsal lunch,' Sephy says.

'The rehearsal lunch . . .'

'Didn't he tell you? You know we fixed a date, right?'

I shake my head.

'That boy is hopeless.'

'Oh, yeah, sorry, he did say something,' I lie. 'I'm still a bit groggy from the flight. So you're getting married when?'

'Thirteenth of June. Saturday.'

Has Zeke decided to tell them in person after all? That would mean I can't say anything for over a month, which would be excruciating. There's no way I can possibly go along with that.

Maverick sets about licking my shell necklace, so I put him gently on the sand, and try not to seem rattled.

'You're looking well,' Dave says, filling the gap in conversation. 'Bet you feel on Cloud Nine after the New Smyrna competition. Bloody well done.'

'We're so happy for you,' Sephy says. 'Your mom must be so proud.'

'Thanks. Yeah, I think she is.'

'Come over for dinner one night. The aunts are in town for the next few weeks. They're helping out with the wedding prep, so you'll be seeing a lot of them.'

'The aunts?'

'Dave's aunts. Nanna's sisters. They're touring Cornwall in their trailer.'

I can't remember Nanna ever talking about her sisters, but if they're anything like her, I know they'll be awesome.

'Sounds great,' I say.

'Dress-wise, you and Kelly don't need to match, honey. I don't care what colour or style you choose, so long as you're happy. Zeke, Wes and Elijah are gonna read during the ceremony and Garrett is the best man.'

Will Sephy even want me to be her bridesmaid once she knows I've split up with Zeke? She doesn't seem like the type to take back an invitation, but if she thinks it's going to be too upsetting for everyone, maybe she will.

From my perspective, yeah, it'll be awkward as hell to stand with Zeke and his whole family through that ceremony, but sitting it out at home will be infinitely worse. They're my ex's folks but they still mean the world to me and I don't want to be excluded.

'Cool. Yeah. I really have to get going. I haven't even unpacked yet. Can you tell Kelly and Garrett I've gone home?'

'Sure you're OK, honey? You look kinda pale.'

'I'm fine. Honestly. See ya.'

She embraces me again, and so does Dave.

'Come over and see us,' she says, firmly. 'I want to catch up.'

73

chapter twelve

I take the long way home and walk down a wide street of bungalows and am confronted by a young girl with a knife in her hand.

'Whoa,' I say, to myself more than her.

She's hacking at a cherry tree so laden with blossoms that her hair is dotted with pink petals.

'Hey,' I shout, and she turns to look at me. I can see rage in her eyes. She can't be more than eight or nine.

She holds up the knife to me – it's a battery-operated carving knife, the kind my mum uses to cut the turkey at Christmas – and says, 'It's gone blunt.'

'What did that tree ever do to you, eh?'

'Get lost,' she says, then rummages through her backpack and pulls out a chisel and hammer, with which she starts chipping out sections of bark.

'Where's your mum and dad?'

'Don't care.'

'You'd better hope the police don't drive by and see you doing that.'

She blanks me and continues.

I hear a whistle, the sort that comes from two fingers in the mouth and a lot of practice, and spot an old lady a few bungalows away. She's sitting in a deckchair at the end of her front lawn, a pair of reading glasses on her head, and another pair hanging around her neck. I walk towards her. At her feet is a flask of tea and a china teacup, and spread on her lap is a pristine copy of the *Newquay Voice*.

In the house opposite, an old man is pruning his privet hedge; like the woman, he also seems to be keeping an eye on the girl. The old lady motions her head for me to join her.

'Been swimming, have you, dear?' she says, and nods at my wet hair. In her voice there is the hint of a Welsh accent mixed in with Cornish.

'Surfing,' I say, feeling awkward.

'Lovely hobby to have.'

'It's kind of my job.'

'Surfing's work these days, is it?' she asks, the corners of her mouth twitching. 'You're having me on.'

'I'm sponsored to surf, so yeah.'

'Enough to pay your bills?'

'Some.'

'Oh, very nice.'

'What's going on there?' I nod towards the girl.

75

'Maid's been breaking her heart for an hour. Won't listen to reason.'

'Why, what's happened?'

'Well, it was her brother, you see. Her whole life she thought she was an only child. Three months ago she finds out she has a half-brother. Now this.'

I obviously look confused because she continues. 'The young lad who hanged himself last night. Word was he came out of the pub at half past nine, carved some letters in the bark of the first tree he saw – that tree right there – and belted himself up. Mr Marten found him – still warm, he was, poor lad – but nothing could be done. Too late, see.'

While I was standing in my garden last night, feeling sorry for myself and summoning the nerve to go inside my own house, this boy – whoever he was – decided to kill himself.

'God, that's horrible. No wonder she's upset.'

'Eighteen. No age at all, is it? Makes you wonder what was going through his head. Permanent solution to a temporary problem is what my father always said, and Lord knows he dragged a cross or two. Best to ride it out and wait for better times.'

'Maybe he was drunk?' I say, as the girl continues wood-peckering the tree with her hammer and chisel.

'Two pints of lager in him, they say. Says his goodbyes to his friends at the pub, like it was any other night. Nobody had a clue. Apparently he'd broken up with his girlfriend and couldn't stand the thought of living without her.'

I think of Zeke. Of what he said to Lily. *I'll love Iris until I take my last breath.* I think of how emotional he could be.

The old woman is staring at me, waiting for a reply to a statement I haven't heard. She shakes her head, perhaps sensing that all is not roses and light with me either.

'You young people and your passions. It all fades with time, that's the truth of it.'

'Shouldn't we stop her?'

'We've tried, of course we have, but she won't have it. I feel for the tree, mind, but I suppose she thinks if the tree weren't there, he couldn't have done what he did.'

'Her parents must know she's missing?'

'Oh, yes, and worried out of their minds, I expect. She won't tell us the number and who knows where it'll end if we call the police? Social Services could come poking their noses in, and that can be a curse as much as a blessing. We're keeping an eye on her and hoping they'll work out where she is. Bound to, sooner or later.'

'What was her brother called?' I ask, wondering if I knew him.

'Darren. Or it might have been Darryl, come to think of it. Came outside when we saw the flashing lights and he looked like such a handsome young man. Dark hair. Nice face. Dreadful to see him like that. Awful waste of life.'

77

'Not Daniel Penhaligon?' I ask this automatically, a reflex born of years of worry. Every time a boy of his age flipped a car, got arrested for fighting or was taken by the sea, my brain would flash an alert. *Daniel?*

'What was it now . . . She did say . . . Might've been a Daniel. I don't recall the surname, though I think it were a long name like that.'

No, it couldn't be. This is just paranoia. My anxious brain taunting me. First I'd worried that Zeke would do something stupid, now I'm worrying that Daniel has. As if my mere existence will automatically bring calamity down on the heads of those I love.

'I've gotta go,' I say. 'Thanks for looking out for the kid.'

I take one of my business cards out of my wallet. 'My number's on there if you want me to come back and talk to her.'

'Thank you, dear,' she says, taking the card. 'I'm sure the storm will pass soon.'

I walk on and give myself a mental whipping for having jumped to the worst possible conclusion even though it doesn't even make an ounce of sense. Daniel would never hang himself. Not after what his dad did. He'd never leave his mum to deal with that pain.

Eventually, I'm back in my street.

I have my key in my hand, but the thought of the ice cream man stops me. If my mum's taken a sickie on account

78

of my big return, Mick might've stopped by.

I ring the bell and wait.

Then I ring it again.

Eventually, I open up and go into a silent house, for the second time since I've been home. I walk through into the kitchen, where no **WELCOME HOME, IRIS** banner is hanging under the herb clock, and none of my family jumps out with an orchestrated 'Surprise!'

The cat from last night steps out of the kitchen litter tray and kicks a flurry of grit across the linoleum. He begins aggressively crying for food, so I top up his bowl from a box of some dark green organic kibble.

'Mum?' I shout, walking upstairs. The bathroom door's open and the light's off.

I don't want to stick my head into her bedroom, just in case disturbing things are afoot, so I shout again, right outside the door. When there's no reply, I go downstairs, sit at the kitchen table and wait.

It occurs to me then that if something terrible *has* happened to Daniel, maybe she's with his mum. But that's crazy, because if that were the case, I'd have been the first person they told.

Wouldn't I? Or would they have wanted to tell me in person?

I decide to ring my mum, but when I look for my phone it's not in any of my pockets or my bag.

It's probably been stolen straight from the beach, and I

kick myself for leaving my bag there unattended. It's normally OK to leave things on the beach early in the morning, especially before peak tourist season, but there's always the risk that some chancer will swipe them.

At least my phone has a passcode on it, I think, relieved that some thieving scumbag won't be able to snoop. And if it's gone, I won't be able to obsess over it any more. Won't be able to watch it *not* ringing.

The landline handset is not in the cradle, and I can't see it on any of the surfaces so I give up. I look in the fridge, pull out a block of cheese and some spinach and open a tin of pineapple and make up a bowl of layered salad, *Hawaii-style*, my nan would have called it, and I feel a pang of sadness.

I leave it cling-filmed on the worktop and raid the cupboard for crisps and biscuits, and then go through to the living room and turn on the TV. After two hours of this inactivity, I hear a definite buzzing and find my iPhone in my sunglasses case, where I forgot I'd stashed it to keep the sand off.

It's a text from Kelly.

Sending you so much love. You'll be OK, Iris. Stay strong.

Thanks. I'm all right. Just don't really want to talk about it.

OK, I get it. Sorry I was hyper today. Stoked to have you back. Hope lunch goes well with your mum. Say hi from me.

She's not even here. Probably off having a 99 with her new boyfriend.

What time did she say to meet her?

She didn't. But she normally has lunch around now.

Delayed at the school I bet. Wait a bit longer and she'll show.

If she was that bothered about seeing me, she could've phoned in sick. Did you hear about some guy that hung himself from a tree in town?

No, I've only just got out of lessons. How awful. What happened?

Don't know. About to look online, but I don't reckon they'll say his name until all his family's been informed.

I wait for Kelly to send another message, but my phone is stubbornly silent. I load up the *Cornish Guardian* online edition, but they don't have anything about the story yet. Kelly's probably on her way to another one of her A-level classes. She won't have time to sit around texting me all day.

Eventually, the silence and the waiting is too much for me. I unhook my old Roxy bomber jacket from the hat-stand and walk the coastal path down to the Gazzle, and across to the Cribbar.

I'm colder than I've been in six months as I stand on the cliff, stare at that familiar horizon and remember what happened at the end of last summer.

Huge waves had broken over the reef as I swam through sucking currents. I can so clearly recall my panic, looking for him, until his surfboard bobbed up in front of me.

Like a miracle. Except he wasn't with it.

I grabbed the board's leg-rope, followed it hand over hand, down into the depths, until my fist closed around his hair.

But, even though I was there, even though I knew what that experience had done to me, I'd completely missed what it had done to him.

Missed it for half a year. In the end, as our relationship was flaming out, he'd had to *tell* me he thought he had post-traumatic stress disorder.

I check my phone again. Nothing from my mum. Nothing from Kelly. Nothing from Zeke.

I feel a cold rush of hopelessness and I walk closer to the cliff. My toes are over the edge and I can feel myself sway as vertigo sets in, the backs of my legs tight with the effort of holding me still.

I hadn't expected to fall apart. I thought I could hold out a week or two before it really hit me, but there is already a pain on the left side of my chest, a burning across my forehead, and my brain keeps flooding with images of him.

I miss waking up in the night, hearing him talking gibberish in his sleep. I miss the heat that comes off his body. I miss being held in strong arms, even though it makes me feel pathetic to admit it. He is every other thought, and I feel helpless and full of shame that I allowed this boy to become everything to me. I loved him incautiously, and set myself up for this pain.

Out of the corner of my eye I see a fisherman coming across the rocks, staring up at me.

He's different – spikier hair, thinner build – but I know straight away who it is. He raises his hand as he recognizes me.

Daniel.

chapter thirteen

My ex-boyfriend picks his way over the rocks and clambers up the cliff to me. He's weighed down by a ballast of three rods, a bucket of dead fish and a tub of worms.

'You're back then,' he says, with scintillating insight, when he reaches me.

I nod and steel myself for the digs, which I know are inevitable. He's wearing a short-sleeved T-shirt, despite the cold, and I see immediately that he's got rid of the tattoo on his forearm, the one that said, 'If it ain't got boobs, fins or sparkplugs, I ain't interested.' He's had the writing covered over with a heavy design of caged demons and razor wire. I wonder if the other one on his lower back has been altered, or if it still says 'Eddie Would Go' – a reference to legendary Hawaiian waterman Eddie Aikau.

'Yeah. Feels like years since I was home,' I say, which is both true because it does and not true because it feels as if I never left.

He nods. The silence is too heavy and I break it with,

'Missed it more than I thought I would. I guess you sorta don't appreciate your home town until you leave it.'

He puts down his stuff and gives me a gentle hug, in which our chests don't touch. I am hanging back and so is he.

'How long you here for?'

'I have a contest in Mexico in a few weeks. Might go early.'

'I bumped into your sister back along. She said you was winning at life.'

Lily and Daniel have always got on fairly well, which is surprising for everyone. Neither of them can stand fakers, which maybe explains their mutual tolerance.

'I wouldn't go that far. Lily was supposed to be coming to Newquay, but she bailed at Exeter.'

'Can't say I blame her.' He shrugs. 'You didn't sound very happy to be in Florida.'

Because, of course, I'd phoned him from Miami one night when everything was going wrong with Zeke. A mistake, in hindsight.

'Sorry. I was having a rubbish night.'

'You all right now?'

I nod, although there is very little that can be defined as 'all right' in any of this.

He looks awkward, standing there with his fishing gear, which reeks so much it's making my eyes water.

'I'm fine,' I say. 'How about you?'

'Can't complain. Caught half a dozen mackerel and cooked one up for breakfast. Loads of driftwood about. Had the fire going all night.'

Daniel always loved going on mini-expeditions, where he'd take off for a day or two and pack nothing except bottled water, a blanket and his fishing gear. He saw it as a test of himself, and he wouldn't eat at all unless he caught and killed something with his own hands. I'd always put this down to his fanboying over Bear Grylls and Ray Mears, but judging by the look of pride in his eyes, maybe there was more to it.

'Nightfishing? Really, Daniel? The charts were mental. You could've been washed off the rocks by a freak wave and drowned.'

'Nah, no way am I gonna drown. I reckon I'll die of a sex heart attack when I'm a hundred and ten. Anyway, rough sea kept the bloody seals away.'

This sort of lunacy is pure Daniel: risking his life just so he can catch a few extra fish.

'Didn't really expect you to ever come back here, to be honest,' he says.

'This is my home town, Daniel. That's never gonna change.'

'Well, *you* have.'

'What's that supposed to mean?'

'Nothing. Your, uh, hair's different.'

I haven't had it trimmed in over a year and it's wild;

a bleached-out mess of frizz and saltwater damage, not helped by the fact that I've totally given up on shampoo and conditioner in order to halve my shower time.

'Yeah, it needs sorting,' I say. 'Good to see you. I'd better get home.'

'I'll walk with you.'

'I can find my own house, Daniel.'

'I'm going near there anyway.'

We turn and walk across the Little Fistral car park and towards Headland Road, neither of us saying a thing. As we follow the pavement, my gaze flicks up to Zeke's apartment.

A sign is in the window.

Newquay Property Centre.

Daniel sees me notice it. 'Take it he's moving.'

'Looks like it,' I say, my heart sinking.

He's selling his place here? He hasn't even told his family about us splitting up yet and he's already been on the phone to an estate agent, cutting his ties?

'Where's his brother gonna live now?'

'I don't know.'

'Probably get a place with Kelly. Two of them's always together.'

I doubt Kelly will be up for paying serious rent when she could live in her mum's house for free, but then people in love can be reckless in all kinds of weird ways. I should know.

We keep on walking and I find myself hoping no one spots us together.

'Why you upset? Didn't you know he'd put it on the market?'

'It's not like I'm his business advisor. The apartment was mostly an investment.'

But Zeke could have made that investment anywhere. He'd chosen to put down roots in Newquay, and now he was digging them up, chucking them on the bonfire.

'Where is he, by the way? The Yank.'

The Yank. Every time. He can't just show Zeke a tiny bit of respect by using his actual name.

'Why do you always have to be such a complete arse?'

'Calm down. I was only asking where the bloke was.'

'Well, don't, all right?'

He looks down at the pavement and I try to get my breathing under control. When I look up, I see him standing there like an idiot, staring at my legs.

'How was the tour?'

'Fine.'

'Must've been good to paddle out in piss-warm water.'

Daniel has such a way with words. I'm not sure how to reply, so go with a nod.

'I saw your heats in Florida.'

'You watched the webcast?'

'Kelly Slater put a link on Facebook so that you could get text alerts when your favourite surfers were up. You were styling. Thought the skinhead girl had you for a minute, but you was surfing like Steph Gilmore. Best buzzer beater wave I ever seen.'

I'd won on the last wave of the heat, snatching victory from Beth in the last few seconds before the buzzer sounded. I hadn't even let myself appreciate what happened there. I'd surfed like a maniac, focused one hundred per cent on each wave.

'What about you though, Daniel?'

'Bit of fishing on my uncle's boat, bit of lifeguarding down Fistral.'

'Sweet.'

He nods. 'Yeah. Though most of the time I just boil a kettle and hand out buckets of hot water to tourists who step on weever fish. One little kid was double-weevered the other day. Both feet. Brutal.'

'You get to drive the jet ski?'

'Yeah, but it's not exactly in the same league as you, with your fancy, you know . . .'

He doesn't finish the sentence. What was he going to say? Surfboards? Boyfriend? Life?

He coughs, changes the subject. 'Bought a carveboard. Thing cost more than my last surfboard. Spent all my savings.'

I've been wanting a carveboard for ages; the ride is supposed to be much closer to surfing than that of a standard skateboard, but I haven't much fancied dragging a carveboard *and* my surfboards around the world. My back aches enough as it is.

'Wow, jealous. I've literally only been to two skate parks this whole year. I'm jonesing for it.'

'Wooden Waves has been refurbed. It's pretty good now. We could go, if you want?'

'Sounds cool,' I say, before thinking through what I'm actually agreeing to.

'You really up for it?'

'Maybe . . . yeah, why not?'

There are so many reasons why not, but I don't allow myself to dwell on them. My head is hot again but I don't know if that's the effect of the virus, or Daniel – who my mum views as another kind of infection.

'When you free? Tomorrow?'

'Maybe in a few days,' I say, then change the subject myself. 'Dan, I heard about a lad who killed himself in Newquay last night. Do you know who it was?'

'Yeah, Cass texted me this morning. Darryl Trevaskis. I only knew him from the Red Lion. He moved here a few months back to be closer to his family. His girlfriend in St Austell dumped him. They was engaged and everything. She got knocked up by his best mate.'

'I can't believe he did that over a break-up. I spoke to some old lady in the street where it happened and she seemed really sad. She went out and saw his body.'

'At least my dad had the courtesy to top himself in

his own home,' Daniel says, with a grim smile, 'and not freak out the neighbours.'

Daniel was there when his mum found the body. His father choosing to kill himself in his own home, and not 'freak out the neighbours' had traumatized Daniel for life.

I look at him, unsure how to reply. 'I should get going.'

'All right.' He doesn't move.

'Bye then,' I say, feeling torn.

Suddenly, he leans forward and kisses me on the cheek.

'Bye,' he says.

Daniel is different. The last time I saw him he was aggro, stocky and cocky, but he isn't that way any more. His voice is quieter. He's lost some weight and a ton of swagger. He's tanned, even though it's so early in the season, and he's starting to get faint lines on his forehead from so much time spent outside in the sun. He holds himself differently. Seems stiller. Calmer. An adult.

I already know I've done the wrong thing in agreeing to meet up with him again. The moment I said yes, his face lit up like I'd just handed him a solid gold board signed by Slater. I don't want to disappoint him, but I sense it already. The threat.

chapter fourteen

Finally, my mum replies to my *Where are you? There's no one here!* text.

So sorry. It's been terrible. A boy died and a lot of his friends are in the Sixth Form. Absolutely dreadful. I couldn't get away for lunch and my phone was flat. Just charged it in the car. I'm going to stop by Sainsbury's on the way home and I have to pick up the dry cleaning, but I'll only be an hour or so, OK?

No worries.

Love you, darling. I feel rotten about last night. I'll make it up to you, OK? Big kiss X

I officially have nothing to do and nowhere to be. I look across the beach to Fistral surf shop complex and take the plunge.

The tide's half in, but there's hardly anyone in the water and nobody at all's surfing. Hundreds of tonnes of sand have washed away, exposing the sharp black rocks of the formerly hidden reef. The Lifeguard building is completely cordoned off with metal fencing, and the base of it – once sand and poles – has been filled in with concrete.

Even the shape of the beach is different, sloping down to the water more steeply and pocked with deep ridges and pools. Two lines of shingle snake down the once golden sands and the red flags are flying on account of a mighty rip and some huge close-out sets.

It looks ugly as hell.

I cut down past the Headland Hotel, follow the boardwalk of the surf shop complex, and stop to hang off the railings to check out the downstairs beach bar area, where some people are watching a giant screen suspended from the building.

The beach-facing door of the Animal store is propped open and I see my friend Caleb staring through the massive window at the sea, probably lost in some far-off tropical realm where the surf's pumping, the line-up's empty and the beach is free of red flags.

'Hey, man,' I say, going into the store, like it's just a normal day in a normal week and not my homecoming.

His eyes turn to saucers and he launches himself at me, a big smile of welcome plastered on his face.

'Iris, no way!'

'Where's all the sand?'

'Mid-Atlantic.'

'It doesn't even look like Fistral.'

'I know. Storms went on for about three months

straight. It was utter shite. So,' he says, mirroring my casual attitude, 'I hear you do airs now.'

I smile. 'Can't always land 'em. But I do stick the occasional aerial, yep.'

'Reckon you could teach me? If you have time, like?'

'Sure.'

'Oh, and what did Zeke say when you told him he has to beef up them skinny legs of his?'

It takes me a moment to remember what he's talking about, and then I shake my head. I have the feeling Caleb has been waiting six months to ask me this.

'No, I didn't actually pass on that message from you, Caleb.'

'The lad's gotta do squats, Iris. There's no other way round it. Tell him, and do the man a favour.'

'He doesn't need any tips from the likes of me.'

'Maybe he does, though. You're surfing like a ninja.'

I laugh and try to shake Caleb's hand, which he allows for about two seconds before he says, 'Nah man, screw that,' and gives me a massive hug.

'So where's Zekers? Downstairs enjoying a vegan cola?'

Before we'd left Newquay, Caleb and Zeke had hung out a bit, bonding over their shared love of Sea Shepherd, beach cleans and vegetarian cuisine.

I shake my head again.

'Ignored all the red flags and gone shreddin'?'

'He's not here. He's back in Hawaii for a bit.'

94

'Lucky git. Whereabouts in Hawaii? Actually, don't tell me, it'll only annoy me. So, what's new with you?'

There's a lot that's new with me, I think, like the fact that I'm now dead inside.

'This,' I say, taking off my old blue plastic Roxy watch and showing him the skin underneath.

Caleb claps his hand over his mouth in fake shock. 'Of all the tats you could have got, you went for that?'

'Yep.'

'Only you would spend your whole life here and then get that the minute you start travelling the world.'

I grin. 'It just felt right.'

'Your mum seen it yet?'

'Christ, no.'

'Least you can hide it with your watch. So, you, um, been upstairs?'

'Not yet,' I say, deciding to pop up to my old workplace next. 'I can't wait to catch up with Billy. How's he doing these days?'

'Yeah, about that . . .'

My stomach clenches. Has something happened to my old boss? He had two little kids.

'What's wrong?'

'Billy's long gone, mate. Shop too. It's a pizza place now.'

My old shop closed down? The flagship Billabong store for the whole country was just gone? To make way for a *pizza parlour*?

'Kelly didn't say a thing!'

'Probably didn't want to stress you out. Not when you had important stuff going down.'

'The store was important to me,' I say.

And it was true, even if I hadn't known how important at the time. I loved hanging out there all day, surfing in my lunch hour, no pressure, looking at the waves from the window, just as Caleb had been when I came through the door.

'I can't believe it's gone! I thought that place would be there forever.'

'You can thank the global economic crash. Hard times. Not selling enough crap to tourists, so they packed in. On the plus side, the avocado pizza up there is trick.' He cracks his knuckles in evident appreciation.

My eyes flick to the shop's main entrance where I see my old maths teacher walk in. Two paces behind him, a look of shock on her face, is Cass.

chapter fifteen

My maths teacher clocks me immediately. He comes over and starts asking me questions about my experiences of competitive surfing, quoting my own contest statistics at me, telling me about the places he'll be surfing in the upcoming school holidays and asking for my opinion. I'm nodding and trying to answer his questions but my brain is busy with Cass, who's standing a few metres away, staring at a shelf of hibiscus-print canvas handbags.

He sneezes, brings a tissue to his nose and blows. 'Man-flu,' he explains, 'but I'm still going surfing in a minute.'

'Nice one, sir.'

Then he's asking me if I'll come in and speak to the kids at my old school. So much enthusiasm is radiating off him; I try to reflect it back. I smile and agree to I don't even know what, until he's touching me on the shoulder – telling me I've done so well and am a credit to the school – and then he leaves to look at a rack of half-price shirts.

I put my head down and look at my feet, which are

roughened by a thousand miles of beach walking – and wait for it. When I look up, Cass is just where I knew she'd be, right opposite me, looking at me intently.

Cass is even thinner than when I'd last seen her, if that's possible. Her collarbones jut out from her chest. Her lips are redder. Hair straighter. Her legs are like a pair of scissors in skinny grey jeans.

'You're different,' she says.

No hello. No how are you.

'Hi Cass.'

'I like your hair like that. All wild. And you've put on weight. I'm not saying you're fat, but you're bigger. Stronger.'

I blink and try not to take it personally. Cass is obsessed with weight. The summer she gained half a stone she said she couldn't rely on her own willpower any more, so she decided a stomach bug would see off the new seven pounds and a bit more too. She took a raw chicken breast from the fridge, and ate it. Two weeks and a short hospital stay later she was finally well enough to eat solid food again.

'I've gained muscle from all the training. Thanks for noticing.'

'You look good,' she says then, out of nowhere, adds, 'He talks about you, by the way.'

I shrug in an attempt to look like I've no idea who she means, which is laughable. Daniel is always the thing that stands between me and Cass.

Caleb walks past us to serve a customer, raising an eyebrow at me as he passes. Cass blanks him totally, as if he doesn't even exist.

'We got back together,' she says. 'Then we split up. But we're on again now. For good. Did you know? Course you did. Kelly would've told you.'

'She might have said something. Sorry it's been so, uh, rocky.'

'You're not sorry. Why would you be? Not after what we did to you.'

'You did me a favour, Cass. Look how much better my life is.'

'Better than mine?'

'No. I just meant better than it was before. I'm happier.'

'You sure? Because you look totally down.'

'I'm tired. I only got back here late last night. But, yeah, life is pretty rad. I've seen some cool places.'

My voice is so flat. I'm fooling no one.

'Daniel's the happiest he's ever been in his life.'

'All eighteen years of it,' I say, and she nods, the needle in my reply slipping right by her.

Cass's little sister Carina walks in, holding two brown paper shopping bags from Fat Face.

'Iris!' she says, swooping on me for a hug.

Carina is three years younger than Cass, but already a

few inches taller and several sizes bigger than her older sister. She's a nice kid and I'm glad to see her. Once upon a time it used to feel like she was a little sister to me too.

'Cass is treating me to some new gear,' Carina says, holding up the bags. 'Since it's my birthday today and all.'

'Oh, happy birthday,' I say, embarrassed that I'd forgotten.

Carina and Cass never went to school on their birthdays. Their mum was so laid-back, she even let them stay home on their dog's birthday. One of those parents who think kids spend way too much time in school and could learn more by being out in the world. Basically the exact opposite of my mum.

'Want to come back to ours for a brew and some birthday cake?' Carina asks. 'Groover'd love to see you.'

Groover is a scruffy terrier with halitosis and a severe drool problem, but I've always loved him. The last time I saw him, the muzzle of his nose looked as if it'd been dipped in white paint and he was limping along Fistral with a tennis ball in his mouth, full of arthritis, but still trucking. He probably only has another couple of years left. I think about playing football with him in their garden, sneaking him bits of pasty when Cass and Carina's mum wasn't looking, and I almost say yes.

'Sorry. I have to be somewhere.'

'Oh, that's a shame,' Carina says. 'But let's catch up

soon.' She wanders off to try on some ditsy-print dresses and I turn back to Cass.

'Bye then,' I say.

'Good luck with the surfing. I always wished I could do that, you know.'

'I thought you hated surfing.'

Carina surfs every board she can get her hands on, but Cass has never even tried surfing once.

She shrugs. 'Looks like it could be fun.'

Understatement of the year.

'So why don't you try it? You'd probably really like it.'

'The boards are so heavy. I don't have much upper body strength. Or lower body strength.'

'OK, but surfing makes you build muscle, like I said.'

'Maybe I will try it then. One day.'

But I know she won't. I can hear it in her voice. She says it the same way I tell my mum I'll one day go on an outing with Newquay's Historical Society. That's her thing, her interest. It'll never be the same for me.

'I am sorry, you know, Iris. I feel like crap for going behind your back with Daniel. I just couldn't stop myself. I know it doesn't matter to you now, but I wanted to say.'

'Why'd you think it doesn't matter to me?'

It had never stopped mattering to me, even when I wanted it to. It all mattered. Fistral. My shop. Daniel. Cass.

'With all the cool stuff going on in your life, I bet you've hardly given us a second thought.'

'It's been busy, yeah, but . . . well, anyway, I have to go see Kelly,' I lie.

'Kel hasn't spoke to me in a year. Don't think she's ever gonna forgive me.'

I look at Cass and see then that Kelly and I matter to her too. We were such close friends once. But too much has happened; it can never be the same.

'There's something else, Iris.'

I wait for her to come out with whatever she has to spill.

'We're getting married,' she says to me, watching for my reaction.

I keep my face very steady.

'Me and Daniel. He's always been the one for me. We're the same, you know?'

Yeah, messed up, I think.

'Congrats.'

She holds up her hand to me and I look at the ring. The same one he'd offered me last spring.

'Nice rock,' I say. 'I hope you're really happy together.'

'Do you?'

'Why wouldn't I, Cass?' I say. 'See you around.'

I look over to Caleb, who's watching all of this with great interest.

Cass grabs my hand and says the last thing I'd ever expect her to say.

'I read that article about you in *Surf Girl* magazine,

about all the places you've surfed, how well you've done, and you know how I felt?'

Embarrassed, I think. The pictures of me were truly terrible. Sunburned face, massive hair and a grease stain down the front of my rash vest.

'Privileged. I felt privileged to know you.'

I'm ambushed by a warm prickling of something like happiness and again I feel the temptation. If I let go of my anger, I could slip back into our friendship, as if nothing awful had ever happened.

'*Don't be stupid*,' I want to say, '*it's just me. Same as ever.*' But it's not and I don't have the words to explain the new me, who is both tougher than the girl Cass remembers, and utterly broken.

She releases my hand and I walk out of the shop. My head is burning again, so I take off my jacket and tie it around my waist.

I hear a voice behind me and see that Caleb has followed me outside. 'Meet me on Fistral tonight at seven. We'll do the beach clean and I'll fill you in on everything that's happened since you left. Oh, and there's some drinks thing afterwards.'

'Who else is gonna be there?'

'Not sure. Some of the surf schools are having a party, so probably quite a few people.'

'Daniel isn't going, is he?'

'Doubt it. Hardly seen him lately. Spending most

of his free time at the gym, by the looks of him. Right meathead now.'

'Yeah, and he's changed that shit tattoo on his arm.'

'You bumped into him already?'

'He was fishing. Couldn't avoid him.'

'Well, you were bound to run into him sooner or later. I'd better get back to work. See you later, mate.'

I pass a few people staggering up from the beach, struggling with the steepness of the incline and picking their way between the rocks strewn everywhere by the storms. One older lady is panting hard, leaning into the slope, her arms set in triangles, elbows out, fists jammed onto hips. I recognize her as Daniel's aunt. She looks at me with surprise, grimaces and turns away. To her I'll always be the stroppy little madam who broke her nephew's heart, irrespective of anything he did.

It's weird to bump into people I know. I've become so used to being anonymous. But on the other hand, at least here I won't have to explain to everyone I meet whose girlfriend I am, what I do for a living and how the heck I got together with Zeke, which will be a refreshing change.

I walk back up Headland Road and sit on the wall outside Zeke's apartment. The curtains are open and I can't see any sign of movement within.

Then I do the thing I absolutely shouldn't do. I still have my key, so I let myself in, walk up the stairs and I open the door on to a pyramid of cardboard boxes. Garrett has already begun packing.

Zeke's personal belongings are still here; I look into an open box and see the photo of me he'd paid a fortune to have professionally framed. I put it back, face-down, and touch the clothes he didn't take with him when we went away: the hand-knitted fisherman's jumper, the bobble hat, the 5mm winter wetsuits, too hot for the seas we'd be surfing.

I feel the softness of an old T-shirt he used to let me wear when I stayed over. I hold a blue and green checked jacket to my face and breathe him in.

Then, I close the cardboard box, shut off my heart and leave before Garrett appears. I walk across the beach and over to East Pentire Headland. When I get to the highest point, an ancient burial mound alive with skylarks and stonechats, I jump up on the bench as I always do and stare at the sea between the headland and the island.

The very first time I came here, I'd seen a pod of pilot whales swim by, all cool and chill. It's been five years and though I've never seen them since, I scan the water for them every time.

I turn my gaze to the south-west, straining my eyes to see past the horizon, and I'm certain that, half a world away, Zeke is looking at the ocean too.

chapter sixteen

An hour later I'm in front of my house, looking at white curtains rippling in the window of my bedroom, at sun-loungers set side by side between Torbay palm trees, where I once stretched out to look for shooting stars with Zeke.

I check my phone again, but there's nothing from him, and no report of him online. Which is definitely unusual, as people are always posting selfies with Zeke on social media. He never says no to his fans.

I scratch a spot on my cheek, which is now more of a weeping sore as I've been digging at it with my fingernail for the past five minutes. What started as a small whitehead has progressed through bleeding crater to hot red patch that feels as if it covers most of my cheek.

I touch my scalp and think briefly about doing the thing I did for a few years after my dad left, but I fight the urge. If I pull out one hair, I know how hard it'll be to stop.

Seeing Daniel and Cass was messed up. They both looked at me like I was a different person.

Once again I can't seem to bring myself to go into my own home. I can hear the noise of the kettle whistling from the kitchen. My mum's in there, waiting for me.

My mum, who'll have been thinking about everything I said last night, and who'll have so many new questions.

My key's in my hand but I ring the bell and take a step back.

The front door opens and I'm surprised to be greeted by not just my mum but my Aunt Zoe. My cousin Cara then slips between their legs and reaches me first, lifting her small arms in a plea to be carried. I pick her up and hold her tightly.

'Where you been? Why you didn't come when I wanted you?' Cara is saying, before I've got beyond '*Hey, Cara!*' No amount of beach-side Skype seems to have made her understand that I was somewhere other than Cornwall.

'Surfing,' I say. 'But I'm back now, little one.'

'I'm not little. I'm three. And I'm getting a sister! Or a brother. But I know it's a sister.'

'You're going to be the best big sister,' I say, smiling at my aunt, who looks the same as ever, despite being eleven weeks pregnant.

Cara takes an edible necklace from her pocket, the kind with pastel-coloured candy beads. She's wearing a once-identical necklace, which is now down to three sweets and wet string.

'I got a present for you,' she says, handing me the intact

jewellery, which I immediately put on and wear across my forehead, hippie-style. 'You got a present for me?'

Cara's weight is tweaking the surf-sore muscles of my back, so I put her down and look through my rucksack, still sitting in the hall from the night before. I hand her a package that I've wrapped in a certain page of a Hawaiian newspaper. On part of that wrinkled page is a small article featuring a group of surfers, one of whom is me. I wonder how long my family will take to notice.

She unwraps the gift with massive excitement. It's a new doll I picked up for her in Oahu. It's Barbie-sized, but instead of a generic blonde skinny chick, it's a figurine based on Rell Sunn, a Hawaiian surf champion.

I also have another gift for her, but I'm saving that one for when it's just her and me. I've collected a handful of sand at every beach I'd been to, sands of all different colours and grain sizes – I even have some black lava sand from a beach on the Big Island – and I've decanted them into plastic travel bottles. My aunt will probably want Cara to keep them as they are for when she's older – like a science collection – but I like the idea of her mixing it all into the sandpit in her back garden, different parts of the world between her toes. I have a feeling that when she grows up, she'll go to all of those beaches.

'You see, Zoe, the wanderer has indeed returned,' my mum says, cuddling me and sniffing my hair, no doubt wondering when I last washed it with actual hair products rather than soap or seawater.

'Not wanderer, conqueror!' Aunt Zoe says.

My mum grins and says to me, 'You're coming to the Historical Society's barbecue next week, so I can show off my famous daughter!'

As if I'm famous. I'd been competing in one small-scale surf tour, which had proved more a gimmick than a respected part of the pro-surf scene. I'm not famous anywhere outside of my own home, but I let it slide.

'I had some lucky rides.'

'You've done amazing,' Aunt Zoe says.

'The point break and reef waves have helped me smooth out my surfing but I've still got a long way to go.' The line given to me by Anders. Smooth surfing was high praise from him.

'Well, we couldn't be prouder of you. We've been watching everything online. Indonesia, France, J-Bay, Portugal, the one in California, and Florida, of course. And that magazine trip you did, in Tahiti. You know the one, what's it called again?'

'Teahupo'o.'

'Oh my God. We Googled it and this woman surfer had her face hanging off after hitting the reef there.'

'She just has a cool scar now,' I say, grinning. I know because she showed me.

'Poor woman. It was all I could do to stop your mother getting on a plane and dragging you home by your board leash. My God, Iris, you looked fearless on that wave. I don't know how you did it.'

'It was relatively small that day and I made sure I didn't look at the breaking waves on the jet-ski ride out there. Knew if I did, I'd bottle it. Waves are only half as big from the back . . .'

'And we loved that picture you sent of all the girls on your tour lined up on the side of a volcano. Nice to see how different you all look. Some of these surf photos you see, everyone all blonde and blue-eyed, really get on my nerves. It's like looking at a summer camp for Hitler Youth.'

'Zoe!' my mum shrieks. 'What a thing to say!'

'Bet you're missing Zeke,' my aunt goes on. 'Your mum said he didn't come back with you.'

I try to keep my voice level, try to keep my body language normal.

'Yeah, he couldn't . . . He's got some other stuff going on.'

Mum and Zoe nod, as if this cryptic explanation is perfectly satisfactory.

'It's a tough time for him. Some of his contracts are up for renewal soon and if he doesn't impress his sponsors, they could drop him. So he might be gone a while.'

Could I have sounded shiftier? I stare at the old Degas ballerina print on the wall and will my mum and my aunt to stop looking at me.

'Ballet dancers make great surfers,' I say, stalling.

'Strong legs, decent upper body strength, low centre of gravity. Good at aerials, *especially* good at three-sixties . . .'

'But Sephy and Dave's wedding is coming up soon? Zeke couldn't possibly miss that, could he?' my mum says.

I risk a glance at her and see that she is indeed looking at me in that sharp-eyed, suspicious way that always puts me on edge. She knows something's up. Knows it without a shadow of a doubt. It doesn't matter what I say or do from this point onwards; she's caught the scent of bullshit.

'Yeah, he'll be back for that,' I say, imagining Zeke not bothering with the reception and instead knocking back beers with his brothers in the basement bar of his stepdad's house.

'Well,' my aunt says, grinning, 'it sounds like you and Zeke have been having the time of your lives.'

I can't speak because of the hot sphere of emotion burning through my airway, so I put my head down and rummage again through my rucksack. I have an escape route; surfing always gives me that. My wetsuit is wrapped tightly in a plastic bag, which is the only way to stop it stinking out whatever form of hot transport I happen to be in. Post-surf neoprene pee stink is an unfortunate occupational hazard, especially now I've run out of wetsuit disinfectant, aptly branded by some marketing genius as *Piss Off*.

'You're not going anywhere, kiddo,' my mum says, sensing what I'm about to say and touching the top of my

111

head. 'You've had months to surf.'

'Fistral's been red-flagged all day, but the lifeguards will be gone now.'

'Iris, we didn't manage to do lunch today and now your aunt and cousin are here, especially to see you. You won't mummify if you don't suspend yourself in brine.'

'How about I just go for a really, really quick surf? Thirty minutes. An hour tops. That all right?'

'No, it's blinking well *not* all right. For the next few hours you're all ours.'

I put down my rucksack, stand up straight. My mum inspects the sore spot on my face. 'I'll get you some antiseptic cream.' Then she kisses me on the other cheek and says, 'I know this is silly, but right now I'm going to pretend you're never going to leave your mother again, OK?'

I used to do a thing with my mum where she'd hug me and I'd just sort of deign to allow it. I tolerated this expression of affection from her, but the whole time I was waiting for it to end because my embarrassment weighed heavier than her happiness.

She hugs me and, for the first time in years, I really hug her back.

chapter seventeen

A few minutes later, while my mum makes tea, my phone beeps to sound the arrival of an email.

Google alert for Zeke Francis.

I take my phone upstairs to my room, lock myself in the en-suite and take a deep breath. I click and bring up a YouTube video. Zeke is driving a car, or a truck maybe, and next to him is a cool-looking girl with dual-piercings in the dimples of her cheeks. She has Angelina eyes and blue streaks in her dark hair. She is painfully beautiful. She's holding the camera and keeps flicking between herself, Zeke and the view outside, which is all lush green tree canopy and mountain shadow in the distance.

The girl has a South African accent but I'm so busy trying to catch a glimpse of the expression on Zeke's face that I hardly hear what she's saying. The video is only short but I re-watch those eighteen seconds until I can see them with my eyes closed.

She starts with, 'So Zeke just arrived and we're already

on the way back to the airport so he can go on a top secret mission to paradise. How excited are you right now on a scale of one to ten, Ezekiel?'

'Uh, could you maybe stop calling me that?' Zeke says, with a tight smile.

'Whatever you say, babe.' She ends the video by bending down and kissing his hand on the shift stick.

If Zeke is going to paradise, he obviously isn't coming to Newquay. Maybe in the height of summer it could be described like that, but in April? No way. So why is he leaving Hawaii when he's only just arrived? The question at the forefront of my mind however, is, 'Who is the girl?'

Whoever she is, Zeke apparently has time to hang out with her, but not to return any of my calls.

My mum knocks on the door of my bathroom.

'Has the aeroplane given you the runs, dear?'

'No! I'll be down in a minute.'

'Oh good. We want to hear more about your adventures.'

Six thirty comes around and my mum is still on a massive maternal bender. Aunt Zoe takes Cara home to get her ready for bed, and my mum says, 'Why don't you get an early night?'

'I said I'd meet Caleb. There's some beach clean thing on.'

I don't tell her about the party that's supposed to be on afterwards.

'There's rain due.'

'The beach still needs cleaning.'

'Have some more casserole before you go.'

I'm hungry, but I'm also keen to escape. I gulp down my second bowl of casserole and its accompanying chewy bread with too much butter, and look at my mum expectantly. 'OK if I split now?'

It feels so bizarre to have to ask permission to go out. Doing whatever I want is something I've come to take for granted.

She sighs. 'Go on then.'

'Thanks, Mum. Why don't you ask Mick over? Watch a film or something.'

'Absolutely not. We only see each other twice a week and I'm quite happy with that. Iris?'

'Yeah?'

'I understand why Zeke didn't come here, but why didn't you go with him to Hawaii?'

I have to meet Caleb. I don't have time for this talk, even if I was ready, which I'm not.

'I haven't been home in ages,' I say. 'I'd better run, Mum, or they'll start without me.'

As I close the garden gate, my back pocket starts buzzing.

'Zeke from Hawaii' is calling me.

I let it ring at least six times. Not to play games, but because I know it's going to be an excruciating conversation and even though I've been trying to contact him, now that he's ringing me I'm not sure I'm ready to hear his voice.

'Hello?' I say, my voice high-pitched.

'Hey.'

'Are you OK?'

'Iris, I can't hear you. You have reception?'

I look at my phone and I have five bars.

'It's your phone that's playing up. Go near a window.'

I hear him breathing as he walks. 'Any better? I'm at the airport again.'

'Where are you off to?'

'Fiji. Some of the team is freesurfing Frigates Pass. Asked me along. How you doin'?'

'I'm fine.'

'You been surfing yet?'

'Tolcarne, not Fistral.'

'How's the water temperature out there?'

'Twelve degrees.'

'Ouch, that's gotta hurt in three millimetres at six a.m.'

'It's not pleasant.'

The line goes quiet and then I say it: 'I'm sorry about how we left things, Zeke. I shouldn't have done it like that.'

'It was a good call. You were right to leave. I'm sorry I gave you such a hard time. I was an asshole and I feel sick about it. We can still be friends, right, Iris? We don't have to hate each other.'

'Course.'

'Um . . . I spoke with my folks, but I didn't tell them.'

'I know. How come?'

'My mom rang me and she was so happy. They've set a date for their wedding. It's in the middle of June, so you'll have time to get back from Mexico. I just didn't want to harsh their buzz, you know?'

'Zeke, you have to tell them.'

'Let them be happy a little longer and I'll do it. That OK?'

'Fine.'

'Thanks, Iris. I appreciate that.'

'Bye then . . .'

'Bye.'

There are things I haven't said. Things I have no right to say.

Things like, *I love you*.

My love for Zeke, which burns so bright, so hot, is both the best and the worst of me.

'Zeke?'

'I'm here.'

'I wish it worked out.'

'Me too. I thought we were gonna go the distance.'

'Same.'

'We'll be OK again, but it's gonna take time. Stay safe, Iris.'

'You too.'

I end the call and I've just managed to deactivate alerts for his name, when he sends me a text message that says, *I'm glad I had that time with you. Go live your life. Move on as soon as you can. Be well and happy. Z x*

chapter eighteen

My head's a mess as I walk down to the beach. This phone call with Zeke has made it sink in. It's actually over.

I walk onto the beach and spot Caleb. He's the only one there. It's already beginning to drizzle and there are huge black clouds hanging over the horizon.

He's sitting on the damp sand, looking his usual untidy self and munching on an apple.

'Wanna bite?' he says.

I shake my head.

'Sure? It's a quality Golden Delicious. I'm working my way through as many varieties as I can. Eating five or six a day.'

'Why?'

'Angling for a job at Newquay Orchard. Second interview next week. Gonna impress them by writing 'em a report with my suggestions, based on flavour, hardiness, popularity and potential profitability.'

Typical Caleb project. Eating an insane amount of fruit

and neatly detailing his findings with graphs and pie charts. I've known him forever, as we live in the same street, and he's always got obsessed with things. He once spent a whole summer trying to develop an eco-friendly sunscreen. He'd experimented using coconut oil, shea butter, zinc oxide and various ingredients pinched from his mum's baking cupboard, which had usually resulted in third degree sunburn.

'Which ones are nicest?' I say. 'Give me your top three.'

'So far: Fuji, Honeycrisp and Jonathan.'

'There's an apple called Jonathan? That's . . . random.'

'Yeah, I'm hoping to track down a Jonamac. Jonathan crossed with a McIntosh. Supposed to be well nice.'

I look around at the deserted beach. Reading my thoughts, Caleb says, 'Weather's put everyone off. They've gone into town. Gonna do the party here tomorrow instead.'

'We can do the beach clean on our own,' I say, relieving him of two carrier bags and holding one out for his apple core.

We look out at the line-up, which is even more blown out and unsurfable now that a squall is moving in. The wind is getting stronger by the second. I wonder if tonight we'll see the tail end of the hurricane Lily mentioned.

'What it's like for tomorrow? Still bad?' I ask him as we walk down the beach together, swooping on cans, plastic bags and cardboard cartons from Fistral's takeaway joint.

'Forecast is showing four to five foot in the afternoon, with a ten-second interval and offshore winds.'

'Beautiful.'

'Hey,' Caleb says, 'you looked a million miles away then. Do you wanna talk about something? Zeke?'

'Not really. Why?'

'Well, he's your boyfriend, so there's that.'

'Caleb . . .'

He stops picking up litter and looks at me.

'Is everything OK there?'

'Yeah,' I say.

'Phew. So he's just away doing cool pro-surfer stuff?'

'Something like that.'

This conversation is agony and I want it to end. It must show on my face.

'You sure? You guys haven't split up, have you?'

'Caleb, if I tell you, you can't tell anyone else. Only Kelly knows. Promise me.'

'Wow, you *did* break up? No way!'

'It's only just happened. All right if we don't talk about it?'

'No worries.'

I can see his brain going ten to the dozen, trying to imagine how it's come to this.

Eventually, he breaks a long silence with, 'It was your

birthday last week, wasn't it? Happy birthday, gurfer.' He says the last part with a grin.

Gurfer. Girl surfer.

'Please don't use that word,' I say. 'And thanks.'

'I know it's not Miami, but sod it, let's celebrate at the party tomorrow. You only turn seventeen once.'

The rain starts coming down really hard and I put up my hood. Now I'm back in Cornwall, I will always have a hood on my jacket, because it will always rain for at least part of each day.

'I'm sort of glad it was cancelled tonight. I'm not really feeling like I want to be around people.'

'Yeah, I get that,' he says. 'But come tomorrow. It'll help. Honest.'

We finish the beach clean and sling our carrier bags full of litter into the metal skips at the back of the North Fistral car park and then head into the beach bar. I look up at the surf shop complex where the camera juts out from high on the outer wall.

I'd been so homesick on my travels that I'd logged onto this webcam again and again, using it like a drug. I'd look through its electronic eye, promising myself it would be the last time.

Maybe, I think, as I walk towards the camera, someone else is looking through it from some far-off country, wondering what it's like to stand in my shoes. Without meaning to, I lift my hand and wave, and the thought occurs to me that maybe Zeke is in the airport in Oahu, on his phone, logged into this webcam.

We walk into the beach bar and Caleb goes to buy us drinks, while I look around, at coffee tables topped with adverts for local lagers, at the wooden-boarded bar weathered to look like driftwood, at the little coffee shop tucked away by the windows, at framed photos of legendary surf stars who have visited Fistral over the years, at tired dogs who've burned their energy playing on the beach, at little kids running in demented circles between pillars and at long-haired surf-boys drinking Corona and chatting about their social anxiety.

I'm pondering a retro, heavily-glassed red shortboard suspended deck-down from the ceiling, when the four flat-screen TVs buzz into life. They're showing a big-wave contest from last year. Suddenly, one of the long-haired surf-boys points to the screen. His mates look up too, and they clink their bottles together, because local hero Zeke Francis has just ridden a bomb.

Caleb turns around, two glass Coke bottles in his hand. 'I've gotta go,' I say to him. 'You drink it.'

'Wait a minute . . .' but I don't wait. I run home.

chapter nineteen

I turn my key in the door. I've been drenched by a sudden downpour. As I stumble into my house, I am faced with my mum, who appears out of the kitchen holding a salad plate of raspberry cheesecake and a mug of tea.

'Thought it'd be cancelled,' she says. 'There's no arguing with the Cornish weather. Come and get comfy with me on the sofa.'

'No one else showed, but me and Caleb did the clean-up. I'm really tired,' I say, brushing past her.

'Everything all right, daughter?' she calls after me, as I run upstairs.

I fling myself onto my bed and try to stop the wheels turning.

Early in our relationship, Zeke gave me a gold-silk eye-pillow that he'd found in Goa. I pick it up and breathe in its scent. It's stuffed with something herbal that makes it smell nice. He said it was a yoga thing, supposed to aid meditation and relaxation. It puts a small amount of weight across the eyes and cheekbones and works like acupressure to trigger a sense of wellbeing, apparently. Zeke told me, without a hint of embarrassment, that when I took it off my face, I'd see more beauty in the world.

I turn onto my back, scrabble to find the remote to my iPod dock and press play. The song that comes on is 'Dissolve Me' by alt-J. The song that was playing as I lost my virginity, a song that is now impossible to hear without remembering. I feel my jaw tense, my teeth grind and I hold the cool eye-pillow to my face and try to soothe the ache in my forehead.

I hear a noise, take out my earbuds and move the eye-pillow. My mum is watching me from the chair by the window.

'Don't get up. Rest!' she says, settling down next to me. I make room for her but don't look her in the eye.

'Is it Zeke? Has something happened between the two of you?'

'Mum, I don't—'

'Oh, it has, hasn't it?'

I open my mouth to answer her, but can't manage it. A fierce rip-current of emotion sucks me out and I have to wait until it lets go. Finally, in calmer waters, I take a deep breath and find the words.

'It happened in Miami, although it's been on the cards for a while.'

'Zeke's staying in Hawaii permanently?'

'He just got on a plane to Fiji.'

'Goodness. Well, I don't know what to say, but I'll listen if you want to tell me what happened between the two of you.'

I take another deep breath and allow myself to remember.

My mum listens, stroking my knee. She doesn't interrupt once.

'So, yeah, it basically all went to rat shit.'

'Well, that's as may be, but no one's died, have they? This is quite normal. Almost all relationships have an end-date. Perhaps there's a better relationship waiting for you? Or perhaps you'll be happy on your own, as I was for all those years. Who knows what will happen? Think positive.'

I nod, and try to think non-doomy thoughts.

'I should have told you about this already. Sorry.'

'Oh, you tell me things in your own good time. I know that. You're a classic INFJ.'

'I-N-what?'

'Myers-Briggs,' she says. 'You know.'

I have no idea what she's on about.

'No, I definitely don't, Mum.'

'When you were little – you remember – I kept making you answer those annoying hypothetical questions. I learnt about it all on that night class. You always came out as an INFJ. It's quite a rare personality type, from what

I recall. Introverted. Intuitive. Feeling. Judging.'

'That's IIFJ.'

'Ah, yes, they use the N in Intuitive. My point, Iris, is that being sensitive and secretive is in your nature, and that's fine. Within reason.'

These words are reassuring to me, even if I consider the rest of her theory a load of rubbish. I've missed my mum so much. I hadn't realized how badly I needed her until now.

'Mum,' I say, eventually, 'I think I was maybe too young to try and live with Zeke.'

'I'm quite certain of it but, stubborn soul you are, I knew you needed to come to that conclusion on your own. If I were you, I'd either take some months off boys, or try to date a few normal ones from now on. Give the surf gods a wide berth. Keep things simple.'

My mum waits for me to reply. One minute passes, then two, and then it becomes clear to both of us that I've said all I'm going to say, and we lie looking up at fake stars on my ceiling in tight silence.

Eventually, I say, 'Are you disappointed in me?'

'Absolutely not! Why would you say such a thing? You've done brilliantly, in very difficult circumstances. I'm incredibly proud of you.'

'Well, thanks for being so nice.'

'I'm your *mother*. There isn't a person on this planet who loves you more than me, whatever you may believe.'

She holds my hand and bows her head towards mine so our foreheads touch. I get a whiff of her cucumber night cream and it makes me tingle with a kind of nostalgia.

'You mustn't beat yourself up. No one expects you to have everything settled at your age. It might sometimes seem as if you insist on making the same mistakes, but eventually you'll remember where the exposed manholes lie and learn to step around them.'

'Seriously, Mum, why are you talking to me about "exposed manholes"? What is Mick even into?'

She begins to laugh, her body shaking with giggles, and I see my mother, the strict teacher and respected member of the Historical Society, but I also catch a fleeting glimpse of a happy-go-lucky girl. She deserves happiness, and if Mick gives her that, then who am I to argue?

'Come on,' she says. 'Let's go downstairs and watch *EastEnders*.'

I give in and follow her. She puts on the telly and gets another slice of cheesecake, which we share. When we've finished, she puts the empty plate on the floor, I lean on her and pull the turquoise fleece blanket over us to get warm.

'I'm so relieved and happy to have you home,' she says. 'I missed you terribly. There were days I didn't even want to get out of bed and face the world.'

'Seriously?' I say, surprised. 'You never let it show in our Skype calls.'

'Of course I didn't. I wanted you to live your dream

without having to worry about your mother's feelings.'

'Um, on that note, I should probably show you this,' I say, unstrapping my watch and showing her the TR7 tattoo underneath.

She purses her lips and frowns. 'I always knew you'd get tattoos, but I hoped you'd choose something creative.'

'I picked a fancy font.'

She rolls her eyes. 'That would have come in handy when you were little. You were always wandering off and getting lost.'

I'm still lost, I think, and coming home hasn't changed that.

'You were so painfully shy, you'd never speak to the people who found you. Not even to tell them your name and address. Nobody had any idea where you'd come from.'

'Well, they'll know now.'

She squeezes my hand. 'Right, you really should get to bed. You look shattered.'

Yeah, I think, *I am.*

chapter twenty

The night passes with a window-rattling storm, but the clouds break first thing and it's blue skies all day. By evening the beach fire is piled high with pristine planks that I strongly suspect have come from the supplies of a nearby building site; the site's metal fencing has blown flat, thus allowing entry to unscrupulous surfrats with a burning desire for top quality pine.

Kelly is working an evening shift at Hendra holiday park and I don't know anyone else here, except Cass's sister Carina, who gives me a cheery wave and then spends the rest of the time deep in talk with a boy I don't recognize, so I stick with Caleb. We're on our backs, following paper fireflies with our eyes until the sparks grow dim and black and flutter to the ground.

Caleb, usually a scruffy beach bum with bleached-and-fraying everything and jeans that hang three inches lower than his boxers, has put on knee-length chino shorts with a white and black polka-dot shirt. He's swept up his hair with products, had a shave, and I have to admit is looking pretty sharp. But also like he's on his way to star in a movie about Wall Street wannabes summering in the Hamptons.

I, on the other hand, am sporting lip balm, wild hair, and jeans so ripped you can see more skin than denim. My jacket smells musty and needs a wash, my checked shirt is faded and I'm wearing nothing beneath it except a triangle bikini top.

When the others leave and try to hit the clubs in town, the fire burns low and Caleb goes to sit on one of the beach's new sandbanks, to look out at the water. I stretch, think it over for a minute, and go to join him.

We've spent all evening talking to each other and I realize how much I've missed him. In the last few years, tangled up in romantic relationships with other people, we've grown apart, but Caleb's cool and uncomplicated, and spending time with him is exactly what I need.

He doesn't acknowledge me as I settle down beside him and I can see he's conflicted. His hand moves closer to mine and I feel our little fingers touch. More than just a casual, inadvertent touch. This feels deliberate.

We keep talking as if it's nothing, as if we aren't both acutely aware of our hands touching, of the thrill of this minimal connection, and eventually he moves his hand on top of mine, and I turn my palm upwards, so our fingers slot together. It's friendship, camaraderie;

nothing more, I tell myself.

'I'm so glad you're home,' he says. 'Wish you never left.'

I narrow my eyes at him. 'You told me to go!'

'Well, yeah, it was an amazing opportunity. But course I wished you'd stayed in Newquay. I used to check out the local webcams at your fancy foreign training breaks, to see if I could spot you.'

'No way! I used to load up North Fistral's webcam on my phone all the time. One night I was in Miami and I thought I saw you walking down to the sea. Whoever it was had a yellow longboard just like yours.'

'What, really? That's mad!'

'Yes, and it was at one of the worst moments of my whole time away. I was totally alone and I wanted to be back here so much. I was dreaming of, like, swimming home.'

'Where was Zeke?'

'I walked out on him after he'd been kissing some random in a bar.'

'Zeke kissed someone else?'

'Yeah – it wasn't great.'

'Girl?'

'Yes, Caleb.'

'Just checking. He's always sort of set off my bi-dar. And he does have impeccable hair.'

'Used to. It's about a centimetre long now.'

132

'How come he was kissing some other bird?'

'For a photo, apparently.'

'So you ditched him?'

'Yeah, walked to South Beach.'

'Check you out. Hardcore.'

'For about five minutes until the panic set in.'

I lean into him and rest my head on his shoulder. I feel his body tense up, and I withdraw, look up at his face.

He closes his eyes and says with a grimace, 'Look, I was never gonna go here, but what the hell. Don't you know?'

'Know what?'

'I had a crush on you for, like, years.'

'Seriously?' I hadn't known. Caleb was just a mate. Until today, he's never shown any sign he's interested in me, nor has he shown any sign of jealousy towards either Daniel or Zeke. Maybe he hadn't been Daniel's greatest fan, but who was? Most people thought Daniel was a complete waste of space on a good day.

'You were always so nice to Zeke.'

'I could see he was a good guy. He does loads for animal rights and eco charities. He's also sort of famous – how could I compete with that?'

As shocked as I am, I'm also pretty flattered, and I can't hide a smile. Caleb is honest. Decent. Loyal. Kind. He's been there for me whenever I needed him. Always.

'Well, uh, thanks for letting me know.'

'Don't worry, we never have to mention it again,' he says. 'But I wanted to tell you.'

We kick sand over the remains of the fire and do a two-minute beach clean, which is Caleb's new thing for when he can't commit to a full hour.

'Do you want to go into town with the others?' he asks me.

I shake my head, so he walks me home and we reminisce until we're laughing so hard that I have to sit on a wall to catch my breath. I don't care about the non-tropical weather, don't care about missing a night on the town, don't care about anything except spending time with someone I've known forever.

We walk back to our street, and I can sense him trying not to ask about Zeke, or say anything that might remind me of him. So he tells me Newquay stories instead, filling me in on everything I've missed, from the guy on his stag-night who arrived off the train wielding a samurai sword and who was promptly rugby-tackled by the Newquay Male Voice Choir, to the leatherback turtles that washed up at Porth Beach alive enough to be rescued by the Blue Reef Aquarium, and the World War Two bomb that some kid dug up on Towan Beach. He retrieves another apple from his backpack, a Red Delicious this time, which I consent to share.

When we get to my door, he says, 'See you tomorrow,' and he gives me a warm hug. God, I've missed Caleb and his hugs.

'Can I come to your house?' I say, suddenly not wanting to leave him.

He looks surprised. 'Course you can.'

chapter twenty-one

Sitting in Caleb's room, opposite a fruit bowl on his desk which is piled high with yet more apples, I wonder how all that fruit doesn't give him severe gut rot, and then I remember something he showed me the summer before I went away.

'You still have that dodgy-looking mole on your stomach?'

He pulls up his T-shirt so I can see a small scar. I try not to notice a new line of hair snaking upwards to his belly button.

'Had it removed. It was getting bigger and the doc was worried it had a weird shape. Thought it might be skin cancer.'

'But it wasn't?'

'They sent it away and I didn't hear anything so it must've been all right. He said I'm supposed to count my moles from now on and keep track of their size, but I can't be arsed.'

'Caleb! You should do it.'

'Can hardly do the ones on my back, can I?'

'I'll help you,' I say, picking up a pen from the pot on his super-tidy desk.

'Really?'

'Yeah. Get your shirt off, mate.'

'Funny.'

'I mean it. I'm gonna ring them all in Biro, number them and take pictures of any that have ragged edges or different colours in them.'

'I'll get me mother to do it, if you're that worried.'

'Caleb, it's fine. Shirt off.'

His fancy shirt has pearly buttons, and I watch as he undoes them and takes it off. He's the only surfer boy in Newquay I know who doesn't have a single tattoo. Doesn't like the idea of foreign chemicals in his skin or something. He can be a proper hippie about stuff. *Your body is your temple, maaan, so keep it pristine*, and all that.

Caleb seems a bit awkward about getting half-naked in front of me, but I can see he's doing his best to hide his shyness.

My brain automatically compares every shirtless bloke I see to Zeke, which is a horrible habit, but one I can't seem to shake. I do the calculation and come up with the total that Caleb is shorter than Zeke, with narrower shoulders, and a softer-looking body. I like it. For one thing, I don't feel as if I'm looking at the cover of *Men's Health* magazine.

137

'Just do my top half. My legs practically never see the sun.'

He has the usual Fistral surfer's tan. Tanned face, hands and feet; untanned everything else.

'I'll do all of you,' I insist, nodding at his chino shorts.

'Haha,' he says, and I squint at him, daring him to say something pervy.

Obediently, he strips them off and I try to control my impulse to giggle as he sits there in his boxers, which look like they've been purchased by his mum from Marks and Spencer.

I bring the pen to his skin and his body does a little spasm of ticklishness. He clears his throat and murmurs, 'Caught me off guard there. Carry on.'

'You good now?' I ask, ringing and numbering my first three moles, and he gives me the green light to continue. I work my way around his back and every now and then he flinches as I touch a sensitive spot, but he doesn't complain.

Caleb's iPod dock is broken, so we sit together on the bed, listening to his iPhone's speaker doing its best with a Bon Iver playlist. The speaker is whacked up to full volume, but the blackbird outside the window is outdoing it.

At mole number 19, I move around and sit crossed-legged in front of him. His chin is resting on his knees and as I reach for his collarbone with the pen, he meets my gaze.

'Sorry about Zeke,' he says. 'It's all right if you want to talk about him.'

'I sort of don't.'

'Fair enough. Can we have a break, though? My foot is cramping up. Need to stretch it out,' he says.

'No problem. OK if I go grab some water?'

'Course. Get whatever you want.'

'You want a glass too?'

'Yeah, that'd be great, thanks, Iris.'

I walk into the kitchen, which is empty of obvious life forms, excepting potted herbs, and I think about the fact that I've known Caleb since we were both bumps.

Our mums had gone to the same antenatal classes and I have a mental photo album of Caleb stretching back at least fifteen years. When it was hot, our mums stuck us in the paddling pool together, naked and cracking up. We'd posed together on our first day of school, uncomfortable in new uniforms and shiny shoes. We'd gone to our Year 8 disco together, proud of the matching Vans we'd bought for the occasion. We'd danced together at our Year 11 prom, while Daniel was too hammered to do anything except lean against a wall and glare at me. We'd slipped out of each other's lives without even really noticing.

I get a few ice cubes from the freezer, slice a lemon and add some sprigs of a herb I can't identify but smells nice, to jazz it up a bit.

When I get back to Caleb's bedroom, his curtains are drawn, his shorts are back on, and he's stretched out on the bed, forearms stacked over his eyes.

He doesn't say anything, but I know he's fully aware I'm back in the room. I set down the glasses on the side, open the curtains a crack and look out for a moment at the lit-up street, dotted with night joggers.

I see Rae, a hippy dippy founding member of the local Zeke Francis fan club, walking with a boy I don't recognize, and wave, but she doesn't see me.

After another minute of silence, I perch next to Caleb on the bed, and for a second I think he has in fact fallen asleep.

Eventually, I sprawl out beside him, my body twelve inches from his. His breathing is shallow, and I know he's awake, because when I cough, he purposely moves his arm so that it's closer to mine.

He's awake and he is waiting for me to do something.

I think about exactly what I'm going to do, then I hook my fingers in the empty belt-loops of his shorts, and pull him towards me.

We kiss for ages, and when I pull back, he asks, 'Is this too weird? Do you wanna stop?'

'No, but, uh, I'm on. I have this implant thing in my arm and it gives me monster periods that go on for more than a week.'

140

'Why are you telling me about your period?'

'Why do you think? Because there is currently blood coming out of me.'

'Okaaay . . .'

'And that might be a problem?'

'Do you have cramps or something?'

Caleb can be incredibly dense at times. Certain things go straight over his head, but the implications of me surfing a crimson tide I thought even he might grasp.

He's looking at me expectantly, waiting for me to provide him answers that I'm pretty sure I've already given.

'I thought you might want to . . . uhh . . .' I say.

'You joking?'

'Or, y'know, *not*.' I'm starting to really wish I hadn't started this conversation.

'Um, it's just blood. It's not like you have mercury stashed up there.'

He's so totally straightforward. It's like every single thought he has comes straight out of his mouth. He'd been like that as a kid, but I thought he might have reined it in a bit now, especially with a girl. Apparently I was wrong.

'Is it uncomfortable for you to, um, do that, when you're bleeding?'

I don't have much experience of it, is the truth, except on one occasion a few days ago in Miami, which was more accident than design. It hadn't hurt, but it did make everything feel more slippery and it hadn't been brilliant

141

for the hotel sheets.

'It's fine,' I say, sliding my fingernail into a flaky patch of skin on my arm, not able to meet his eye. 'I was just worried you wouldn't be OK with it.'

'Course I am. If it doesn't hurt you, it's not gonna hurt me.'

I remember how uncomfortable Zeke had been about my periods. How he hardly mentioned it, pretended it wasn't happening.

He'd grown up with brothers, though. Caleb has three older sisters. The sight of sanitary towels and tampons was probably a daily occurrence for him. He isn't bothered by something that some other boys would have found retch-worthy. That in itself makes me want to kiss him harder. I bat away every thought of Zeke. Refuse to let myself see his face, or hear his voice, or remember the touch of him. I'm doing nothing wrong. I'm single. Caleb's single. We've known each other for years. Zeke told me to move on. I knew this would happen with someone eventually and I'm glad it's with Caleb. My body responds to him more with every passing second. Then, I let go of my thoughts altogether.

'We should do that again,' he says, grinning at me.

I turn over to him, and say, 'Not now?'

He laughs. 'No, I was thinking maybe tomorrow.'

'Oh. Yeah, maybe.'

'Hey, Iris,' he says, 'this wasn't gross for you, was it? I mean, we've been mates forever.'

'Things change.'

'What about Zeke? I know you don't want to talk about it, but now we're sort of together, so . . .'

'Caleb, we're not together. Come on.'

'Not "together" together, but, you know, sleeping together.'

I jump off the bed and lace up my bikini, without even bothering to try and cover myself up. That horse has bolted.

I look over my shoulder, but Caleb's gaze is on the ceiling, which is plastered with Sea Shepherd posters. He's not looking at me, but is trying to preserve my modesty, which is also very Caleb.

'Thanks for a nice evening,' I say. 'I mean it, Caleb. It was cool.'

'And sort of head-bending,' he says, venturing a glance at me.

I smooth my shirt over my stomach and say, 'I'll let myself out. Night, then.'

My head throbs as I walk to my house. I've slept with Caleb. And I know exactly why I did it. I was testing myself. To see if I could accept a future without Zeke in it.

It's fine, I tell myself. *This is not falling apart. This is moving on.*

chapter twenty-two

I'm still asleep when the landline rings. Looking at my phone, I see it's only just gone 7 a.m. I hear my mum walking downstairs from the bathroom, complaining about her knees, as she goes to answer it. No one ever rings this early in the morning and my hackles are up.

I hear my mum's harsh teacher decibels, *'Well, I suppose you'd best speak to her then.'*

I go out to the landing and meet my mum halfway down the stairs. She hands me the phone. My heartbeat throbs, my brain pulses in hot blood as I remember the night before, and I can't think for panicking.

'Hello,' I try to say, but the words croak out in a whisper. I clear my throat. *'Hello.'*

'Is that Iris?'

It's a girl and she has a South African accent. I get a clear visual of blue hair and cheek piercings.

'Who's this?'

'Kristin. I'm here with your boy Zeke.'

'He's not my boy.'

'Hello? Can you hear me? Speak up. The line is bad.'

'Put him on.'

'He can't talk because he spent the whole day getting loaded at the airport, cos our flight was cancelled, and now he's passed out on a couch in our hotel bar.'

'Who are you?'

'I told you. Kristin. I work for Billabong.'

'How did you get this number?'

'This is his phone; I took it from the back pocket of his pants.'

I see it clearly. Zeke, hammered and face down on a sofa. Who knows if alcohol is the only substance he's consumed?

'Can you check he's breathing?'

'Breathing? The dude's snoring. He's been talking about you for three hours straight. He's a mess. You need to call him.'

'I did. He told me to move on.'

'Hang on,' she says. I hear heeled footsteps, then a moaning sound. I almost hang up, and then there's Zeke's voice.

'Iris? You there? It's me.'

He sounds hammered.

'I can't stop thinking about what happened,' he says, 'and, man, I wish it had gone down different.'

NO, I think. *Not this. Not now.*

'Zeke, your friend Kristin called my landline and my mum's here. I have to go.'

'Sure, sure. Hey, my sponsors aren't gonna bail,' he says, voice artificially happy, like a painted-on mouth. 'Anders said I have some image rehabilitation to do, but nothing major. I still have a career.'

'That's great.'

'Iris,' my mum mouths, 'who is it? Is it Zeke?'

'I'll always care about you, baby,' he says, in that cringey drunk voice I hate.

'I have to go,' I say, and hang up.

chapter twenty-three

I'm in no fit state for civilized society, so I head for Kelly's house. When I get there, she's in the kitchen reading the paper and Garrett is making her a fry-up for breakfast.

He slides across the kitchen in socked feet and offers me a fist-bump. 'How's it going, Little Sis?'

'Don't call me that, Garrett. Cheers.'

'That good, huh? How are ya?'

'Fine. You?'

'Good, good. Trying to explain the difference between sausage, which you eat sliced on pizza, and dogs, which you eat in buns. Kelly just ain't getting it.'

'Oh, I get it,' she says. 'I get that you're completely bloody wrong.'

I look at Kelly, who makes me a cup of overly sugared tea, which I drain in seconds.

'Do you want Garrett to set aside some sausage and bacon for you?' she asks me. 'I know you've been cutting down on meat, but just in case you're peckish . . .'

I say yes even though I've hardly eaten meat since hooking up with Zeke. He never said he thought I should be a veggie, but I knew he was serious about animal rights and the health benefits of vegetarianism, so I became one too. Daniel would have said I was trying too hard. Trying to be something I wasn't. Maybe I was.

When we've finished, we go out into the morning light of Kelly's garden and I water the potted fruit bushes, while Kelly and Garrett sit together in the hammock and scroll through Tinder profiles. Kelly recently dropped the bombshell to me that she and Garrett had decided to try out a polyamorous lifestyle, but so far that had involved a lot of talk and not much else.

When I raise my eyebrows at this, Kelly says, 'I know it looks dodgy, but we swap phones. I sort the girls and he sorts the blokes.'

'Have you actually met up with anyone?'

'That'd be telling . . . Ah, sod it. No, not yet, but we're messaging a few. Well, quite a lot, really.'

'But you haven't met any of them in person?'

'No, but oh my *God*, Rae and Daniel flashed up on the first day!'

'Daniel's on Tinder?'

I shouldn't be shocked, because it's not as if Daniel is known for his dependable moral compass, but why now when Cass is wearing an engagement ring? And Tinder doesn't seem like his style at all. He's all about connecting with people in meatspace. He used to sneer at the very idea of internet dating.

'Yep, and get this: in one of the Facebook pictures he linked to, he has his arm around *Cass*. So, so shameless.'

'Aren't they engaged?'

'Why are we talking about this?' Garrett interrupts. 'I could care less about Newquay's dumbest shitbag. Hey, what about this guy? He's in good shape. Swipe right?'

Garrett shows the screen to Kelly for a second opinion. There's a burly young guy in the image, flexing a muscle.

'Uggh . . . gym selfie. Definite no-no,' Kelly says, and flashes her own screen at us. 'How about her?'

Garrett and I dutifully look at a picture of Kyla, twenty-one, who has curly hair and heavy grey eye make-up.

'Ew, no way, her kid's in the picture. Who does that?'

'What sort of thing are you looking for exactly . . . ?' I ask.

'We'll know it when we see it,' Garrett says, not sounding confident about this at all.

'He's chicken,' Kelly says. 'I keep suggesting we meet people and he's all, "let's wait and get to know them better." Totally wussing out on me. What was it you said yesterday, Garrett? "One in every hundred people is a psychopath – probably more around these parts." Bloody cheek of it!'

'It's the technology. I don't like it. This is not the way

149

I do things.'

'It's easier than just creeping on cute strangers in bars,' Kelly points out. She seems to be quite into this poly thing. More than Garrett, even, which is a surprise, as I assumed he was the one driving this.

'Always worked for me.'

'Yeah, I bet.' Kelly rolls her eyes at him and he places his hand quite casually on her left boob. I take this as my cue to leave.

Garrett scrambles off the hammock. 'Spend time with Kelly,' he says. 'I have to go see a man about a dozen kayaks.'

'Babe, do not sign anything,' Kelly says, looking completely exasperated. 'You're already skint.'

Sephy had set up trust funds for her sons, which Zeke and Wes have barely touched. Garrett, on the other hand, burned through his at an alarming rate, thanks to his tendency to invest large sums of cash in businesses that tanked within a year.

'Hey, it's not as if I'm flat broke. I have a few bucks left over. You'll see. This is the one, Kel.'

'Uh-huh.'

They kiss and Garrett leaves. The wind has come up and it's chilly, so I put down the watering can and we go inside.

'So,' Kelly says, 'I have something to tell you.'

'Sounds bad.'

'It's not. There's another reason I'm screening the girls,' she says. Then, after a pause, 'I think I'm a three on the Kinsey scale.'

'I have no idea what you just said.'

She sighs. 'You know when I was visiting you in France?'

'Yeah.'

'I spent the night with Beth.'

'My Beth? Beth on my tour? Beth who hates my guts?'

Beth with the grade 2 haircut and washboard stomach. Beth who I just beat in New Smyrna. Beth is a unit. A dauntless competitor, feared for her strength, self-discipline and mastery of various martial arts. In addition to the deadly skillset, she has a gruff manner, a bone-dry sense of humour and I've desperately wanted to be her friend since I met her. A feeling that has not been mutual.

'That's her. I should've told you before. Sorry, mate,' she says. 'Why are you looking at me like that?'

'You're my best friend and I didn't even know you had a thing for girls as well.'

'What do you mean, *as well*?'

'As well as blokes.'

'Ohhh. Seriously, though? How many evenings did we spend with our clothes off, tickling each other?'

'So what? It felt nice.'

She smiles, and shakes her head at me.

'You really didn't know?'

151

'No.'

'Ask me questions.'

'OK, um, so, when you're out, you're like looking to see which girls you fancy as well as which boys?'

'Nope, not at all. It's not like on any given day I could go either way. Some days I feel super-straight, and some days I feel one hundred per cent gay. I don't know if it works like that for other people, but that's how it goes for me.'

I nod, and wonder if my sister's experience of bisexuality is the same. Not that I could ever ask Lily. The thought of her being sexually active makes me want to gouge out my brains with a melon baller.

'What does Garrett say? Have you told him?'

'He's actually super respectful about it. Told me to do whatever I need to do to be happy. *Go forth and experiment*, were his exact words. Basically, he's poly and his brother is gay, so it's not like he's going to be judging anyone.'

'Really? He was a right horrible git to Wes when he came out.'

Kelly frowns. 'He's done a lot of thinking about that. He realizes how awful he was. Honestly, Iris, he feels so bad. He's spent loads of time getting to know Elijah. They're mates now. And . . . cards on the table, I think he probably leans towards bi himself.'

I'm struggling to keep up with this. 'Really? What makes you think that?'

'Apart from the pink T-shirts he wears? Joke. No, I can't say why, without severely compromising his privacy, but let's just say I have my suspicions.'

'So, he was all right with you hooking up with Beth?'

'I think so.'

'Christ, Kel. This is mega. Beth never said a word to me.'

'I asked her not to. You were competing with her. You didn't need any distraction.'

'Why her, though? I mean she's cool and all, but . . .'

'I don't know, exactly, but there was this instant connection. Same thing happened with Garrett. Sort of a recognition. The strongest feeling that I knew her already. Who knows, maybe I've been tumbling around time with her for a millennia or two already. Beth, me and Garrett. Imagine that. Jesus.'

I smile.

'Have you told your mum?'

'No, I'm waiting until she's dead. Of course I've told my mum. She thought it was really interesting and asked loads about it.'

Kelly has always been really close to her mum, who's much younger and cooler than mine. Kelly's mum does long-distance charity bike rides, and goes dancing with lads from the local RAF base on a Saturday night. Lads twice her size and half her age, who usually appear bleary-eyed at Kelly's breakfast table on a Sunday morning. Kelly's mum says it's best to leave judging to old gits in white wigs.

Since Kelly is being so open about answering questions, I go with, 'Has Garrett asked to be, um, involved?'

'Nope. Not even a hint. And I mean, Beth's gay, so it's not like there's any chance of a threesome, which I wouldn't be up for anyway. If I'm with a girl, I'm with a girl. I don't much like the idea of lezploitation, either.'

I look at her blankly.

'The exploitation of lesbian activity for the titillation of men. I'm emailing you some links. You've gotta do some reading, girl. Anyway, since we're having some real talk, how about you?'

I deploy my confused face.

'You know what I'm asking,' she says, and I feel my heart rate ever-so-slightly increase.

'No idea, Kel.'

'Have you never thought about girls? Not even when you're . . . having some private time?'

I hesitate too long before answering.

'Haha, I knew it,' she says, offering me a high-five, which I half-heartedly return.

'But, I mean, I don't think I would ever actually, y'know, with a girl.'

'Don't knock it until you try it. Just because society tells us to be straight, doesn't mean we have to listen.'

'Have you been hanging out with Elijah lately?' I say, 'because you're sounding a lot like him,' and she whips me in the side of the head with a tea towel.

'Human sexuality is complicated, Iris. Don't live your life simplified.'

'OK, you've definitely been hanging out with Elijah.'

I try to digest all of this, but it's difficult. This is real talk and I've been light on that in the past half a year, surrounded by strangers and non-friends.

'I actually have something to tell you too,' I say.

'Spill it.'

'I did it with Caleb.'

Her eyes widen.

'When you say "did it" you mean had-sex-with, right?'

I front it out, try to act casual, and nod.

'Blimey, you don't hang about, do you? Wanted to get one in the bag before you make it up with Zeke, eh?'

'No! God, Kel, it wasn't like that at all. And I'm not getting back with Zeke.'

'Whatever you say. So how was it?'

'Strange, but nice strange, not messed-up strange.'

It had been awkward, but then sort of comforting. I'd been tired-but-wired for days. Afterwards, at least for a little while, I lost the wired.

Despite the fact that it's still morning, Kelly goes inside to the fridge, opens a bottle of her mum's Prosecco and fills two glasses. She hands me one, which she immediately clinks with her own.

'I'm not toasting this, Kel,' I mumble. 'It's not like

I've just passed my theory test.'

'Nope, it was definitely the practical.' She grins, and then raises her glass again. 'Here's to new experiences!'

chapter twenty-four

When I get back home I find I have the house to myself, and a note from Mum saying she's gone to the gym. I get the coffee machine going and make myself a double espresso, after which I can't stop fidgeting, so I strap on my trainers and run to Fistral. It's about time I got back to my training.

I give myself the run to think about Zeke and remind myself I have nothing to feel guilty about. He's probably slept with ten girls in the past twenty-four hours. I think of his Oahu relatives, his aunt, his cousins, his grandfather, the way they welcomed me into their family, and doubts tap on my forehead like a teaspoon. For a few yards, I dare myself to run with my eyes closed and pretend I'm back there.

'Be present,' my yoga teacher has told me over and over. 'Don't rush to the airport. Don't think about finding your seat on the flight. Don't worry about hailing a cab. Don't worry about all the things you did wrong yesterday. Be here now.'

Barely more than a week ago I'd gone for a run across New Smyrna Beach with Zeke. He never liked to chat when he was working out, but as we ran across those seven miles of sand, I wanted him to speak to me, to distract me from my own thoughts. I told him things, silly things, about stuff I'd done as a kid, about the people I knew in Newquay and their weird ways. 'Uh-huh,' he said. 'Is that right?' Followed every time by, 'No kidding . . .'

I was offended, hadn't realized he was struggling so hard to keep a lid on his own thoughts that he couldn't mop up mine.

Halfway into my Fistral run, before I turn and swing back again, I stop for a break and sit in the shadow of the surf complex. Jammed between rocks, something catches my eye.

I curl two fingers around it and manage to loosen it. A GoPro camera, completely ruggedized and waterproof. When I get home I take it up to my room, where I plug it into my computer.

I see crystal clear images of the bottom of the sea floor and watch for a minute as fish of varying sizes zoom past the lens, and then I rewind to the beginning, where a girl and her boyfriend are hamming it up for the camera, messing around on finless alaia boards, which are spinning out on the waves. The time stamp says it's from two years ago. Had it been rolling around the ocean for that long? I hadn't even heard of Zeke then. I wonder if the couple is still together.

I put the GoPro on my shelf and vow to put the pictures up on Facebook so that I can find the owners and give it back to them, when I'm startled by the sound of my front door slamming.

I walk cautiously to the landing and look down the stairs to see Lily.

'Hey, sis!' she says. 'Guess what?'

'You're back in Newquay?'

'Yeah, and I just had the most delicious coffee with Zeke's brother.'

'Which one?'

'Resolute Blend, I think it was called. They wouldn't sell me the beans, alas.'

'I meant which brother.'

'Oh! Garrett. He was talking to some guy in The Box and Barber. I hadn't noticed quite how attractive he was before. Yikes, those arms . . .'

'LILY. He's Kelly's *boyfriend*.'

'Yes, but they have some casual deal going on, right? You said so in Florida.'

'Do not go there. If you sleep with Garrett, if you even flash him your boobs, I will never speak to you again.'

'OK, fine. Blimey, Iris, you're so uptight. So, have you got a new boyfriend yet?'

She says this jokingly but it hits me right where it hurts.

'Why are you even here, Lily?'

159

'I told you I wasn't staying in Exeter long. Wow, I thought you'd be a bit happier to see me. Wait, *have* you got a new boyfriend?'

'No.'

'Well, something's happened with someone. It's written all over your face.'

'I've been sort of hanging out with Caleb. That's it.'

'Good! I like him! He's so down to earth and stable. Stable in a good way, not a boring bastard way. Say hi from me and remember to use a condom. I'm really not ready to be an aunt. Right, I'll just have some toast and then I'm off to meet Stan.'

'Stan followed you to Newquay?'

'Yes, he's only here for today though. He drove me down. We're going river-SUPing at the Gannel. I thought it was about time I learnt a new skill.' She turns and moseys off towards the kitchen. Lily has never really enjoyed surfing, but I imagine stand-up paddleboarding will suit her better. For one thing, up high she'll have a better view of all the talent in her general vicinity.

Once Lily's left, I text Caleb and he comes to meet me at my house. I'm still sweaty and gross from my run but he kisses me anyway.

It's not the same as before; he's kissing me but he hasn't relaxed; he doesn't seem to be breathing either. It's like he's psyched himself out.

I close my eyes and, without meaning to, I think

of Zeke. I think of his hands caressing my back, his mouth on my ear, his breath between my shoulder blades.

I summon my nerve and try to keep my voice steady as I say, 'So you like me, and I like you.'

'You like me?' he asks, taken aback.

'Caleb, how can this be a surprise to you? We've already slept together once. Maybe we should do it again.'

He looks surprised. 'Really? You left so quick last night and when I didn't hear nothing from you this morning, I was worried you thought we'd moved too fast.'

'Well, don't worry. It's all fine.'

I absolutely want to sleep with him again. I want to put as many experiences as possible between me and Zeke. Layer all the rainbow chalks over my past, so my experiences with him will mean less. I'll sleep with a new person every week if it means burying each memory of Zeke.

'Is this a pity thing, cos of me saying I had a crush on you?'

'No! Caleb, I'm basically telling you I'll have sex with you in a minute, if you fancy it. Don't you want to or something?'

He raises his eyebrows. 'I mean, yeah, if you do, but not here. Your mum scares the hell out of me. I'm still not over the time she gave me a week's detention for hacking into her network and sending out the Cove Guardians' newsletter. Plus, I might need a drink first.'

'Thanks a lot.'

'Not like that. But talking about it is sort of putting me off.'

'I hereby rescind my offer.'

Caleb laughs. 'Want to stay over at mine tonight and we'll see how it goes?'

'What about your mum?'

'I asked her and she says it's all right.'

There's an instant cooling in my veins. I experience some version of this whenever I realize someone's had a conversation about me, but it's a million times worse now, because Caleb's mum might know I've slept with her son.

'You've talked to your mum about me?'

'Not really. Just said that we're hanging out. She doesn't know what happened.'

'OK, cool.'

We leave my house, go to the corner shop and Caleb manages to buy a bottle of gin on special for a tenner. When we get back to his house, his mum is watching a *Top Gear* re-run in the front room, both feet propped up on a brown velvet footstool. Caleb holds the gin bottle against his hip to hide it and rushes me up the stairs so I can't talk to her.

We sit down on the edge of the bed in silence, which Caleb breaks with, 'Can I kiss you?'

I laugh. 'OK. Since you asked so politely and all.'

'Oh, I'd better brush my teeth first. Had Monster Munch before I knew I was seeing you,' he says.

Well, he's considerate, I think, remembering Zeke's complete lack of self-awareness in this regard. It never seemed to occur to him that his breath might be a bit whiffy after chowing down on an entire bag of Doritos or one of his favourite Mexican dishes, which also tended to result in epic farting, which he was also completely unashamed about.

When Caleb's finished, a white smear of Colgate on the corner of his lip, I also start feeling a bit self-conscious, so I go and swill some toothpaste around my own mouth and give my face and underarms a bit of a wash. At least my period has finally finished, I think, dabbing my armpits with the hand towel.

When I come back, he's at the window, looking outside.

'Do you want me to take off your clothes?' I say, trying to sound casual and worldly.

'Er, OK. Do you want me to take off yours first?'

'Knock yourself out,' I say, and then wait while he fumbles with the tie of my jogging bottoms. Then the clasp of my sports bra utterly defeats him.

Zeke's fingers barely seemed to touch my bra and bikini straps before they fell to the ground, but then he'd had a lot more practice at removing this particular type of clothing than Caleb, who is making it seem a task worthy of Mensa.

Eventually, after he's somehow managed to graze me with the clasp, I undo my bra myself, by which time he's sweating and looking terrified.

I take pity on him. 'We don't have to do this. Not if you don't fancy it.' I'm not even sure I fancy it, but sheer bloody-mindedness is pushing me on.

'I do,' he says. 'Honest. Pass the gin.' He takes a huge gulp of it, and then another.

'Don't worry,' I say, 'it's OK if you're not feeling it.'

'I'm feeling it. Believe me. Too much.'

He reaches over and kisses me again, but I hold back.

'Seriously, Caleb, don't feel like you have to. We can watch TV with your mum if you'd rather.'

'Maybe we can stop chatting about it? Let me put some music on my phone.'

He puts on 'Never Ending Circles' by Chvrches and I get up and draw the curtains. When I turn around, his T-shirt is off and he's perched on the edge of the bed, looking nervous.

Caleb has another drink, and we get back to kissing, which is feeling progressively less weird by the minute.

We block out the fact that his mum's downstairs, carry on kissing for at least half an hour. Then I give him the nod and he frantically searches through his pants drawer, rubbers himself up and we're sleeping together again.

It doesn't feel as strange as the first time, and when it's over, I feel calm.

164

Caleb goes to sort himself out and when he comes back, he looks at me sheepishly, as if he expects me to tell him off. 'You hungry? My mum bought popcorn. Maybe we could watch a film?'

All the way through *Final Destination* he keeps darting looks at me, until I get fed up and say, 'What gives?'

'Just checking you're all right.'

'Why wouldn't I be? Because I'm a girl and I'm supposed to care more about this than you? Sexist bollocks.'

'OK, OK.'

I was stupid to feel upset the last time. I'm single and I can do whatever I want. I don't need to be defined by my past. I will go out and experience other things, other people. I will move the hell on.

I don't let Caleb walk me the thirty steps home, but go straight to my room and fall asleep.

I am not going to over-analyse. So what if I sleep my way across Newquay? I won't be made to feel guilty. I won't be judged.

chapter twenty-five

It's later that afternoon, and Caleb and Kelly are chugging down super-fancy milkshakes in The Beached Lamb cafe, when I look up and see Cass.

I feel my body stiffen. Kelly picks up her phone and blanks Cass completely. It's so total and sudden that even I feel awkward. Caleb obviously picks up on this horrendous tension and decides it's the perfect time to use the loo, but he touches me gently on the shoulder as he brushes past me, a gesture that I'm sure Cass will have noticed.

'How are you, Iris?' Cass says, a V-sign to Kelly's ice wall.

'Fine,' I reply.

Carina is at the bar ordering and she gives me a wave when she sees me. When she's done, she rushes over, her face all excited.

'Hey, how cool was that Angola vid?'

'Huh?' I say, frowning at her.

'The point break? It's just been posted to Billabong's

YouTube page. He caught like a two-minute ride and I'm not even kidding.'

'Angola?' Kelly says, looking up from her phone at Carina. 'Who's in Angola?'

'Who do you think!'

'*Zeke's* in Angola?' I ask.

'Yeah,' Carina replies. 'Didn't you know?'

I shrug, and Cass and Carina exchange a look that clearly conveys, *Trouble in paradise?*

'He's supposed to be in Fiji. He probably got some last-minute magazine gig.' I think back to what that Kristin girl had said about their flight being cancelled. Maybe he changed his mind about joining the other guys in his team and took a better offer.

'So you didn't even know?' Cass asks, her eyes widening.

'We don't speak to each other every day. We're not joined at the hip, like *some people*,' I say, looking at Cass. 'Anyway, it's probably some old trip from the archive that they've dug out on a slow traffic day.'

Cass's eyes spark with irritation. 'Me and Daniel are not joined at the hip, Iris.'

'Didn't say you were.'

Carina coughs nervously and looks at her phone again.

'The YouTube page says it was put up three hours ago. Dunno when it was filmed, though. There's a desert, a beach, and no one else for a hundred miles by the looks of it. I reckon he's there on his own.'

'He can't be alone. Someone must be filming him surf,' I say, wondering if the lovely Kristin is there with him.

'Honestly, there's not. He's got this new video get-up. Strapped a sensor to his arm, and he has some swivelling video camera thing on the beach that follows him as he rides a wave.'

So he can meet his sponsorship commitments without having to be around people. I can't think of anything more lonely.

Cass and Carina's drinks arrive and they go to the dark, chill-out area at the back of the cafe, strewn with colourful floor pillows and low tables, like some exotic Moroccan place.

'It's so stuffy in here,' I say to Kelly. 'I'm just gonna step outside for some fresh air.' She nods, and I leave before Caleb gets back. I can feel my face is showing stuff I don't want it to, and I'd rather she and Caleb didn't see it.

I go outside to the wooden chairs next to our bikes and sit there for two minutes, convincing myself of all the reasons I shouldn't watch the video clip. They mostly revolve around the idea that it will only make me more upset to see him, but as far as upset goes, I'm pretty maxed out as it is now I know Zeke is completely alone on a remote beach in Western Africa. So what I'm doing is burying my head in the sand, and if I've learnt anything from the past few months, it's that avoiding problems never makes them go away.

I hook my phone into the Wi-Fi, and load up the Billabong site. Normally I'd check out Twitter, Instagram and Facebook as soon as I go online, but I know if I do that, I'll never get to the Billabong site. It'll be too easy to get sucked into a chain of clicks that ends with me deciding that watching a video of Zeke surfing isn't such a great idea after all.

I don't even have to search the site; it's there on the homepage, but I load the video and I close it before it starts. Then I load it again and do the exact same thing. On the fourth attempt, my finger still hovering over the top corner X, I let it play out. As expected, my heart contracts at the sight of him. I order myself to get a grip, and open my eyes again.

The video starts with Zeke speaking to the camera, saying something about the beauty of Angola. His hair is short, so the video must be new, not some trip from years ago he'd forgotten to tell me about. The camera scans the desert behind him, and the clip cuts to him shredding a bright blue left that seems to go on forever. The wave is only two feet high, at most, but Zeke throws in cutback after cutback, floaters, carves, and he finishes with a perfectly executed air. There's not another soul in the water. It looks like the loneliest place on the planet.

At the end of the clip, Zeke walks out of the water. He's wearing a pair of yellow boardshorts I've never seen before, and as he approaches the camera to turn it off, I see something else that's new. On his chest he has brand new ink. As he walks closer, he throws a hang-loose shaka with one hand, and I see a close-up of his skin.

Over his heart is a tattoo of a blue iris.

chapter twenty-six

Curious, or more likely worried, Kelly has followed me outside and looks over my shoulder at my phone screen.

My thoughts are all over the place. Why has he had that tattooed on his chest? To mark part of his past? Or because he wants me to be part of his future?

I turn to her, tears in my eyes.

'What's wrong?' she says. 'Has something happened?'

'Zeke has a tattoo of me. Well, not of me. An iris flower.'

'Wow. That's gotta mean something.'

'He's alone on some remote beach in Africa, Kel.'

Thinking of this causes me physical pain. He has no one to talk to. No one there to help or support him if something goes wrong.

'Oh, mate,' she says, hugging me. 'Try not to worry. I'm sure he's all right. He probably just wanted time away from it all to think things through.'

We go back inside and I watch Caleb dribble

milkshake right down his white T-shirt.

'Everything all right?' he asks us.

'It's fine,' Kelly says. 'Me and Iris are just going to go for a bike ride,' she says, looking at me for confirmation. I nod.

Halfway along a quiet street, we turn away from the road and into a narrow break between houses. This path is hidden to everyone but locals. It looks like nothing more than an access path to a back garden, but it heads towards a secret sanctuary of untouched beauty looking out to the Gannel river valley. As kids we used to come here when we wanted to hide from the world.

We leave our bikes against the rusted metal gate at the end of the path and climb the stile. Not into a nature reserve, but a building site.

My guts twist as we come face to metal with an abandoned digger silhouetted against the sky, its bucket hanging motionless in the air.

'Yeah, they're building a few houses on this side of the valley,' Kelly says.

'How many?'

'Three hundred and fifty.'

A new gravel road cuts the old field in half and at the end of the road the foundations of a dozen houses are already laid and waiting for their bricks.

There are badgers living in this field, foxes, hares,

endangered newts in the stream that slopes down towards the river. The next time I come here it'll all be coated in concrete.

A movement in the digger's cab catches my eye and I see that watching us from the driver's seat is a buzzard. The window has been left open and the bird pecks something from the black leather beneath its talons and gulps. It stares at me a moment longer, hops onto the window seal and takes flight, swooping low over still grasses and cubes of stacked breezeblocks to the other side of the valley, where it settles on a fencepost.

Kelly puts her hand on my back and I lean forward and cry. Afterwards, I sit there, congealed tears sticky on my skin, too tired almost to blink.

I have travelled every corner of the world, seen the most beautiful panoramas and met the most extraordinary people and now I want to turn back the clock so none of it happened.

'Better?' Kelly says.

'A bit.'

'OK,' Kelly says, 'it's about time you told me what really happened in Florida.'

'It's gonna put you in the middle, Kel. You're gonna have to keep it all secret, especially from Garrett.'

'I don't care. Tell me.'

So I start talking.

* * *

Saturday night in New Smyrna, still excited after the awesomeness of my early rounds, which I'd blitzed, I walked into the bar, where Zeke was drinking craft beers with some of the local pro-surfer posse. I heard the noise of them before they saw me, so I held off, pulling out a bar stool, and I watched Zeke help himself to a shot glass from a circular tray containing at least thirty of them, arranged in a flower shape. He downed it and then took another. And another. As I got closer I could hear he was making an idiot of himself, clowning around and talking rubbish. I hadn't expected him to get so drunk. We'd put our argument on the backburner while I surfed my contest, but we hadn't resolved anything, and I'd assumed he'd be on his best behaviour.

I saw a tall guy approach Zeke before he did. The man had messy grey hair and was carrying a camera around his neck.

Zeke was sitting beneath a plastic palm tree listening to the group of lads explain a complicated drinking game. He was totally absorbed in this and the guy had to literally put his hand on Zeke's shoulder before he noticed him.

'Can I help you, dude?' Zeke said, drunk but trying to be polite, although I could tell he was weirded out by some strange old man touching him. The other lads fell silent, waiting to see how this would pan out.

'Yes.'

'Do you want an autograph or something?'

'No, I do not want an autograph.' The guy had a slight accent, German maybe, and his English was overly formal.

'What then?'

'I would like to buy you a drink.'

Zeke stared at him. 'Thanks and all, but I think I'm good.'

I could tell Zeke was wondering if the man was hitting on him, something that happened fairly regularly.

'May we speak for a moment outside?'

Zeke rocked back on his chair, misjudged it and only just stopped himself from falling to the ground. The guy tried to steady the chair by holding Zeke's shoulder, but Zeke swatted away his hand, got to his feet and squared up to the guy.

'I'm not interested.'

The guy looked confused, and leaned forward to say something that only Zeke could hear.

Whatever it was, Zeke didn't like it.

'Back off,' Zeke said, and his hand went to his hair, as it always did when he was stressed. He spotted me at the bar and his face turned red. He hesitated, then walked towards me and put his arm around my shoulders.

'Let's go,' he said.

He leaned into me and I took some of his weight as we walked towards the exit. Before we went through the door, I glanced back at the man, who looked crestfallen, and mouthed, '*Sorry.*'

'Try to take it as a compliment,' I said.

'I need to surf,' Zeke replied, skimming past my words.

'*Now?* You're hammered.'

'If I don't get in the ocean, I'm gonna do something stupid.'

'More stupid than getting wasted in the middle of my contest, Zeke?'

'Yeah.'

'Come on, Zeke, it's crazy to surf if you're drunk. Especially at dusk. In bull shark central.'

'Fine. Whatever. You're the boss.'

'You can pack that right in,' I said. 'That's not cool, Zeke.'

'Huh?'

'That passive aggressive crap. Just stop it, right? I'm not the boss and neither are you.'

'Sure you ain't.'

When we woke up at the crack of dawn the next morning, he was all apology. Mortified and desperately disappointed in himself for getting so wasted and acting out.

'What did that guy even say to you to make you so angry?' I asked.

'I have no idea,' he said, not looking me in the eye. 'I don't remember half the night.'

When I went out to get coffee later that morning,

the man was walking towards our trailer. I went back to warn Zeke.

'That man from last night. He's here,' I said, quietly.

Zeke sat bolt upright. 'What? Where?'

'About five feet away. Waiting for you outside.'

He leapt out of bed and pulled on his jeans, without bothering with boxers, and grimaced when he caught a few hairs in his zipper, which under usual circumstances I'd have found hilarious.

'*Motherfucker.*'

'Why the panic? Who is he, Zeke?'

'An attorney from Manhattan,' he told me.

'Wait, why would some New York lawyer follow you to Florida?' I stared at him, silently demanding an answer.

'He wants to talk with me,' Zeke said.

'About what?'

He closed his eyes. Said nothing.

'About the drugs?' I asked, tentatively. It was a painful subject, which I generally tried not to bring up, because it hurt him to remember, but Zeke had used hard drugs in the past. At first to have fun, then to get him through tough times and tough competitions. To paddle into unimaginably huge and scary waves. To get the covers of surfing magazines. This was not public knowledge, although certain people in the surfing community knew and did their best to keep it to themselves. The World Surf League commissioner and legal team, however, did not

177

know. At least, that's what I'd assumed.

He shook his head.

'So what is it, Zeke?'

'If he doesn't beat it, I'm gonna break his face.'

I held both Zeke's wrists to stop him from going outside.

'Zeke, he's some fancy lawyer. Talk to him in the wrong tone of voice and you'll get yourself in trouble. Just tell him to leave.'

Neither of us were keeping our voices down, and I was acutely aware that the man could probably hear everything.

'He's not gonna sue me, Iris. He says he's the brother of my mom's first husband.'

Zeke hardly ever spoke of his biological father, who walked out on the family when Zeke was still a baby.

'Wait, that guy's your *uncle*?'

'I guess so.'

I took a moment to consider this piece of information. The accent wasn't German, then. One of the only things I knew about Zeke's paternal family was that they were Danish.

'Is he for real?'

'Maybe. I don't know. He wants me to agree to a meeting with his brother, I guess my biological father.'

'Wow, that's a lot, Zeke. What are you going to do?'

'He's pretty insistent that we all get together to have

some big talk but I don't give a damn. I don't want anything to do with him or his douchebag brother.'

'You have to hear him out. What if your dad's really ill or something? This could be your last chance to meet him.'

'Dave is my dad. He raised me.'

We were interrupted by gentle knocking on the window.

'Stay here,' Zeke said.

'No, I'm coming with you.'

'Damn it, Iris, for once in your life can you just do what I say?'

I sat on the bed, shocked at his tone of voice, and watched as he pushed open the door and ran outside into the hot Florida morning.

Something on the formica table near the window caught my eye. It was a little black plastic film canister, the sort Zeke used to collect his dog-ends in, rather than littering the beach.

He had no use for this. He'd given up smoking. Or so I'd thought.

I popped the lid and detected a distinctive stench straight away. I tipped out the canister onto my hand and looked at three roaches. Not the insect kind. The butt of a marijuana cigarette kind.

After all our rows over the past few days, our heartfelt conversations about the danger of drugs, the need to get a proper prescription for antidepressants from the doctor rather than buying dodgy street pills, and the need for him not to hide things from me, Zeke had been secretly smoking weed.

The door swung open.

'He's gone.'

'Yeah, you know what else is gone? My trust in you,' I said, opening my palm. 'Way to hide your drugs from me AGAIN, Zeke. Two different kinds in a week. Good going!'

'Mary Jane ain't drugs. You have a problem with a doob?'

'When the person smoking it is a recovering drug addict, I do. Oh, and probable current alcoholic.'

'I'm not an alcoholic, Iris. Get real.'

'Where did you even get marijuana?'

'In the bar.'

'You smoked it while I was asleep?'

'Yeah, I had insomnia. It helped. I can't believe you're making a thing out of this. Even my mom smokes pot. It's like the family herbal tea.'

'It's illegal.'

'In some places.'

'Including here.'

'You know what, Iris, I'm done with this conversation. Whatever I do is wrong. You want me to be this perfect guy and that's never gonna happen.'

'I don't expect you to be perfect. I'm just not too keen

on you waiting for me to fall asleep and then taking drugs on the sly!'

'It's not like I was hiding something. If I was, would I have left that on the table?'

'I don't know, Zeke. Maybe you meant to dispose of it and forgot because you were so incredibly stoned.'

'I don't need this,' he said. 'Think what you want. I'm out of here.'

He started looking through his backpack.

'Where do you think you're going?' I asked.

He retrieved a smallish tin from the bag, held it aloft and tapped the lid.

'For a walk and a dope smoke. Come with, if you want.'

I realized then that it would never end. Drugs would always find their way into his life. He would always be addicted to something. Lots of things, probably. Life with him would never be simple, never predictable. When it came to it, he would lie, bury the truth, pretend, and it would never stop.

'So Zeke *is* on drugs again?' Kelly says, not sounding too surprised. She's probably been waiting for this to happen. She saw her dad whirl through spirals of addiction and counter-spirals of sobriety. She knows better than anyone what a terrible, unbeatable disease it can be. She always hoped for the best but never, ever counted on it.

'Yes. And it's not just weed; Zeke has been self-medicating for post-traumatic stress disorder.'

'Wow, really? He has PTSD? From when he almost drowned?'

'Yeah,' I say. 'And I didn't even realize until recently. Even then, he had to tell me. You sure you want to hear the rest, Kel?'

'Tell me.'

So I do.

His uncle kept coming back. One of the last times, I watched Zeke jog up to him and when the guy said something, Zeke frowned.

The man left and, without saying a word to me, Zeke dialled his mum and deliberately put her on speaker phone, so that I could hear all of this play out.

'Hey, baby. How are you?' Sephy sounded happy, relaxed.

'Not much. Oh yeah, I ran into my uncle. For like the fifth time. He's basically stalking me at this point.'

'Which uncle? Dave's brother?'

'No. Erik Matthiesen. The brother of my biological father.'

'*Oh shit.*'

'He seemed pretty pissed, since you apparently hate everyone in his family and haven't let any of them see us, or let us see any of the cards or letters they sent.'

'I don't hate anyone. What did you say to him?'

182

'What do you think I said to him, Mom? My whole life you told me that my biological father ran out on us. Is that true? Because this guy is saying we did the running.'

'OK, you're not getting the whole story here, baby. Not at all.'

'The whole story? You had nineteen *years* to tell me the whole story!'

'Do you even want to hear what I have to say or do you just want to shout? I mean, I'm down with that, if that's what you gotta do, but wait for me to turn down the volume on this phone. You're hurting my ear.'

'This is not funny, Mom. I'm serious.'

'I know, and I'm trying to have a two-way conversation with my son, but you don't seem to be interested in what I have to say.'

'Did we leave his brother? This Kurt guy?'

'Yes, we left him.'

'So how is it you told us he was the one to leave? Like, every damn time?'

'I thought it would be easier for you kids to handle.'

'You think that made it *easier*? We thought our father wanted nothing to do with us. Not great for a kid's self-esteem, you know?'

'If I'd told you I'd ended it, you would have never stopped asking to see him. You didn't know the situation. You'd have wanted me to work it out with him, no matter what. But it wasn't that simple.'

'Did he beat you?'

'No.'

'What then?'

'There are other ways of hurting people, honey.'

'So he hurt your feelings? Wow, that's a terrific reason for destroying a family and taking kids away from their father, for like all fuckin' time.'

'You don't know everything, Zeke.'

'So tell me already.'

'There are things that need to be said in person. Come home, honey.'

'No, and FYI: Newquay is not my home. Oahu is my home.'

He ran out of steam. Stood in silence.

'Zeke?'

'What, Mom?'

'Don't tell Garrett or Wes about this. I want to talk to you all together, OK?'

'Garrett is gonna go nuts when he hears about this.'

'Let me worry about that. Concentrate on you for now. Hold it together, Zeke. It's not so easy to explain, but you know I would never do anything to hurt you or your brothers. And I would never have left my husband unless I had good reasons. You were so little. You don't know how things were. I love you, baby.'

I looked at Zeke. I knew he had been through a lot, but his life hadn't been awful. He'd been loved. He'd had his mother looking out for him and his stepdad was completely brilliant.

'Love you too,' Zeke said, 'but I'm pissed, Mom.'

'I know, baby, and hey, everything happens for a reason. If I hadn't of left your father, I'd never have met or fallen in love with Dave. If not for Dave, you would not have met Iris.'

'Cos that worked out so good,' he said, his eyes shining with tears, before hanging up on her.

'I'm so sorry,' I said.

'Why? It's not on you. You didn't do this. Let's go.'

We locked up the trailer and walked down the street. We were close enough to be holding hands but we weren't.

'I mean I'm just sorry that you're having to go through all of this upset.'

'Right, I'm upset. I was lied to my whole life. By my own mother, who's full of lectures on the importance of disclosure and honesty.'

'You've got to wait and hear everything before you go hating her,' I said. 'For all you know, the bloke could have been having an affair.'

'So, she should have forgiven him.'

'Whoa,' I said. 'She should have forgiven him? For cheating on her and betraying her trust?'

I was stunned that Zeke saw it this way.

'She had three kids. So what if he banged someone else? She should have just dealt. What kind of mother breaks up a family because her husband plays away one time?'

I couldn't believe what I was hearing. I looked at his face, which was flushed with anger and hurt.

'Are you for real?' I asked.

'It's just sex. It's not everything. If we were raised without our father just because he bumped uglies with someone who wasn't my mother, how is that justified?'

'Uh, it's totally justified,' I said. 'If my husband – the father of my children – had an affair, I would leave him in a millisecond. He wouldn't see me for the dust I'd be kicking into his lying, cheating face.'

'If you were older and had kids, you wouldn't feel that way.'

'Yes, I would, Zeke.'

'Why are you getting so worked up?'

'Maybe because you seem to be fine with infidelity.'

'If that's what happened, then the guy's an asshole, but my mom had a family, she had responsibilities to more than her own feelings. She had three sons to think about, and it sounds like she didn't think about us at all.'

'You don't know the facts. You've written Sephy off already, which is horrible, by the way, since she's your own mother and has done nothing but love you and look after you since you were born. And you did have a dad in your life. You had Dave. He was there for you since you were little, so I'm not really buying this "*I had to grow up*

186

without a father" malarkey. Your mum is amazing and she did her best for you. There's no way she should have had to put up with a cheating husband.'

Zeke looked stung by this.

'Just because your mother is such a hard-ass that she threw out your dad for being, like, *weird* and not earning enough money, or whatever, it doesn't mean every mother should be that way. Some moms make sacrifices for their kids.'

As always, my face had its way of telegraphing anger. I felt the movement of my jaw, the grind of my back teeth.

'I can't believe you just said that. You don't know anything about my dad, or my mum, so keep your nose out, yeah?'

'But it's OK for you to be telling me what I should feel about my family?'

'I didn't randomly bring them up. You were arguing with your mum two minutes ago. And P.S. if you didn't want me to know about this, then you shouldn't have put her on speaker phone, should you?'

'You're right, I shouldn't have. This is family stuff.'

'And I'm not family.'

'What are you, my sister? No, you're not family. You're my girlfriend and we hardly know each other.'

'We *hardly know each other*? Seriously?'

'I thought I knew you, but I guess I was wrong.'

'Yeah, I'm nobody to you. I saved your life at the

187

Cribbar, but who cares?' Garrett may have done the CPR, but I found him underwater, freed him from his leg-rope and got him to the surface. 'You're basically only alive because of me.'

'You know I appreciate that so much, but what am I supposed to do? Give you some kind of a medal?'

I couldn't help laughing at him. He was being so ridiculous. As if he'd lost control of his mouth.

'No, but saying we hardly know each other is total rubbish. Also, I lost my virginity to you, dickhead, so making out that we just have this tiny little relationship is pretty hurtful to me.'

'Here we go. I was waiting for that one. I was the jerk who deflowered you, so I have to keep kissing your ass for the rest of our lives?'

'No. You're deliberately misunderstanding.' I paused as I realized just how much I sounded like my mother, and took a breath. 'I'm just saying that you mean something to me. You'll always be really important to me because you were my first love.'

'Huh? You loved Daniel. You've told me enough.'

'Not like this.'

'It's not my fault you were a virgin. I never asked you to be a virgin. No one did. That was all you.'

'Was I *supposed* to be shagging around? I was sixteen when we met.'

'OK, fine. Whatever. Sorry.'

'You seem to be saying sex is this little thing that doesn't really matter, but I don't feel that way. Not at all.'

'You're a chick. It's different for guys.'

'It's different for guys? How is it different for guys? And by the way, that is probably the most douchey thing you've ever said to me.'

'I'm not trying to be a douche, I'm just pointing out that it's different, because girls make it all about feelings.'

'And you don't have any feelings? You're one of the most emotional boys I've ever met!'

'I have a ton of feelings. But I can separate them from sex.'

'Why would you even want to?'

'Because sex and love are two different things and I know that?'

'You *think* that. That's just your opinion. You're not the authority, even if you have shagged like two hundred girls. In fact, that makes you less of an expert in my opinion, because your experience is so messed up.'

'I'm messed up?'

'I said your experience was.'

'Because I'm a complete manwhore and have to apologize for that for, like, ever.'

'I've *never* asked you to apologize for anything you did before you met me.'

'Even if I did, you still wouldn't be satisfied because I don't have a time machine and I can't go back and make

189

myself not sleep with anyone so that I could be a virgin for you.'

'Like you'd ever even use that time machine.'

I knew that I was just making things worse. Needling him. But I couldn't control it either. This was how it went. We couldn't stop tearing strips off each other. Soon we'd be down to bone marrow.

'I can't change my past! It's done. It is what it is. It's not like I cheated on you.'

'Apart from kissing that girl in Miami.'

'That was a PHOTO KISS!'

The argument blew itself out and we walked to the end of the street in silence. Then, he grabbed my hand, apologized for everything he'd said and begged my forgiveness.

'I've gotta sort out my head,' he said. 'I'm going crazy here. I have to go.'

'Where?'

'I don't know. Someplace else.'

Someplace else.

'Where?'

'Home.'

I felt the same. But my home was in Newquay, not Oahu.

I turn to Kelly. 'I had to come back. I couldn't stand it any more.'

'Absolutely the right decision. The only decision, really. But, is that argument really why you broke up? And what about the uncle? Did he sort it out with Zeke?'

'Not exactly.'

I was on the beach, waiting for Zeke, when I looked up and saw a man walking towards me, a tall man with artfully messy grey hair. Zeke's uncle.

He had ditched the suit and was wearing a tan jacket, white shirt and jeans when he came up to me. I looked up at his face and took in the thin-lipped mouth and piercing blue eyes.

'Hello, Iris. How are you today?'

'How do you know my name?'

'It is online. You are Zeke's girlfriend, yes?'

'What are you doing here?' I replied, coldly. 'Haven't you done enough damage?'

'I would like Zeke to come to dinner, to talk at length, but he continues to refuse.'

'That's up to him, not me.'

'Will you help to change his mind?'

I stayed silent.

'It is not what you think. Bring him to me, so we may talk.'

'Look, he's told you he's not interested in playing Happy Families. I know him, and I know he can't handle this,' I said, feeling my blood run cold, because Zeke was already in a dark place. Another blow and he could fall apart completely. He was suffering a debilitating mental illness, feeling the lure of drugs, worrying about losing his sponsors, about losing me. His family was the last of his castles. 'Please just leave him alone.'

'I'm not leaving. Zeke has family he knows nothing of, but it is time. He will grow used to the idea,' Erik said, not understanding a single thing.

I spotted Zeke at a distance and he came jogging over, evidently annoyed. 'Your uncle's here. Again,' I said, pointing out the obvious.

'You don't get the message, huh?' he said, looking up. 'What the hell do you want from me?'

Erik took Zeke's arm and led him a few paces away. He was pleading with him, then he said something I couldn't make out, and I saw Zeke recoil. He swung around to look at me and his eyes were wild.

Then, out of nowhere, he took a swing at his uncle, his fist smashing into the man's nose. Hitting it hard enough to make it spurt blood.

I couldn't believe it. I knew Zeke had a temper but I never thought he would lash out like this at a member of his own family. Erik had tears in his eyes as he turned away from us, pulling a Kleenex out of his pocket and mopping up the blood. I watched him walk out of sight. I couldn't bear to turn to Zeke and face him, or this. When I finally did, Zeke was leaning forward, hands on his knees, hyperventilating. I led him to our beach blanket, put my arm around him, waited for an explanation.

'He's a liar,' he said, but he could barely get his words out and his face was contorted.

'Zeke,' I'd said to him. 'What was that? You just assaulted your own uncle. *Who is a lawyer.* Talk to me.'

But he wouldn't talk to me. Wouldn't even try. I knew then that it was over. Knew it had to be.

'Everything I did just made things worse, Kel. Made him unhappier. Made him do crazy stuff. He was better off without me.'

'I don't know, Iris . . .'

'You weren't there! Look, you can't tell Wes and Garrett any of this, right?'

'OK.' She sighs. 'What a total bloody mess.'

'Tell me about it.'

'Remind me of Erik's surname?'

'Matthiesen.'

'And he lives in New York?'

'Yeah, why?'

'Leave it with me.'

'What are you gonna do, Kel? I'm not even supposed to have told you.'

'I'm not sure yet. Don't worry, I'll keep you out of it. Plausible deniability.'

'Kel, I really don't think you should get involved.'

But Kelly is already involved, because the Francis family is important to her too and if fighting needs to be done, she'll be first in the arena.

'Iris, relax. I will handle this.'

'How though?'

'Trust me. I promise I won't make things worse.'

chapter twenty-seven

I wake up in the small hours of the night and check my phone. While I was asleep, Caleb had sent me a few messages on WhatsApp with links to stupid stuff on YouTube. I watch the videos and send him a thumbs up. I expect him to be deep in the Land of Nod but he replies straight away.

There's a wild swim on at Fistral in a couple hours. Wanna go with me?

Shouldn't you be getting your beauty sleep?

I necked a load of Red Bull and Pro Plus while I was finishing my apple report. No way I'm getting back to sleep now. How come you're up?

Stressing. Wild swim sounds a bit yummy mummy, Caleb . . .

Nah, there'll be a big group down there. All sorts go. They meet twice a week and go really far out. No one wears a wetsuit either. It's hardcore.

I can do hardcore . . . What time is it?

6 a.m.

OK, I'm in.

* * *

We're early, the first to arrive at the beach, and we sit on the sand watching the sky turn pink around us. Before long we're surrounded by twenty or so swimmers of various ages, from young teenagers to white-haired pensioners.

The only swimsuit I could find was my sister's and it's old. It's her cozzie for doing laps at Waterworld and the chlorine has faded it and stretched it thin. Looking at that swimsuit I feel the same hit of nostalgia that I get from old photographs.

A woman called Eliza – who I recognize from long Sunday afternoons spent drinking Rattler at the beach bar, tons of friends and one bored border collie at her side – is the organizer of this wild swim; we strike out together, a colourful group of seals.

After all the obsessing and remembering, an hour of swimming with Caleb, rising and falling with the swell, is just what I need, and I splash out of the bracing saltwater refreshed and breathing easier. Some of the lads Caleb knows from his dad's building company have brought bodyboards with them, and ask us to watch them, since they have plans to do beach circuits as part of their training for a Half Iron.

'We all right to borrow them?' Caleb asks, with a winning smile.

It's been ages since I've been on a bodyboard; I'd given mine away as soon as I'd mastered stand-up surfing.

The blokes say it's fine, and we're away.

I've forgotten how much fun bodyboarding can be. Caleb and I are rushing through the whitewater, squealing as we swerve to avoid jellyfish, and surfing so far in, no fins to worry about, that we're almost beached.

After an hour, the guys come back from their circuits and wait for us to get off their boards, which we do reluctantly, me vowing to buy my own decent bodyboard at the next opportunity. Speed bumps, spongers, dick draggers and shark biscuits are some of the less offensive names people called bodyboarders, but screw looking cool. Bodyboarding is great fun and I can't believe I'd forgotten that.

'Feeling better?' Caleb says.

'So much better. Thanks, man. Appreciate you bringing me out here this morning.'

'Um, Iris, I think you've got a bit of sand . . .'

I look down and flick at one of the pale areas on my swimsuit, but no sand comes off, because what I'm flicking is, apparently, skin. The friction of my bodyboard has worn away the fabric over my nipples in two neat patches.

Certain things are impossible for me to do with any semblance of dignity; running for a bus, walking barefoot over shingle, and holding my hands over my nipples while talking to Caleb, were just three of them.

I feel my face flush in embarrassment, even the skin of my throat is burning.

Caleb can't stop laughing. He's gasping as if he's about to succumb to an asthma attack.

I run to our giant beach towels and throw one over myself, including my head.

'Never speak of this,' I say, from underneath the towel.

He touches my head through the rough fabric and I can feel how he's arranged his fingers, 'Scout's honour.'

And then I laugh, a real laugh, and I realize it feels like forever since I've done that.

chapter twenty-eight

I stay over at Caleb's house that night and we're just on our way to get vegan courgette cake and a jar of mint leaf tea, which Caleb is somehow into, when Kelly texts me.

Guess what? Beth's here!

In Newquay?!?!

Yesss! She was in London.

That's who you were visiting?

Um, maybe. Anyway, since I've had like a hundred percent attendance this term, I'm skipping school today and we're going out.

With Beth? She scares the crap out of me, Kel.

I think of Beth's buzz-cut haircut, her full sleeve of tattoos, and the look of ruthless determination in her eyes as she paddles out.

It'll be fine. She's on holiday.

She's clearly here to see you.

Um . . . I think she also wants to check out Fistral, since your final contest is here.

She still sore about me beating her in Florida?

Dunno. Probably.

This is gonna be so awkward.

Nah, it won't. Meet us at the Gazzle in an hour. Wear your wetsuit. Don't bring a board.

Caleb is off to his second interview with Newquay Orchard, so he kisses me quickly on the lips and gets on his skateboard.

Two hours later, I'm standing on a cliff-face.

'You've cut yourself, Kel,' I say.

'Hmm?'

She's ahead of me, a few metres further down the cliff-face, and I'm following her step for step. Beth, Wes and Elijah are further on, easily keeping up with the instructors and nimble as mountain goats on the dark, slippery rocks.

'Seriously. You're leaving little pools of blood all over the cliff.'

Kelly looks at her palms with some surprise, and then shows them to me. They've been shredded by the barnacles sticking to every rock. These aren't shallow scratches either, they're pretty deep slices that will take a week at least to heal, and sting like mad in the meantime.

'Christ, I didn't even notice.'

I climb down onto the same ledge as her. I've been coasteering a few times. Usually dragged along by

Zeke, who tends to be drawn to any activity with the potential to prove fatal.

I wasn't as keen. I'd been freaked out by the rock-climbing element, which was done without ropes. As long as you make sure you have three points of contact with the cliff-face before moving, it's supposed to be fine, but that isn't easy when the sea grass growing over the rock-face falls away in your hands.

I look down at the slashing rocks below, which would probably break our backs if we fell, even with the safety gear we're wearing.

'Maybe the saltwater numbed the pain,' I say, looking at my own hands, which are also scratched, although not nearly as bad as Kelly's.

Elijah clambers back up to us, Wes right behind him.

Earlier, when we were setting off, I'd mouthed to Kelly, 'How come you invited Wes and E? Won't it be awkward?' she'd replied with, 'It's fine. Elijah's my best male friend. I want him to get to know Beth, and you haven't caught up with Wes yet. Also, queer coasteer!'

'What's happened?' Elijah says, moving carefully around me so he doesn't accidentally knock me off a cliff.

'Don't worry. It's nothing.'

Wes takes a look at her palms and whistles. 'Man, that's gonna hurt tomorrow. Should've brought some wetsuit gloves.'

Beth has followed the boys and joins us, looking

worried. 'You need to be more careful, babe. Don't grab on so hard.'

Kelly gives her a bright smile. 'That's not what you said this morning.'

Beth grins, and Wes and Elijah exchange glances.

'Anyway, a few cuts aren't gonna kill me,' Kelly says.

I think of Zeke, who once said something similar to me, after he was dragged across coral heads during a particularly nasty wipe-out at Pipeline. Part of his calf was practically hanging off.

'This jump might,' Beth says, turning to our instructor, a chilled-looking guy called Jonny-Lee, who doesn't seem surprised that Kelly is dripping blood all over the place.

'The danger just makes it more fun,' he says, grinning. He's mastered the art of cliff-climbing. When he holds out his hands, I see he doesn't have a single graze on them.

'Laugh a minute,' I say, but Kelly is silent. I look at her face and she doesn't seem to be feeling it, which is odd because she's always up for an outdoors adventure. True, coasteering's a bit dangerous, but we're here with qualified instructors, wearing flotation vests and safety helmets.

'Good idea then?' Elijah says.

'What's better than jumping off cliffs and getting washed through gullies?' I say, deadpan.

'Well, surfing,' Kelly says, pointing out the obvious.

'But that's work now, isn't it? And Beth's never been coasteering.'

We start climbing down to an outcrop that's about thirty feet above the water. A finger of granite juts out and the instructors wait patiently for us to make our way down.

The owner of the coasteering school is an ex-marine called Vaughan, who has short dark hair, a thousand tats and the sort of puffy face that makes him look like he's in the middle of an allergic reaction. Elijah and Wes know him as he lives in the flat below theirs, and they feed his guinea pigs while he's off on his many extreme sports holidays.

'We're losing the tide fast, girls. So Jonny-Lee is gonna jump in. If he doesn't hit the bottom, you're up next.'

Beth turns to Jonny-Lee and says, 'Mate, you get danger money for this?'

'Nope,' he grins, and jumps.

Jonny-Lee survives and Vaughan says, 'Listen now. Make a star shape to keep yourself nice and vertical and then bring your legs together and cross your arms before you hit the water. Give us the thumbs up when you surface so we know you haven't broken owt, OK?'

'So we just step off——?' Kelly asks.

'Noooo. I *really* wouldn't recommend it,' Wes interrupts. 'You see that light green patch of water right below? Rocks. Gotta clear those.'

'Yeah,' Vaughan says. 'One foot in front, toes hanging over the ledge, other one behind and use your back foot to push off *hard*. The further out you get the better. Remember to give us the thumbs up when you land so we know you're not hurt.'

He tightens the straps down the front of Kelly's flotation vest and then double-checks the chinstrap of her helmet.

Kelly looks at me and Beth, and I know she wants to back out.

'Skip it, babe,' Beth says. 'Just do the small jumps.'

'But you're all doing it.'

'We don't have to,' I say. 'We can climb down instead – although, I mean, that'll actually be harder than a one-second jump.'

Jonny-Lee is treading water and looking up at us, probably wondering what the delay is all about.

Vaughan turns away from Kelly, giving her time to think about it.

'Wes, off you go, mate.'

Wes does the jump exactly as he's been instructed and with no issue. He gives us the thumbs up, then bobs in the water, waiting for us to jump.

Elijah volunteers to go next and takes a bit of a run-up. Not only does he jump, he pulls up his knees, puts his arms around them and goes for the bomb. He makes the most insane splash and surfaces after a few seconds with both thumbs up. I see Wes laughing and he swims over to punch Elijah lightly in the head.

'E, you tosser!' Vaughan says. 'Girls, don't do that. Nice and straight, like I said. Kelly. You ready?'

'I've never jumped from this high.'

Vaughan tries to calm her down. 'It's easy, love.'

'You reckon I can do it?'

'Course you can,' Vaughan says.

'You'll be fine,' Beth says. 'Don't think about it, just do it.'

I blink and Kelly's jumped.

Her legs must have been tired from all the climbing because she falls like a stone, hardly making any forward momentum.

Vaughan inhales sharply and Beth looks completely horrified, evidently thinking it's air ambulance time. Wes reacts as soon as she's airborne, swimming towards the rocks, Elijah in his wake.

Kelly surfaces really quickly. She's light and her flotation vest has kept her from falling too deep. But her thumbs aren't up.

Beth pushes me aside, jumps and begins swimming like a maniac in Kelly's direction. I watch as Wes and Jonny-Lee reach Kelly first. Wes rests his hand on her shoulder, saying something I can't make out.

I kick off hard with my back leg and get a huge endorphin rush as I slice through the air and make a massive splash. I hold my breath for what seems like ages, and think of Zeke pinned underwater at the Cribbar, until I finally break the surface.

When I see Kelly, her thumbs are up. She must have just forgotten. Before I can ask if she's sure she's OK, Beth hugs her, a bump of swell lifts them together and Beth's mouth touches Kelly's nose. Then Kelly links her arms around Beth's back and gives her a real kiss. I don't know where to look, because I've never seen Kelly with a girl before and it feels as if I should say or do something to let her know I'm cool with this.

'Nice one,' is the best I can manage, and Kelly laughs.

'I know you all love this,' Kelly says to us, 'but that's me done.'

'You don't want to do any of the sea caving?' Elijah asks, disappointed. 'Cos that's the best part.'

'I've had enough,' she says.

Vaughan comes down then. He doesn't starfish it or go for the bomb. Like a massive show-off, he dives perfectly and comes up looking totally relaxed.

'Ready for some cold, black wreckers' caves?'

I shake my head. 'Kelly isn't feeling it, so we're gonna bail.'

'You sure? You paid for another hour.'

'Yeah, we're done,' I reply.

'Whatever you say. It's a twenty-minute open water

swim to get back, and then we can dry off and get an ice cream.'

Kelly makes a face at the mention of the ice cream and I hope she's not on some stupid diet. It's probably just all the time we've spent bobbing around in the water. Even after years in the ocean, it can still mess with my stomach and balance. Some nights, especially when I've been surfing big waves, I've been on my board so long that in bed I can still feel the movement of the sea.

We swim back, Elijah and Wes quickly getting ahead, making the most of their lanky legs and extra wingspan, Beth just behind them. I hang back with Kelly, who seems low in the water, even with her flotation vest. We pull ourselves up onto the rocks below the Gazzle car park, strip off the gear and change into our normal clothes, which we'd left in the coasteering school's minibus.

Elijah and Wes go back to their flat to change and get started on a video game marathon, and Kelly sits down on one of the boulders marking the cliff edge.

'So, Mexico,' Beth says to me.

'Yeah, I haven't bought my ticket yet. Need to borrow some money off my mum. What day are you going on?'

'Dunno,' she says. 'Haven't booked it.'

'Skint?'

'No, but I'm trying to convince Kelly to come along with me.'

'Oh,' I say, wondering for a moment if Garrett will be

worried about this. I'm also pretty worried from a personal point of view that if Kelly comes to our contest, she'll be cheering for Beth instead of me.

Kelly shakes her head at this suggestion. 'I cannot just go skipping off to Mexico. I have a life.'

'You wanna fly over together?' Beth asks me. 'Once you've got the money together?'

'I'd love that,' I say, filling with warmth and smiling at her. Now she's seeing Kelly, maybe she'll stop giving me such a hard time. Perhaps, I think, we might even become mates.

'I'm gonna go check out this Fistral Beach that everyone keeps banging on about,' she says. 'You two fancy a surf?'

Kelly shakes her head, staring at her sore hands, which have stopped bleeding. 'I need a rest. Iris?'

'Nah, I'm good,' I say, looking at Kelly, who has gone very pale, possibly because of a massive sugar dip after all the physical exertion. Beth leaves and Kelly drinks from a bottle of water that Jonny-Lee gave her, while I go and queue at the ice cream van.

Mick greets me with, 'Daughter of the finest teacher in Cornwall: what can I get you? On the house.'

'Thanks, but I'm getting stuff for my friend too, so I'll pay,' I say, completely unable to look him in the eye and trying to erase my mind of the sight of him naked.

'I said it's free, so free it is.'

'Thanks.'

I have my usual Twister and Coke combo and get Kelly a cone with all the sauces, sprinkles and a Flake.

The sugar rush will help Kelly come around a bit, I think, since we've all burned way too many calories.

'Thanks,' she says, taking the ice cream. 'Freebie from your mum's fella?'

'Yep, this is on Mick.'

'He's not bad. Glossy hair, especially between the eyebrows.'

We shoot the breeze for a while, and Kelly eats down to the cone before suddenly she sits bolt upright, puts her hand over her mouth and almost pukes, but somehow manages to swallow it down.

'Cop a lot of seawater?' I ask.

'Some,' she says. Then she gives me a serious look. 'I actually wondered if I might be pregnant.'

'*What?*'

'I don't think I am. Least I hope not. Last thing I need is Garrett Francis knocking me up. Can you imagine how hectic that kid would be?'

'Kelly, you need to do a test!'

'Chill out. I already did a test. Two actually. They're not accurate until the first day my period is due, so I'll do another one in a few days, assuming I'm not already on the blob by then.'

My heart is racing at the thought of Kelly being

pregnant. I don't know how she could possibly make the life she wants if she has a kid.

'Don't worry so much, Iris. I doubt I am. We've always been double-careful, if you know what I'm saying,' she says, and changes the subject. 'So, you haven't asked any more about me being bisexual.'

'Oh, right, yeah. I wasn't sure if you wanted to talk about it.'

'Why wouldn't I? I'm not ashamed. Ask me anything.'

'Um, so, what sort of girls are you into? Apart from Beth, I mean.'

'You know how I generally fancy boys who look a bit like girls? Well, it turns out I also generally fancy girls who look a bit like boys. Therefore, in answer to your question, my preference is apparently for fem boys and butch girls. Not sure what that says about my psyche.'

'Uh-huh,' I say, having no idea of the proper response to this. 'Does Garrett know you call him a fem boy?'

'Yeah, and he loves it. And have you *seen* his cheekbones? Could shave my bikini line on 'em.'

Judging by the deviant expression crossing her face, she's about to launch into some hideously explicit story involving the breaking of public decency laws.

'Take your word for it. You coming over to mine for a bit?' I say.

'Nah, I have to go and buy a new dress for our big night out.'

'What big night out?' I groan.

Monday night is locals night, on account of loads of Newquay residents having to work bar and club jobs over the weekend. It's generally even messier than a Saturday night, as everyone goes a bit wild after long, tedious shifts dealing with the drunken general public.

'You'll see. I'll come to yours at six o'clock, so we'll have plenty of time to get ready. Byeeee.'

chapter twenty-nine

On the way back from the Gazzle, Garrett texts and asks me to come over to Dave's house, so I drop my plan to chill out with some trash TV and walk to his house. I'm dreading it just being the two of us, but if I start avoiding him, he'll know something is up. When I get there, there's a silver bullet caravan on the front lawn, almost identical to the one Zeke and I had stayed in during our time in New Smyrna, and Garrett comes out of the garage, a gnarly-looking power tool in his hand.

'Yo, Iris, how's it going?'

'Not bad. Nice caravan.'

'You mean the trailer? Yeah, my aunts have some cool wheels, huh? So, what have you been up to today?'

'Coasteering.'

'Oh yeah, I forgot about that.'

'Are your folks in?' I ask.

I'm worried that if Sephy's around she'll rope me into some big family meal, which I am very much not up for.

212

'Nah, gone to get plumbing supplies. Some connector broke off in my mom's hand and there was water all over the show. They've been gone like five hours.'

'What you doin' anyway?' I look over Garrett's shoulder and see he has a workbench out and some piping in a clamp.

'Been cycling all over this town, one hand on the handlebar, one on my surfboard. Yesterday a gust of wind took the board and hit the mailman in the ass.'

I can't help smiling. 'Ouch. Bet he loved you.'

'Not so much. Anyways, I promised the guy I'd make a surfboard rack for the bike. The only way the dude wouldn't sue me.'

'Seems like a job and a half. Kudos. I wouldn't have a clue.'

'Put down two thousand dollars for the bike, so I figure I should save a few bucks by making the rack.'

'Two grand for a pedal bike! Garrett. No.'

'Hey, if the rack turns out good, I can sell them; make a bunch of money.'

I roll my eyes. He can't help himself. He's always looking for the next scheme, which generally means the next way to lose a small fortune.

'What happened to your motorbike?'

'Nothing, but there's something about getting somewhere on your own steam, y'know? By the sweat of your own brow. Plus, Kelly says it's good for the polar bears, and there's no arguing with that chick.'

Kelly has been into green causes since watching some documentary on climate change, and I kind of like that she's recruited Garrett. He doesn't seem like a natural eco-warrior – more of a weekend warrior. Still, I can't imagine Garrett asked me here to talk about global warming.

'Here, can you lend a hand?' he says.

'I'm not very crafty.'

'You ride a watercraft every day.'

'Not the same thing.'

'All you gotta do is hold this piece in place while I saw.'

'OK.'

He sets to work. 'So Kelly's seemed different lately,' he says.

'Has she?'

'She's gone super quiet. Stopped wanting to——'

'Talk?' I say, desperately hoping the next word will be that.

'Suuuure,' he says slowly, raising his eyebrows and enjoying my embarrassment.

'Christ, Garrett, I can't talk to you about stuff like that. Gross.'

'I'm just kidding. I don't expect a diagnosis. But I thought you might be able to tell me if she's mad at me.'

'She hasn't said so.'

'She's super into Beth, right?'

'I dunno. Maybe. I thought you guys had an open relationship? All that Tinder stuff.'

Garrett puts down his saw, takes a second to consider this and sits down on the garage beanbag. He leans back, hands resting on his thighs and closes his eyes.

'Kelly told you that? She said we have an *open relationship*?'

'Maybe she didn't use those words, but she definitely said you were poly.'

I sit on a small stepladder and wait.

'The Tinder thing is make-believe. Nothing's gonna happen there.'

'Does she know that?'

'Sure. It's just the fantasy.'

'Hmm,' I say, feeling quite sure he has this wrong.

'But nobody's talking monogamy and forever afters. Kelly is going to college and one of these days I'll be going back to Hawaii.'

'You're going back to Hawaii? Like, soon?'

He sits up. 'I don't know when. But, sure, at some point I'll go back. It's home.'

'Doesn't mean you have to live there.'

'You never missed Newquay when you were away?'

I shrug, try to look cool, try to seem as if I hadn't missed it every single day. 'But what will happen with you and Kelly, if you go back to Oahu?'

'I don't know. That's not so easy to figure out,

215

especially when she won't talk about it.'

'You could still make it work. You could LDR it – do Skype.'

'Eww, *Skype*,' Garrett says, as if Skype is a half-dead rat carrying bubonic plague. But then, I think, Garrett's version of a Skype chat is probably quite different from mine. In that mine wouldn't involve lubricant.

'You don't think you could do a long-distance relationship?'

'Do *you* think I could do a long-distance relationship? Because maybe everything I know about myself is wrong . . .'

'All right, no need to take the mick,' I say. 'I just think it's a shame that you guys are giving in to the idea of splitting up.'

'What else is there? It's not like I'm gonna marry the girl.'

'What's wrong with Kelly?'

'Nothing. But she's seventeen. She's barely legal.'

'You're only twenty. It's not that big of an age gap.'

'Soon be twenty-one. What, am I gonna take her home and buy her and Beth milkshakes while I sit at the bar with a beer?'

'I don't know. Yeah, why not?'

'Iris, why do I have the feeling you want me to marry Kelly?'

'I don't want anyone to get married. I just don't

want you guys to break up.'

There's been enough breaking up already.

'And I want my girl to be into me again. We used to hang together all the time. Like right from Day One. Kelly told you how we got together?'

'I was there the night of the house party. For your stepdad's fiftieth birthday. I sort of got the drift that you liked each other. I remember you dancing on a table together to Stevie Nicks.'

'But did she tell you about the next night, down at the beach?'

'No, I don't think she did,' I say, racking my brains. 'Did you take her surfing or something?'

'Or something. She'd never even been on a proper board. I was surfing and when I came out of the water she was waiting for me. At least, I think she was waiting for me. She was sitting there with a book, like *Fifty Shades of Lame* or something like that, but she wasn't reading, she was watching the surfers. I didn't notice her at first; I was worried about this really gnarly little ding I'd just put in the nose of my board and was trying to remember where I'd left my solar repair kit, when she shouted my name and I went over and said hey.'

Kelly would have been all over that. It was the sort of daydream she'd spent a lot of time working on during our first few years of secondary school. She always liked surfers, especially ones with sick bods and cool accents.

'Yeah, and?'

'Then I asked for her number, since she'd left the party while I was taking a leak. I didn't have a pen or my phone, so I scratched her cell into my board wax.'

'That is actually quite romantic,' I say, smiling as I imagine Garrett digging his fingernail into Sex Wax to scratch out a phone number, and wondering why Kelly hadn't told me that.

'Then she gave me a handjob in the dunes.'

'GARRETT,' I say, completely blind-sided.

'There was a moment. We'd been kissing for like forty-five minutes.'

'Garrett, seriously, too much information. Waaay too much information.'

'My bad.'

'When we were little we used to practise our recorders in those dunes. We played roly-polies there. I never thought Kelly would be doing *that* there.'

'Real pretty view of the ocean.'

He smiles as he says it, but there's anxiety written on his face too. Kelly's getting to him.

'One more thing I gotta ask you,' he says.

Here it comes, I think. He knows.

'Zeke still sober?'

This is not what I expected him to ask. 'Erm, he's drinking quite a lot of alcohol.'

'I was talking about crystal.'

'He's not on meth. No way. Why'd you ask?'

'Two weeks ago he signed over the apartment to me.'

'*You* put it up for sale?'

'I'm having a few financial issues.'

'Hot air balloon business didn't take off?'

He grimaces at the pun.

'Turns out Cornwall is one of the poorest areas of this whole country. Who knew?'

I consider answering this diplomatically, but go for, 'Only everyone who lives here.'

He shrugs. 'So . . . will you talk to Kelly for me?' he says, giving me serious eyes.

'I'll try,' I say, extracting myself from the stepladder. 'I've gotta get going.'

'See you tonight.'

'You coming out with us?'

'Nope, guys are banned, but I think I'm supposed to be giving you a ride to Perranporth.'

'See you then.'

'Say hi to Zeke from me if you speak to him today. I can't get him to pick up.'

'OK.' I rush out of the garage, because if I stay any longer, I know I'll crack and when I do it'll be like the San Andreas Fault.

chapter thirty

The plan is that after Garrett drops us in Perranporth, we're going to hang out at the Watering Hole for the evening, a gorgeous beach bar at the foot of the dunes with dozens of tables set outside on the sand. I can't wait to get there and chill out in front of the legendary Perranporth sunset. It's going to be a mellow one, and when we're done, probably around eleven, Garrett's going to pick us up. Beth is already on the way, having decided to walk the coastal path rather than accept a lift from Kelly's boyfriend.

Kelly insists she's going to help me with my make-up, since the only bottle of foundation I have is now at least three shades too light and I haven't bothered to buy more, even though it means my zits are permanently on show.

She marches into my bedroom holding a box that has several pull-out layers packed with different make-up products. This is her mum's 'posh kit', which Kelly's absolutely forbidden from using as it has about a grand's worth of stuff in it. All the very best cosmetic brands and brushes that her mum uses when she's making a bit of money on the side by doing wedding and prom make-up.

'Is Beth staying with you tonight?' I ask, knowing how this sounds.

'Nope, she has her own accommodation.'

'And where's that?'

'She won't say.'

Kelly starts giving me the once-over, appraising my skin tone, as she sorts through the products and stacks them on my dressing table.

I get off the three-legged wooden stool my dad made in one of his more practical moments, and go to get one of the comfy chairs from the kitchen with the padded seats, since it's clear I'll be stuck on it for ages.

'Are your eyelashes actually white?' Kelly asks, looking thoroughly unimpressed.

'Bleached out from the sun. Sorry.'

'Can't you wear waterproof mascara when you're surfing to protect 'em?'

'Nope. It ends up smudged under my eyes and it's not as if anyone cares how my eyelashes look when I'm in the middle of a contest heat. Anyway,' I add, 'I won't wear make-up in the water out of principle. My contribution to ending the sexualization of female surfers. So . . . what does Garrett think about Beth being here?'

'Not bothered. Long as I spend some time with him, he's happy.'

221

'*Are* you spending time with him?'

'Yeah. Why? Did he say something?'

'No.' I've bottled it. He wants me to find out what she's thinking, but I don't want her to feel like I've been gossiping about her behind her back, especially to her boyfriend.

'Want me to do your hair first?' she asks, picking up my water spray and a detangling comb. 'When did you last wash it?'

'Like with shampoo?'

'Yes, like with shampoo.'

'I haven't really been doing that, unless I had some swish event, because I've been in the sea so much. Didn't seem much point if it was gonna get salty two hours later.'

'So you've just stopped washing it altogether?'

I shrug and she makes her horrified face.

'Maybe I should cut it?' I say, mulling it over.

'When did you last have a trim? I can cut it for you now if you like?' she offers, retrieving gold-tipped scissors from her mum's box of tricks. 'You could totally rock a pixie cut.'

'No,' I say, panicking as she lifts the blades. 'I'll sort it out another day.'

'Your choice,' she says, 'but since you're gonna wash it with actual shampoo tonight, how about pushing the boat out and treating yourself to a blob of conditioner?'

222

'OK,' I say, sighing and dragging myself to the en-suite.

An hour later I have a face full of make-up and clean, straightened hair that hangs like a curtain almost to my navel.

Kelly is appraising me as if I'm her life's work. I'm still only in bra, pants and towel; I have yet to decide what to wear.

'So show me everything you bought on your travels,' she says, walking purposefully towards my wardrobe.

'I didn't buy much that was fancy.'

'Come on, you must have something.'

'Well, there was this one dress I bought in Miami.'

'Done. You're wearing that.'

'You haven't even seen it yet.'

'You bought it in Miami! It's gotta be cool.'

I pull the thin silver dress out of my wardrobe. My mum looked at the label and took it to the dry cleaners. If it had been up to me, I'd have probably binned it. It was the dress I'd worn on my seventeenth birthday, the night I ended up in the Everglades. The worst birthday ever.

'Wow, girl,' Kelly says, looking impressed. 'That had to cost a few quid. Do you have shoes for it?'

'Yeah.'

I pull out my stilettos and chuck them on the bed. 'But we're going to a beach bar, so I'm wearing flip-flops. I'll give you the hair and make-up, but I need to be able to walk tonight without sinking, OK?'

'Fine. Y'know, you scrub up pretty well when you make the effort.'

I throw one of the flip-flops at her. 'I make plenty of effort, thanks very much. Just not at painting a new face each morning.'

Garrett gives us a lift in Dave's new car, which is all slick German engineering and leather interiors. He breaks the speed limit on several occasions, weaving along the winding Cornish roads like he's on a race track.

'Knock it off, Garrett,' Kelly says from the front, while I brace myself with one hand on the back of her seat.

'Hey, so Titans is probably gonna run today,' Garrett says, sounding depressed.

'Titans?' Kelly asks.

'Titans of Mavericks,' I say, thinking back to the gold envelope Zeke had received while we were in Miami. An invitation extended only to an elite band of big-wave surfers. 'They changed the name of it. It's the contest in northern California that Zeke was invited to compete in.'

'Bummer that Zeke's in Africa,' Garrett says. 'I reckon he had a real shot at that thing.'

'He's probably had enough of potentially lethal waves beating him up,' Kelly says. 'And who can blame him?'

'It's the opportunity of a lifetime,' Garrett says. 'You don't turn that shit down.'

'You do sometimes,' I murmur, and Kelly turns in her seat to look at me.

Still not giving up, Garrett continues, 'Old folks say that right at the end, when it's too late to change anything, you only regret the things you didn't do. Little brother's always gonna regret passing up Mavericks.'

'Yes, well, he'll live,' Kelly says. 'Which is the main thing.'

'It's not the number of breaths you take that's important,' Garrett says, 'it's how you use the oxygen.'

Kelly looks at him and frowns. 'Er, I imagine Zeke will use it for breathing.'

'You use it to power your body,' Garrett says. 'And Zeke's should be powering through Mavs.'

Beth hasn't arrived in Perranporth when we get there, but we queue up at the Watering Hole to buy pints of Coke padded out with too much ice, which we fish out and leave on the soil of a potted palm to melt in the heat of way too many punters. This purchase is purely because Kelly has one hipflask of Malibu in her handbag and another one of vodka. We go sit at a table outside and watch the surf building in the bay as the swell rolls in.

'God, I missed this,' I say.

'I bet you didn't give us a second thought. Too busy living the dream.'

'I missed you. Every. Single. Day.'

225

Kelly gives my hand a squeeze and turns her back to hide the fact that she's topping up my Coke with an inch of booze.

When we're halfway through our hipflasks, which happens surprisingly quickly, we bump into our friend Jack. He has his own promo company, and we get talking to him and two of his brand new friends from Sydney.

'Check it out,' one of the Australian lads says to me, motioning to his crotch. He roots through the front of his trousers and flashes a squashy plastic bag of pink wine with a black spigot in one corner, which he's tucked into his waistband.

'Ooh, what do you have in there?' Kelly says, looking on with great interest.

'Ahh, it's just goon. Help yourself,' he says to us.

'No thanks,' I say. I've sampled enough of the stuff during my time in Australia with Zeke to know that in my case at least it led to extreme puking and killer hangovers. The only good thing about goon, as far as I could tell, was that once you'd drunk all the wine, you could blow up the bag to make a pillow, right before you passed out on the floor.

'You want some?' he asks Kelly.

'Like my head's going anywhere near your penis,' she says, nodding at his crotch. 'Mind you, the night is young,' she says, winking. 'Ask me again later.'

The Sydney boys look really shocked at this, which

makes me smile. No matter how cheeky a boy is to Kelly, she always manages to outdo them.

'You don't have to drink it from my undies,' he says, fishing out the whole wobbly bag and passing it to Kelly. 'I'm James, by the way.'

'Oh, all right. I'll have a bit. If you insist.'

I watch as she positions it above her head and lets the flowing wine fall into her mouth, no longer showing any concern about the glass collectors seeing her consuming non-bar purchases.

She drinks for a good long time and then belches.

'Lush,' I say, and she hands the bag to me.

'Try it,' she says. 'It's really nice!'

'Go on, then,' I say, and tilt my head backwards. Which is, I think afterwards, the point of no return.

chapter thirty-one

Once the goon kicks in, Kelly sees fit to tell everyone we meet that I'm a famous pro-surfer and that if they Google my name, they'll see for themselves. She also takes it upon herself to pull my Billabong business cards from my wallet and hand them out to every lad we meet, which results in me getting various cryptic text messages over the next two hours from unrecognized numbers, and rank photos from three different senders, plus one link to an amateur porn site.

After a while though, I get used to being treated like a minor celebrity and even start to like it a bit. People seem really interested in hearing about my travels, the waves I've surfed, and they have loads of questions.

Beth still hasn't arrived and Kelly is flirting furiously with another Australian traveller, despite her advanced state of inebriation.

I'm about to interrupt when the goon guy, James, approaches me again. He has a fresh bag of cheapo wine now, which he tells me he has just purchased in the corner shop, this time in a silver bag. I watch as he crushes the outer box it came in and walks a few metres to chuck it in the huge beach bins. As he leans over, I can't help noticing that his jeans have ridden down quite a lot.

'Hey,' he says, on his return. 'I didn't know you were a pro-surfer. My mate's sponsored too. Mostly local brands. He's here somewhere. You have to meet him. He's surfed heaps of crazy waves. Even Shipsterns.'

It feels good to be with someone who's seen a bit of the surfing world and speaks my language. My little area of Cornwall is full of interesting travellers and it's about time I got to know them.

'Wanna get out of here?' I say.

'Hell yeah,' he says in an over-the-top American accent that makes me think of Zeke.

'Cool.' I take his wrist and start walking towards the exit.

'Wait, where are we going?' he asks.

'Somewhere quiet.'

I'm not entirely sure what I have in mind, except that it will start with a deep and meaningful conversation with this Aussie boy who, after half a bottle of Malibu and a fair bit of wine, I'm starting to find very attractive. We walk to the dunes, away from the noise and light of the beach bar.

'Hey, I'm only in Newquay tonight. We're leaving for London early tomorrow, so . . .'

He raises an eyebrow at me. This is a question. No, a proposition.

'Let's go back a bit,' I say, suddenly having second thoughts. 'It's too dark here.'

'Nah. Come on. *Seize the day*,' he says, and pulls me into a savage kiss.

He is not seizing the day. He is seizing me.

He's pulled my stupid long hair backwards so that my face is tilted upwards, which is hurting my neck like hell, and he's kissing me hard. His breath smells of cigarettes, goon and some spicy snack that he must've eaten at the shop. He loosens his grip and I manage to wrench myself free.

'What's the problem?' he says.

'*You* are,' I say, breathless with anger.

Then, suddenly, Beth is with us and she's pushed him hard, sent him tumbling backwards and he's landed on his arse. She's looking at me with concern, asking me if I'm OK.

'I'm fine. No thanks to him.'

'Hey – you brought *me* out here!' he says, scrambling to his feet and looking affronted.

'Who cares? You could see she wasn't up for it,' Beth says. 'What the hell is wrong with you?'

'Just go,' I say to him. I'm completely unable to control my own shaking.

'Whatever.' For a moment I think he's actually going

230

to leave. Then he turns back to me. 'Hey, I Googled you earlier, *Iris Fox*,' he says, getting out his phone.

'He can use a search engine!' Beth says. 'Give the boy a prize.'

He ignores her and smiles at me, his eyes glinting maliciously. 'Your friend made out you're this radical charger with heaps of progressive moves, but you're shit. You can't even do airs and your bottom-turns are crap.'

Then he holds up his phone screen to me and I see the page of some hater forum, *Fugly Gurfer Fails*, with a bunch of GIFs of my most embarrassing wipe-outs, incomplete manoeuvres and failed attempts to land airs.

I feel my face flush, and pain grips my chest. I know this feeling. Humiliation.

'Well, *mate*, she just beat me in a contest,' Beth says, her voice tight, 'and I grew up shredding Maroubra, so I'd say that makes her pretty special. Now piss off before I break your arms.'

Beth is a black belt in karate and I'm quite sure she's capable of breaking any part of him.

He looks her up and down, his eyes skimming over her black vest top, which reveals serious muscle and sugar skull tattoos, and I see the moment he decides it's not worth the effort. 'Yeah, whatever you reckon. Have a nice life,' he says, and then adds, '*Bitches.*'

He doesn't go back to the Watering Hole and we watch him take off across the beach and towards the car park. The tide's coming in, so he has to wade around the rocks.

'Christ, Iris,' she says. 'You OK?'

'Yes. I think so.'

'What he do to you?'

'Nothing . . . I don't know. Kissed me. Pulled my hair,' I say, looking at a clump of it sitting on some marram grass. 'I'm fine. Let's just go and find Kelly.'

I can't say anything else and take a moment just to get a handle on my breathing.

'I'm glad you were here,' I say, eventually.

'Took me a minute to recognize you with your hair like that. I saw you leaving the bar and was worried you might be a bit Adrian Quist, so I followed to make sure you were OK.'

'Adrian Quist?'

'Pissed. Reckon we should call the police?' she says. I can tell Beth's been drinking a bit today too. She probably stopped at one of the other pubs along the way.

'No,' I say. 'Please.'

'Why not? There's some wannabe rapist running around. Let's get the shithead locked up.'

'I don't even know his surname. Anyway, he's leaving tomorrow.'

'Come on, we'll call your mum and ask her to pick you up.'

'No, I'm not telling her anything. She worries all the time as it is. And please don't tell Kelly either, will you?

232

I'll tell her myself tomorrow when she's sober.'

'OK, but I still reckon you need to report it to someone.'

'What would I say? He kissed me and pulled my hair? I just want to forget it.'

When I get back to the bar, Kelly hasn't even noticed I'd left. I sit with Beth, not able to think of a single topic of conversation. Kelly dances for a bit, then goes off to the loo and comes back with a huge grin on her face.

'I AM ON THE BLOB, LAYDEEZ AND GENTLEMEN!' she announces to the bar. 'No Garrett Junior on the way! Woo!'

'Thank Christ for that,' Beth says, looking relieved.

'Kelly told you about the pregnancy scare?' I say. I thought Beth would have been the last person she told.

'Course I told Beth,' Kelly says, staggering between us. 'I like totally love her, Iris.'

Beth rolls her eyes, then mouths to me, *That right there is Adrian Quist.*

Then we watch as Kelly climbs on a table, puts on her sunglasses and starts rapping along to Flo Rida's 'My House'.

Within the hour Garrett shows up in Dave's car to give us a lift home.

Kelly sits with her head lolling back against the headrest and witters on about her most amusing drunken conversations of the night and me and Beth sit in silence in the back, her hand on mine on the middle seat.

When we get to the mini-roundabout by the River Gannel, I get my phone out of my bag, open an iMessage and write, *Zeke, can you call me?*

Then I delete every word and put my phone back in my bag.

Garrett drops me at the end of my street and I run through the dark to my house. The TV is on in the living room, where I can hear Lily laughing at some soft-core porno by the sounds of it, and I run straight upstairs, crawl into bed and count the stars.

But there's a soft knock at my bedroom door.

chapter thirty-two

'Fancy going for a hot chocolate at the Lewinnick? Mick's taken Mum to the cinema, so I'll drive us in her car.'

'They'll be closing soon.'

'No, they're open late for some BID function. Raising money for the air ambulance's new night-time flying hours. Little Lapin are playing and there's free cake!'

Newquay's Business Improvement District group are always putting on community events and it usually means running into loads of people you know and having to make small-talk with them. I couldn't handle that.

'I'm not up for it, Lil.'

'Come on! Your favourite local band is playing and there's *free cake*, Iris! Plus, the Lewinnick's hiring. I was thinking I might talk to Paulie and try to get some hours. Tide me over while I'm here.'

'If you do, you'd better not ask me for ID,' I say.

She laughs, stops in front of my bedroom mirror and slaps on some of the make-up Kelly left here and then drags me to my wardrobe and gets me to change into jeans and a T-shirt. I groan, tell her I can't be bothered, but Lily insists and I give in. It's not the worst thing in the world to have Lily with me when I'm feeling like absolute crap.

She throws a yellow and grey scarf around her neck and I reach for my bobble hat. The night sea breeze is going to be nippy at the Lewinnick, perched as it is right on the cliff. Lily chats in the car, she talks so much that I can hide in the shadow of her personality, follow her brain from thought to thought and not form my own.

When we get into the bar area, the band has already left and there are only around a dozen people there, lots of faces I recognize, but no one who's likely to interrogate me, which is a relief. Lily goes to investigate the cake table, but there are only a few crumbly bits and bobs left, which she makes the most of anyway.

Suddenly my phone goes off. Kelly's ringing me. Weird, as I assumed she'd be passed out by now, wrapped in the arms of Garrett. Or Beth.

'Everything all right, Kel?'

'Titans of Mavericks is on,' she says, her voice all breathy. 'He changed his mind! Zeke is competing!'

Oh my God.

'What's happening? Has he ridden a wave yet?'

'Yes! He was just up on some crazy bomb and broke his board. He's fine. I think he's going to try to get another one.'

236

So while I was being mauled by some halitosis wino, Zeke was competing in the world's highest profile big-wave contest.

I look at my watch. Zeke will be on Pacific Standard Time so it's only afternoon where he is. The evening hasn't even happened for him. I wish I could say the same.

'He's supposed to be in Angola,' I say. I can't believe he's actually gone through with it. Zeke is confronting his worst fears and risking his life by braving the terrifying energy unleased in the Mavericks bowl. I feel sick at the thought of him facing that heavy, super-violent wave, which has killed other professional surfers in the past: blokes who were older and more experienced than Zeke.

'Yep, looks like he's on a whistle-stop tour of the world,' Kelly says, with a sigh.

Once he heard Mavericks was green-lit to run, he must have changed his mind, rushed to the airport and jumped on the first flight to San Francisco.

A waitress begins noisily stacking plates in front of me.

'Where are you, Iris?'

'Lewinnick with Lily.'

'Get them to put it on the screens!'

I tell Paulie, the manager, about the contest and he flicks through the obscure sports channels until he finds it and whacks up the sound. He's a surfer too and I know he'll want to stay up to watch this.

The live feed keeps cutting out, but it's interspersed

with clips of Zeke wiping out horribly on his previous ride – a giant, evil-looking wave. I can only imagine the panic Zeke must have felt as that wave detonated around him. It must have brought back the worst memories. The feed cuts to him furiously paddling half a surfboard back to the channel and swapping it out with a new board.

He air-drops on another bomb, somehow remains vertical, and this time it all comes off perfectly. There are some ugly bumps and kinks on the wave, but he rides it out and the whitewater never catches him. Even the commentators are awed.

Every patron left in the Lewinnick is up on their feet, cheering him on, and a few of them clap me on the back, as if this is my achievement.

I slump down next to Lily, and we mainline complimentary hot chocolates from Paulie, and watch the rest of the contest in silence. When it's through, I feel exhausted. In the past twenty-four hours my emotions have scrolled through sadness, embarrassment, terror, and relief, now that I've seen Zeke do the thing he needed to do. Win.

I don't want to stick around for the prize-giving ceremony. I haven't seen the podium part of this contest before, but I know I don't need to see Zeke hold a trophy above his head. Don't need to see him handed a fifty-thousand-dollar cheque, or start a champagne fight with the other guys. I definitely don't need to see a former or current Miss World put a flower wreath over his head and watch him get hugged and kissed by a dozen girls in hot pants and tight T-shirts.

But, even though I'm shattered, I can't take my eyes off the screen, and I watch Zeke carried by six guys on his board. The crowd roars and it's Zeke's name that they're shouting and cheering. They're treating him like a rock star. An old man with a microphone wipes a tear from his eye and says, 'That was the best surfing I've seen since Greg Noll charged Makaha.'

It is the most surreal feeling. Zeke has done it, has officially made the big time. Watching him holding the wooden wave trophy, a smile of total disbelief splashed across his face, like he's just this second discovered he has the ability to fly, I feel overcome with emotion. I'm both stoked for him and absolutely crushed.

He takes the mic to make his victory speech, his hands shaking.

'I wanna thank my family, my sponsors, my agent, my coach and all the other wavesliders who hang with me. Special thanks to my mom for teaching me to surf and my pa for all the awesome pep talks, my brothers Garrett and Wes for shredding so hard and making me wanna do what they do. And . . . yeah,' he says, his face becoming very still, 'I also want to thank pro-surfer Iris Fox from Newquay, a little town in Britain, who helped get me here today.'

My heart clenches and I feel as if I've been punched. In

his moment of glory, his thoughts have turned to me. And not just his thoughts, his words: he's name-checked me to the entire international surf community.

I should never have even been in those dunes at Perranporth. I should have been with Zeke in Half Moon Bay, California.

A cheer goes up in the Lewinnick at the mention of Newquay. 'And to everyone else who turned out today: you guys rock. Appreciate the support so much. Oh and my man Jimmy, you got no reason to have your head down, buddy. You surfed awesome out there! You too, Alonso. Proud of you guys. Now let's go celebrate.'

'I'm out of here, Lil,' I say, and she doesn't try to convince me to stay. She just looks at me with sympathy and follows me out.

'I'm sorry, Iris. That had to hurt.'

'I shouldn't have left,' I say. 'It was a massive mistake.'

'You had good reasons for coming home. Remember them.'

'Yeah, cos coming home's turned out to be so totally amazing,' I say, my voice cracking.

'What is it?' she says. 'Something happened earlier this evening, didn't it? You're upset.'

'No. It's two a.m., Lil, and I just want to get to bed.'

chapter thirty-three

I sleep in until 11 a.m. and pour myself a drink that's half orange juice and half gin from the bottle that Caleb let me keep, before I've even eaten my cereal.

Then I text Kelly, who's sent me eight messages making sure I'm OK after seeing Zeke take a major contest.

I'm happy for him. But I have to tell you about something else, Kel.

What?

I went outside with one of those Aussie blokes at the Watering Hole and he wouldn't let go of my hair.

I don't get what you mean, Iris? Was he messing around??

No, it was heavy. Felt like he was sort of trying to force himself on me.

WHAAAT?

He didn't do anything except pull my hair and kiss me, but it freaked me out. Don't stress about it. He's probably left Newquay by now. Beth was there and gave him shit. I told her I'd tell you about it, so now I have and we don't have to mention it again.

Iris. This is serious. Come over.

I don't want to. I'm fine. I just need to forget it. See you tomorrow.

I don't want to think about last night. Luckily, I am well-practised at regurgitating my feelings and locking them in a sealed box, deep under the floorboards where I will never look.

I know Kelly would tell me that this is not a long-term solution, that eventually I'll have to deal, that feelings always need to be felt, but I'm not ready to do that and I don't know when, or if, I ever will be.

Anyway, at least it won't be long before I'm out of Newquay. I'll soon be packing for my Mexico trip, hunting for my warm water wax, mossie spray and fin keys. No chance of running into anyone then. It's the penultimate contest and I have to get serious about my training. I'll need to be mentally and physically prepared, with a spine of steel and my game face on. I don't have time to think about Aussie goonheads with bright smiles and black hearts. Or a soft-spoken, wide-shouldered boy from Hawaii who holds my heart in his back pocket. I'll be with Beth and the other girls from the tour and we'll focus on one thing only. Surfing.

My phone lights up with a call from Anders.

'Hey, man. How's it going?'

'Iris, thank God you picked up! Sorry to hear about your break-up with Zeke. That sucks. So, anyway . . .' the line breaks up and I only catch about twenty per cent of his words. '. . . they assessed it and there's just not enough time. Couldn't be helped.'

'Sorry, I didn't catch that. What did you say?'

'Mexico. Severe hurricane damage all along that stretch of coast, including all the competitor accommodation and the surf centre. No time to fix the damage before your contest. Health and safety concerns.'

'Wait, you mean it's delayed? They'll do it later, right?'

'Cancelled. To be perfectly honest, the competition hasn't exactly been a raging success. Dwindling interest. I imagine they'll be relieved to cut one of the locations.'

'Awesome.'

'Don't feel too down about it. Think of all the experience you've had. All the travel. Better than spending the winter in stormy Cornwall. And if you win Fistral, you'll have taken the whole competition, and who knows what opportunities will come your way.'

He's right. I have to stay positive. I've worked hard in training and I'm more proud of my win in Florida than anything else in my life.

'Thanks, Anders. I'll concentrate on the final.'

'Exactly. Not to pile on extra pressure, but everything comes down to Fistral, so don't screw it up.'

'I'll try not to.'

* * *

243

Downstairs Lily is already awake and lounging in the kitchen in a white Lycra vest and shorts. She's wearing make-up but not wearing underwear so I can see both her nipples and her pubes, but she doesn't seem the least bit embarrassed.

'Who was that on the phone?'

'Anders. Mexico's been cancelled.'

'You can't cancel a country, Iris.'

'My contest there. Obviously. Hurricane's damaged that whole coast.'

'Bad luck. Sorry.'

'Thanks.'

'Look, I left my scarf at the Lewinnick. I'm going to get dressed and walk over now, if you want to come? We'll get some decent breakfast. I'll treat you,' she says.

I look into the fridge and see we're low on pretty much everything.

'Yeah, breakfast would be good,' I say. I can feel my blood sugar is crashing and I already feel wobbly enough as it is.

We walk to Pentire and eat a fried breakfast that makes me feel queasy. The hot bartender guy comes to clear away our plates, and as Lily puts down money for the bill, a bubble of emotion pops somewhere in the vicinity of my chest and I make an ugly sort of sob noise.

'Lil,' I say, tears coming into my eyes.

'Iris, what is it? I know it's not just Zeke winning

that competition thing. Something's happened. At Perranporth, right?'

'Did Kelly text you?'

'No. I have eyes, Iris. What went down? Did you have an argument with Caleb?'

I shake my head. 'No, Caleb wasn't even there.'

'What happened?'

I can't bring myself to say it. I have to change the subject. 'I can't believe Zeke actually won Titans of Mavericks.'

'Forget Zeke for a minute. Tell me about last night.'

'It's no big deal.'

She looks at me, hawk-eyed, and beneath the kohl-rimmed eyes and pale orange lipstick, I see my mum. She's waiting for me to tell her the truth.

'It was just, something happened with some random Aussie bloke and . . . I didn't want it to.'

Without another word, Lily leads me away from the Lewinnick and we follow a rabbit path to our favourite sunbathing spot, which looks across an expanse of ocean to Fistral Beach.

We sit down on the springy grass, cross-legged, facing the water, and she says, 'Tell me everything.'

It doesn't take me long to get through it and when I finish, she puts her arm around me.

'Does Mum know?'

'No. She'll only worry.'

'Do you want to make a police report?'

'I don't know where he was staying, or even his surname, and he's leaving Newquay today. He's probably already gone.'

'Report it anyway.'

'They'll think I'm stupid for going outside with him.'

'No. You had every right to go outside. "Outside" is not, by default, a male space. This is not your fault.'

'Yes, but I was the one to suggest it,' I say, cringing at the memory. 'It wouldn't have happened if I'd stayed inside.'

'It might have. Inside, outside. The space is not the problem. The mentality is.'

'Just leave it, Lil,' I say. 'It's nothing.'

But it isn't nothing, it's something, and it keeps swirling over me, like I'm trapped on the seabed, watching a barrelling wave roll over the surface, high above.

She sighs deeply. 'I should tell you something, Iris, that you aren't really going to want to hear.'

Colour flushes into her cheeks and she takes a moment to compose herself.

'Right. Every girl in my friend group has been sexually assaulted at some point in her life. Some were abused in childhood, some were raped in adolescence, and others were assaulted by strangers, or people they thought they knew. It is more common than anyone admits and not one of my friends was to blame. You hear me?

NONE of them was to blame.'

Lily is an extrovert, with a crew of tough-looking girls she's picked up at art college, the indie band scene and her various international travels. I can barely take in what she's saying. 'They were all assaulted? *All* of them?'

'Every single one. Including me.'

'Oh my God, Lil,' I say, staring at her in total shock. 'You never said. When did it happen?'

She exhales, shakes her head and then says, very clearly, '*Which time?*'

As we walk together into town, Lily tells me about the most recent incident, which happened late one night at a train station in Paris, but she dwells mostly on the French police officers who had been completely kind and professional when she had reported it.

'I'll tell you about the rest of them another day,' she says with a grim smile, as we arrive at St Michael's Road.

'OK,' I say, not wanting to push her for details that might cause her pain.

She gives me a hug and then saunters off towards the health centre to book a long overdue smear test. 'Gotta keep on keeping on,' she says. 'So say the cells of my cervix.'

When my mum doesn't come home for lunch, I go back up into my bedroom with its smell of damp, dust and dirty skateboard, and drink a highball of my mum's schnapps. My phone beeps and it's Daniel, asking if I fancy the skate park today.

Yeah, what time? I text back, my main thought being, *Just screw it all.*

Got a bit of work down the harbour. Say, 5 p.m.?

OK.

I sit on the bed, kick off my shoes and meditate myself into a state of something verging on calm. Then I lie face down, feeling my chest push into the mattress.

Not so long ago I'd been in this room with Zeke. Sneaked him in at night and sent him off to do the walk of shame as the sun came up. Except he was never ashamed. He was happy.

He'd helped me pack my bags for our travels in this room, told me we were going to have the time of our lives. Soon he'd be back for the wedding. I wouldn't just be looking at him on a screen, which had been hard enough. I'd be looking into his eyes.

My phone vibrates again.

Don't be late.

His message is peppered with three winking smilies, just in case I haven't caught on to the fact that he's joking. I've never known Daniel to use an emoji. He always said they creeped him out.

I sleep for a few hours and when I wake up, I feel a bit better and think about getting ready to meet Daniel. Most of my travelling gear is still in the washing basket at the top of the stairs. I look over at my wardrobe, trying to remember which clothes I've left behind and wondering if any of my old gear will still fit. I go over to it, touching all my old things, faint whiffs of me emanating from the fabric.

It will look dodgy if I make too much of an effort, but I don't want him to see me looking rubbish, either. Finally, I settle on a loose T-shirt with various profanities graffitied on the back, and some splash-dyed leggings with my old Vans trainers. The T-shirt is tighter on my arms than I remembered, but the leggings are loose in the waistband.

Surfing is changing my body weight distribution, moving it closer to the V-shape of male surfers. Online haters say this makes me look 'blokey' but I don't give a toss because a stronger upper body and leaner lower body make it easier to catch and ride waves.

When I finally get to the skate park, a sea fog has rolled in and half of the place is lost in grey. I walk around the metal bars and through the entrance, narrowly avoiding a football that two of the lads are kicking from ramp to ramp.

'Can you stop that?' I say, and one of them says sorry but the other one tells me to get stuffed, and carries on.

'Charming,' I say, carrying my skateboard around to the half-pipe, where I see Daniel. He has his back to the board-fence and is sitting down, legs in the classic manspread. When he sees me, he grins. Even though it's been a long time since we were together, I feel my heart go out to him in the old way.

'Better late than never,' is what he says to me. 'You didn't tell your mum you was meeting me, did you?'

'Left her a note to say I was going for a skate.'

'Still hates me then.'

I glance at him, wondering if he's really going to knock out his 'boo-hoo, I'm so misunderstood' routine.

'Yes, she still hates you, Daniel. Stabbing Zeke in the leg may have something to do with it. As well as you cheating on me with my friend.'

'I know. I didn't mean to stab him, though. I only wanted to scare him a bit,' he says, and he sounds earnest enough. 'I was drunk and slipped. I feel shit about it. The cheating weren't an accident. Sorry.'

'Yeah, I can see you're dripping with sorrow. And you should feel terrible. If you'd clipped the artery he'd be dead.'

'I'd do anything to go back and change that night. I never carried a knife again. Threw it in a drain right after.'

'Got rid of the evidence. Smart.'

'Well, yeah, but I knew I crossed a line and I was never gonna do that again. I know I'm lucky I wasn't arrested,' he says. 'Why didn't he press charges?'

'Don't ask me. I told him he should.'

'Probably be bad for his clean teen thing. Getting stabbed by some local dirtbag.'

Daniel was spot on. Zeke couldn't afford to be caught up in any kind of scandal. Not after his history with drug use. He couldn't risk that coming out.

'He's not that clean,' I say, thinking about all the things I've learnt about Zeke in the past year, 'but, yeah, something like that. Plus, he gives everyone a lot of chances, even when they don't deserve them.'

'If I hadn't done it, you'd never have got together with him. He'd have been gone, instead of chilling out here all summer.'

'Daniel, I don't think he's going to thank you, somehow.'

'I know. I'm just saying that it's cos of me that the two of you got together.'

'Change the subject, Dan. Seriously.'

A group of about thirty kids gets off a bus in the overspill car park and starts filing towards the skate park. Some of them have penny boards, some of them have BMXs and, even worse, some of them have scooters.

Daniel and I lock eyes.

'Great,' he says. 'Youth club tournament.'

'Let's go somewhere else then.'

'Yeah, but like where?' He spins his cap around so it's on sideways and says, 'Wait, I know. Follow me.'

We cut down past Waterworld, through a back road to

251

Wildflower Lane, and I watch him scramble up through a gap in the hedge.

'Really, Dan?'

We're at the back of Newquay Zoo. It shut an hour or so before, but there could still be staff members and keepers wandering about.

'Yep. It's a zoo and we're the only people here. What's not to like?'

Daniel leaves his carveboard in front of the hedge, swings up onto the high wire fence and jumps over. 'Throw my board.'

'No way. Weighs a ton. You should've carried it over.'

'Come on,' he says. 'Lob it!'

'Sod off. Come and get it if you want it.'

'Stash it then and climb over.'

'Is this not super-lame? Also, this fence is like fifteen feet high.'

'You're lighter and fitter than me. If I can do it, you can do it. And it's ten feet.'

'Wait a minute,' I say, hiding our skateboards in the undergrowth.

I do my best to climb the fence without getting my trainers stuck in the wire mesh holes. From the top it seems like a very long way down.

'Oh, balls, I don't want to jump,' I say. 'If I break my ankle I'll be out of the competition.' I think of all the nagging I'd get from Anders. The disappointment I'd bring

252

to everyone who's worked so hard with me.

'So you're staying up there all night? Don't be such a wimp. Jump.'

I turn and let my body hang down from the top of the fence so I won't have as far to drop, and then I let go.

Half a second later, Daniel's arms are tight around my waist.

253

chapter thirty-four

'Caught ya,' he says, breathing into my hair.

I wriggle out of his arms and turn around.

'Get off,' I say. 'Why are we here?'

'Come on, let's go wake up the lions.'

'How about we let sleeping lions lie. Where are we now?' I ask, looking at the holey ground beneath my feet, where some critter has obviously been tunnelling.

'Racoons, it used to be, but I think they've been moved somewhere else now.'

A little creature pops its head out of a hole and bolts.

'Meerkats!' we say at exactly the same time, Daniel looking even happier about it than me.

'Let's stay here for a bit,' I say.

We get settled and sit in silence, until he asks, 'What was it like surfing in all them foreign countries? Weren't it hard not speaking the language?'

'Yeah, until I figured out that learning the words for three things in every language made life a lot easier. One:

Hello. Two: Sorry, I don't speak this language. And three: Where's the loo?'

Daniel smiles and swings his small rucksack off his shoulders.

'You bring any drink?' I ask.

'Yep.' He hands me four cans of weak lager. 'I brought a picnic.'

'*You* made a picnic?'

'Nah, my mum did. I told her I was seeing you and she went straight up Asda and spent like an hour putting it together.'

'Bless her. She shouldn't have gone to so much trouble.'

'She loves it. Want some of these?'

I nod and he passes me some Jacob's cream crackers, which his mum has covered with real butter and sandwiched together.

He opens a pack of mini-Scotch eggs, and when I shake my head, he burns through them one by one until he's eaten the whole lot.

'She was gutted when you left Newquay. Kept Googling you so she could find out when you was competing in surf contests. Glued to the webcasts. At first it was to watch you, but then she got into the men's tour too. She has a crush on Owen Wright. Thinks he's hot because he's like six foot eight and ripped. Oh, and blond. She likes long blond hair on men, which is just weird if you ask me. Unless you like your blokes looking like birds.'

I think about Kelly's preferences and then I think about Zeke's hair and how much I'd loved it long and sun-bleached. How sad I'd been when he'd shaved it off during a low moment. Daniel must have guessed what I was thinking.

'Not that there's anything wrong with long hair, like. Not having a go at the Yank. It's fine, if you like that sort of thing. Just didn't think my mum would.'

'Don't worry,' I say. 'I know you weren't having a dig.'

'Saw he did well at Mavs.'

'Yeah.'

'Even richer now than he was before.'

'Money isn't everything, Daniel,' I say.

'So when's he coming to Newquay?'

I shrug. 'I don't know. Not yet.'

I look at my feet, can't meet his eye.

'You've broke up?'

'I can't talk about it, Dan.'

'He cheated on you, didn't he? Knew it. Or did you cheat on him?'

I don't answer.

'That article I heard about?'

'Thanks for trying to warn us. Really appreciate that. Anders is on the case.'

Daniel unfurls his hand and reaches out to touch something on the side of my head. 'Leaf insect,' he says.

256

It flies off and lands on a wall. It was so light I hadn't felt a thing. Daniel doesn't withdraw his hand.

'Forget that bloke, Iris. He doesn't give a toss about you. You popped your cherry to him and he doesn't even care. He's probably got two girls on the go in his bed right now.'

'Get lost, Daniel. You don't know anything about him.'

'I know enough. I liked his fan page on Facebook, and you should see all the girls on there making a play for him. Hundreds every day. Fake saddoes, plastic everything, going, "*Zeeeeeke, you're so gorgeous!! Here's my cell number — call me and we'll bang sooo hard!*" It's disgusting. And what does he say to them? Nothing. Oh no, sorry, one time he replied to someone who posted a photo meme about him and Stephanie Gilmore needing to get it on and produce uber-surf kids, and he said, "*I have a gf.*" That was it: *I have a gf.* He didn't even mention your name.'

So Daniel follows Zeke's Facebook page? I'd seen that meme and it had irritated me beyond belief, even though I pretended I didn't care.

'He can't say anything else, even if he wants to.'

'Not even to respect you?'

'He has to act professional online. He can't be getting into arguments with fans. And if he made a fuss about me, they'd only be on my back too.'

Daniel grits his teeth, tries not to say the thing that's

257

eating him, and fails.

'Why would you want to be with someone like that? It must be horrible. You're just a nice normal girl and all these birds with perfect looks are constantly trying to pull your bloke. How do you put up with that?'

My face must have fallen, because he says, 'I didn't mean it that way. I'm not saying you're ugly or nothing. It's just there are always gonna be better-looking people out there. I should know,' he says, 'one of them stole the love of my life.'

Hearing him say this is like a blow to the chest; I feel winded.

'I am not the love of your life, Daniel. You're engaged to Cass.'

'Only because she found the ring and put it on. I couldn't hardly say no, could I? And yeah . . . you are.'

I look at him and there are faint beads of sweat on his forehead, even though it's chilly in the evening wind.

'Daniel, I'm not.'

'You are.'

'You just have history with me. We were so young, and it was intense, and part of me will always feel something for you, but it's not the same thing as being the love of someone's life. You can't even figure out who your great love is until you're old, at the end of your life, looking back. That's what Zeke's nanna used to say.'

'Don't tell me what I feel. You being gone has been

shit for me. I've thought about you every day since you left. You're the last thing I think about when I go to sleep at night and the first thing I think of when I wake up in the morning and I have these dreams about you. I'm admitting that even though I know it's sad. You're the only girl for me.'

'Daniel, no. I'm sorry, but you're not the guy for me.'

'Fuckin' yeah I am. I'm more the person for you than he'll ever be.'

'Dan—'

'I know you. He doesn't.'

'Um, yes he does. And he's the one who's been sleeping next to me for half a year, just in case you've forgotten that, so actually he probably knows me a lot better than you do.'

'Because he's shagged you? So what? That's not knowing someone; that's just friction, sweat and jizz.'

'It's not "nothing" to me.'

'You really want him to be the only person you ever sleep with? His number is probably like two thousand and yours is one. You really happy with that?'

'He's not the only person I've slept with,' I say. The words are out of my mouth before I've even thought about them.

'Who else you slept with?'

'None of your bloody business.'

'Who?'

'I know Zeke's number and it's not two thousand.'

'What, then?'

'Couple of hundred.'

'Two hundred birds?' Daniel leans back, laughing and shaking his head. 'He's gonna be shagged again when the CSA catches up with him. He's probably got twenty kids out there.'

'I'm leaving,' I say.

On the way out of the zoo, my landing's not as soft. I jar my ankle and manage to get a metal splinter in the palm of my right hand. Most of it comes out, but a piece of it is still jammed deep under the skin.

Daniel's right behind me and sees me testing out my ankle. He takes one look at my face and says, 'How bad is it?'

'Jarred not sprained, and like you even care.'

'Come to my place and I'll sort you out.'

'No, I'm going home.'

'Don't go home. I'm sorry for being such a git. I don't know why I can't stop talking shit around you.'

'Apology not accepted.'

'Please, Iris. Just for ten minutes. My mum's dying to see you.'

He puts his arm around me and I breathe in the old familiar smell of him, which is Lynx Africa, lager, and some nice musk unique to Daniel Penhaligon.

I wriggle out from beneath his arm but agree to walk to his house. We find his mum in the kitchen, folding clothes from the tumble dryer. The house smells like fabric softener and baking.

When she sees me, she drops the clothes on the floor and starts crying.

'I can't believe you're really here! How are you, Iris? How's the big time treating you?'

'Good, thanks, Mrs Penhaligon. Bit of a rough few days, but I'm OK.'

'Coming home's always hard. So how was the skateboarding park? Do any fun tricks?'

Daniel hands me a glass of water and two ibuprofen, and then says, 'Skate park was swamped with groms, so we broke into the zoo.'

'What are you kids like? She's only been home five minutes and you're already getting her into trouble. Some things'll never change, eh?'

My ankle's feeling OK but my splinter is still bothering me. Daniel sees me picking at it with my fingernail and gets the First Aid kit. He cleans my hand with an alcohol wipe and sets about trying to get a grip on the remains of my splinter with tweezers and a sewing needle. Both me and his mum watch his every move. He's incredibly gentle.

He finally fishes out the tiny bit of metal and holds it up for us to see; we inspect it before he bins it, and his mum gives him a pat on the back.

Then she says, 'Daniel, run and get some more teabags from the corner shop, will you? We've only got two left.'

'Don't go to any trouble,' I say. 'I don't need tea. I'm fine with water.'

'Shush, now. You're not leaving this house until you've had a decent cuppa. Come on, Daniel, get your bum moving. We're gasping here.'

Daniel complains a bit, then picks up his car keys from the kitchen table.

'And you ain't blimming driving neither, so you can put those keys down. Honestly, the boy will spend three hours in the gym, most of it on the bloody treadmill, but he won't walk five hundred yards to the shop.'

'I thought you said you was gasping?' Daniel grumbles. 'I was only trying to save time.'

'We can wait five minutes.'

Once the door has closed behind him, Daniel's mum touches my wrist and whispers, 'Saw a bit of Mavericks. Your Hawaiian boy did so well. I suppose he's on his way here now, is he?'

I look at her kind eyes and know I won't be able to lie to her.

'No.'

'You're still together, though?'

I shake my head and she gasps.

'Oh no. How could he? He must be mad.'

She assumes Zeke broke up with me, because she,

like everyone else, thinks I could never leave him. She's trying to be sympathetic, I know that.

'Thanks, Mrs Penhaligon.'

'Call me Pam. Oh, sweetness. I always said to Daniel that it would be a sad day if you two ever split up, and it was, believe you me. I hoped you'd be my daughter-in-law one day and I knew if that happened, I couldn't have done better. Neither could he.'

I smile at her. I'd forgotten how totally lovely Daniel's mum is, despite the aggro front she can put on at times.

'He's engaged to Cass.'

'That's not real. She'll be throwing that ring in his face by the end of the week. Mark my words. So, does Daniel . . .?' She stops herself from continuing.

'Does he what?'

'Have a chance?' Her voice is tense and I hear how much she cares.

'With me? I don't really think of him that way. We're friends, just about, but that's it.'

'Babe, I know you probably don't want to hear it but he thinks the world of you. That boy has a lot of love in his heart. Dickhead ways, no doubt about it, but big love too.'

Yeah, I want to say, *I know all about Daniel's dickhead ways*, but she's still clutching my wrist and searching my face for answers.

When I'm silent, she carries on with, 'The good and the bad go side by side. I don't mean only in Daniel. In life.

Youngsters today want the smooth with the smooth and it just don't work that way.'

Daniel walks back into the kitchen with a box of Tetley teabags under his arm.

'Everything all right?' he says, looking from me to his mum and back again.

'Fine,' I say. He splits open the teabag box, and sticks a bag in each of our three mugs before putting it away in the cupboard. 'Mum, there's five hundred in here already.'

She waves him off, as if the number of teabags she has to her name is entirely beside the point.

'You two go in the front room and I'll bring you a brew and some of my new cupcakes. Bacon and egg custard.'

Daniel pulls a face but I know he's going to eat them, pretty much whatever they taste like. He leads me into his sitting room with its dusty Venetian blinds, faded surf prints and sagging leather sofas, things given to Daniel's mum for free after his dad died. The local cafe was undergoing a revamp and they let Daniel's mum come in and choose whatever she wanted.

'Your mum's lovely,' I say, smiling.

'When she wants to be,' Daniel replies, 'which ain't all the time. You wanna try living with her.'

She calls in to me, 'Well done, by the way, Ris. You were amazing in America. And I loved the photos of you at Pipe.'

Daniel turns to me. 'She got all excited about the

Triple Crown Pipeline contest last year and tried to set up a "Pipe party". Hardly anyone responded to her Facebook invitation. Probably thought she was talking about crack.'

She pops her head around the door again. 'I read on your site about the local lad who ran you over when you was paddling out at one of them exotic places. "Malibu strike to the shoulder", right? Lucky you didn't break something, babe.'

I was lucky, but it was like Zeke's shaper used to tell me all the time: surfers have to take their slaps. If you're gonna cry every time you eat shit, get jacked up by fibreglass or sliced open by board fins, you'd best stick to ping pong.

She brings in the tea tray and we sit together, eating our crazy cupcakes.

'It's just part of being in the ocean,' I say. 'The injuries and accidents happen to everyone. Sometimes a surfer screws up and hurts somebody. Everyone does sooner or later. We don't mean to, but we all make mistakes.'

'Wanna go up to my room for a bit?' Daniel says. 'I've got some amazing prints of Teahupo'o up there. One of the new Fistral lifeguards was out there and got the shots himself.'

'I'd better be getting back.'

'Not yet, love,' Pam says. She goes into the kitchen and returns with another batch of cupcakes. Purple ones.

'I call these The Three Bs. Blueberry, brie and beer.'

'Not for me, thanks. I'm stuffed.'

I get up to leave but Pam blocks my way and says, 'Oh, go on Iris, you've gotta see the photos before you leave. You won't regret it.'

chapter thirty-five

As we go up the stairs to Daniel's bedroom, I think of how often I've climbed these steps. How much my life was altered that day, several years earlier, when we'd first really taken notice of each other. I was on the beach watching the local crew do their thing. This one little grom of six or seven was messing about on a longboard, doing headstands, rodeos and coffins, and generally pissing about.

I was knee by knee with Cass and a few other girls, because we'd been doing a tideline survey for a school science project, but I wasn't really listening to them chatting away as they flicked through a guidebook and tried to identify different kinds of seaweed. I was appreciating the show this little kid was putting on, when I saw a huge sleeper set way outside the line-up. Most of the surfers had seen it and were on full RPM to get further out to sea and out of the way, but that one little grom was looking to shore, maybe trying to check in with his parents or maybe just seeing who was watching him. He'd no idea what was coming his way.

I jumped up and started shouting. The boy looked at me in confusion, unable to hear what I was saying, as I ran through the waves towards him. A wave knocked me off my feet, so I swam for it, and came up shouting, because I knew if that kid didn't immediately start paddling hard out to sea, he'd be in a gnarly impact zone.

I looked back to the shore but it was just before tourist season and there was no lifeguard cover. I could see someone running towards the Lifeguard building to get the permanent rescue board, and then I turned back to the kid, who finally spotted the sneak set and paddled hard.

But he wasn't going to make it. He wasn't going to punch through and get over the back of the waves. They were going to land on his head and give him the worst beating of his life. As the first one hit, I saw him sucked over the falls and then a swarm of whitewater rushed towards me.

Suddenly a dark figure was paddling a board through the impact zone, towards the boy, who had surfaced but was now floating face-down in the water. I watched the figure hook his arm under the boy's neck, get him onto the board and start delivering rescue breaths. As the next wave hit, the rescuer, an older boy, held on, and the whitewater knocked them both twenty metres towards shore. I could see the little boy's skin was already turning blue, and watched as the older lad used his fist to bang on the boy's chest, between breaths. The third wave knocked them both off the board but they were far enough in for me to help drag them both to shore.

The boy had already begun to come around, coughing and spluttering, and I looked into the distraught face of the lad who'd saved his life.

Daniel. I hardly even knew him. He was just a boy with intense eyes who spent a lot of time hanging around on his own.

Some of the men from the Quiksilver surf school, who were on the beach training before their big spring opening, got the kid on the rescue board and carried him away.

Within ten minutes the air ambulance was landing on Fistral Beach.

'You all right?' I said to Daniel. He'd swallowed some seawater too and had to step away to be sick.

'I think so,' he said, his voice shaky.

And that was the start of it.

chapter thirty-six

He opens the door to his room, which he always keeps locked, and I tell him that I need the loo. I take my bag with me, drain my bladder, wash my hands and splash cold water on my face, which sends my mascara streaking down my cheeks.

Walking across the landing to Daniel's room, my body seems to be moving in a different kind of way, nervous and reluctant. I open the door to see Daniel lying on the bed and staring at a lit candle. He pauses to send a gust of his breath towards the flame and watches it flicker. Then, when it's perfectly still, he does it again.

He hasn't heard me come into the room.

'Dan. I mean Daniel,' I say quietly. 'Looked like you were miles away. Like somewhere in the vicinity of the asteroid belt.' What am I even talking about? Daniel looks at me, curiously, and then, maybe realizing I'm nervous, he gets off the bed, flicks on Radio 1, takes something from the stash of junk food he keeps in an old biscuit tin on his desk, and chucks a Smarties tube over to me.

'Help yourself.'

I use my thumb to prise off the lid, and shake a cigarette into my lap. His mum absolutely hates smoking on account of most of her blood relatives dying of lung cancer, so I don't blame Daniel for hiding them, despite the fact that he's eighteen. Her house, her rules.

I hold one in front of him, rolling it in two fingers.

'In here?' I say.

'We'll open a window.'

I light it on his candle, inhale and cough.

'Thought you hated smoking?' he says.

'I do.'

I take another drag, cough up another storm, and then offer it to him.

'Don't wanna deprive you, like. I'll get my own.'

'No really, Dan, take this.'

I walk around his room, trying to figure out what's changed in the year or so since I was last in here. The Teahupo'o photos are nice, but I don't want to look at them, because for all I know, Zeke's the tiny surfer on the giant waves. Or maybe it's one of his teammates and he's there in the line-up waiting for his turn.

Daniel still has the same wrestling duvet cover set that he got one Christmas before I knew him. It gives me a pang of nostalgia when I see it. He doesn't care about fashion or style. If he likes something, whether it's a duvet cover or a surfboard, he sees no reason to change it just because other people think it's lame.

He tidies a few things, puts some energy bar wrappers in his wastepaper basket, and throws his discarded clothes into the bottom of his wardrobe. Then he gets back on his bed, and says, 'Come over here if you want.'

He leaves the rest of the cigarette to burn out on the top of an empty can of Relentless, and I sit down, watching the smoke unfurl. Then I stretch back and lie beside him.

I don't even fight it. I want to feel human warmth and connection. Just to lie next to Daniel in silence. I turn onto my side, lean my head against his shoulder and wriggle until I'm comfortable. Then I put one arm over his chest. Suddenly it's three years earlier, I'm fourteen again, everything's simple and I have no expectation weighing down on me. All I have to do is lie on a bed with Daniel.

We stay like this until the sun goes down in its spectacular inferno, which turns the pale walls of his bedroom a vivid pink.

Suddenly, the radio begins playing Taylor Swift's 'We Are Never Ever Getting Back Together', which seems to go on forever and feels excruciatingly awkward.

Daniel sits up and says, 'Wanna walk to the beach to see the sunset properly?'

'No, I just want to stay here.'

The colour fades and we watch the room fill with

shadows. My sugar and nicotine buzz ebb, and I fight back yawns. Daniel doesn't move, and neither do I, so we stay there, our breathing shallow, our bodies fizzing with possibility at their shared borders.

chapter thirty-seven

My bladder gets me up and when I return, Daniel's sitting on the side of his bed, staring at his feet.

'Sod it,' he says. 'I got you a present.'

He leans over and pulls something out of his bedside table and shoves it into my hands.

It's wrapped in a folded Tesco bag and I can feel that it's hard and cold.

'Open it,' he says.

It is, by all appearances, a number plate.

'For your ride,' he says. 'Kelly told me you got some sick wheels for your birthday. Got it off a bloke down the pub yesterday. Cost me three hundred quid, but I reckon it's worth it.'

It doesn't say Iris.

It doesn't say Surf.

It doesn't say Newquay.

What it says is even better.

FI57RAL

The grom in me wants to rip it from his hands, punch two holes in it, thread a chain through and wear it as a necklace.

'Are you sure you didn't buy it for you, Dan?'

'Got it for you. Birthday present. And . . . peace offering. It's yours.'

'But it's so expensive. I'll pay you for it.'

I don't technically have enough money in my bank account to cover it, but there's always instalments and I figure I'm bound to make some money sooner or later.

'Like hell you will. It's a present.'

I look into his eyes. 'I love it,' I say. 'I absolutely bloody love it.'

'Sure it's not a bit crap to buy a girl a number plate?' he asks. 'I didn't know whether to give it to you.'

'Daniel, it's amazing. Completely amazing. There's millions of cars out there, but only one of these.'

He coughs, looks even more embarrassed and says, 'Well, don't go bawling or nothing.'

'I'll try not to.'

I get my lip-balm out of my bag and dab my mouth. This is mostly an excuse to turn my back to him. I need a deep breath and a moment to myself.

'Hey,' Daniel says, touching my lower back gently, 'you remember the time we swam across the bay and got caught in that blue jellyfish bloom?'

An abrupt change of topic, even for Daniel.

'Yeah, my legs got stung so bad, and when we got out of the water you wanted me to let you pee on them.'

He laughs. 'It wasn't some kinky golden showers thing. I thought it'd help with the pain.'

I hadn't let him do it, but there was a short sea cave interlude where I crouched in the darkness with a piece of driftwood, attempting to funnel my own urine onto the worst of the stings while Daniel kept watch outside.

'Remember when you were obsessed with grey aliens,' I say, 'so we sat in Fistral dunes staring at the sky for half the night to see if we could spot a UFO?'

'Some copper and his missus saw like eight of the buggers the night before. It was all over the local news.'

'They were looking at the laser show from the circus,' I reply, smiling.

His phone vibrates and he holds it up to look at a text exchange.

He laughs and puts a hand on my stomach. I watch it slide slowly downwards.

I take his hand and put it back on the duvet. As I do this, my sleeve rolls up and he sees an old bruise on my forearm, from the final heat at New Smyrna when I wiped out and caught it on one of the rails of my board. It ached a bit but is nothing compared to my air-training bruises.

'What's this?' Daniel says, looking at it.

'Surf injury.'

He gets up, lights another cigarette and passes it to me, but I decline.

'Do you want me to walk you home? Before your mum starts stressing?'

'I don't have a curfew. I can go home whenever I want, and I don't need a chaperone to walk to my own house.'

Daniel exhales and when he speaks, his voice is hesitant.

'Do you want to stay the night, then? As friends, like.'

I think about it for the whole time it takes him to finish his cigarette. Daniel doesn't interrupt my thinking, doesn't press me for an answer.

'What about your mum? She'll know I'm here.'

'She won't care.'

I get my phone out, check for messages and voicemails but I only have a few spam texts from EE. Nothing from my mum. Nothing from Kelly. Radio silence from Zeke.

Daniel's phone beeps and he starts texting someone again, as I pull up my mum's number and message her to say I'll be back in the morning.

Why aren't you coming home? What about film night?

Sorry, I forgot.

You're not with a boy, are you?

No, I lie. Just catching up with Kelly.

Don't stay up too late nattering.

I'll make sure I'm in bed by midnight.

'Do you wanna wear a T-shirt of mine?' Daniel asks. 'It's cold out tonight.'

'Thanks.'

He fishes a white Nike T-shirt out of a drawer and hands it to me. I turn my back to him, and strip off. I sense he's watching me get undressed, and I'm glad I'm wearing my old ratty supermarket pants. His T-shirt comes halfway down my thighs and I pull it down further as I turn around, so he doesn't think I'm trying to be alluring.

'Ready to go to bed?' he asks, and then blushes hard because that's a question that can definitely be taken two ways.

'All right,' I say, wondering when he'll get undressed. As if reading my thoughts, he takes off his Rip Curl T-shirt and throws it over by his door. He stopped wearing Billabong stuff the moment I started seeing Zeke. No way would he spend money on something Zeke was paid to wear.

I catch a glimpse of him and see he's definitely been working out. Before, he was sturdy, but now he's leaner, with decent muscle definition. I try to act cool and unbothered as he takes off his jeans.

Zeke has fairly dark skin from his mother's side, but Daniel's is darker still. I think back to the Cuban guy I met in Florida. Seb. Lovely Seb. He and Daniel could be brothers.

Daniel steps back, as if to say, 'After you,' and I climb into his bed and pull the covers up to my neck. He waits a couple of seconds and then gets into the bed too, perched pretty much as far away from me as he can manage. Both of us are looking at the ceiling. I don't want to turn away from him towards the windows, and I don't want to turn towards him either, because both of those things would feel really significant.

'Night, then, Iris,' he says.

'Night, Dan.'

There's a heavy moment in which I am aware of nothing but my own noisy breathing and suddenly it's gone and we're both turning towards each other and my mouth hits his brow-bone, his eyelid, the side of his mouth. Then Daniel is on top of me and my hands are reaching for his boxers and he is pulling up my T-shirt, my cold skin connecting with his hot skin.

I feel powerful and experienced and I'm not afraid of a thing. This is reality. The Zeke part of my life is over.

chapter thirty-eight

It's what we've been building up to for years, but it didn't happen because of Cass and because of Zeke. The contradictions swim together in my blood. It's both sweet and agonizing; it feels right and also like a monumental disaster.

I have to get through it. Get it out of my system. Get it done with. So I can move on.

I won't think of Cass, even though I know this would hurt her desperately. Or Zeke, who would never understand it. Or Perranporth.

I'm trying not to think of all these things, when the panic kicks in.

'Daniel, stop.'

'Huh, what you sayin'?' he says, failing to stop.

'I said STOP. GET OFF.'

He rolls away and we lie there in the cold grey light, thoughts of Zeke rushing at me like whitewater.

Daniel's making a horrible grunting noise, then

stops abruptly.

I can smell it in the air and it turns my stomach.

A voice in my head is telling me, '*You did it with Daniel. Daniel who almost killed Zeke.*'

Another one chips in and helpfully points out, '*It was thirty seconds before you stopped it. That doesn't even really count.*'

'Wow,' Daniel says. 'Thank you.'

His thank you is a knife to my heart. It's the worst possible thing he could have said, because it makes it seem as if I've given him this gift he's been waiting for.

'What?' he says, aware, for once, of my blatant unhappiness. 'What did I say wrong?'

'Nothing. Forget it.'

'How come you stopped? Was it like chafing or something?'

'No.'

'This is mega, Iris.'

'No, it isn't.'

Remorse sits in my gut like a block of radioactive ice. I lie there, minutes ticking by, my brain flooded with hideous thoughts.

Daniel, next to me, has cleaned himself up with toilet paper, revealing the fact that his stupid 'Eddie Would Go' lower-back tattoo is still intact, and rolled over to go to sleep. He snores loudly and unrelentingly about three seconds after closing his eyes.

I'm trapped, because movement from me will wake him up, and I'm not ready to speak to him. So, I stay there through some of the most miserable hours of my life until the sun rises and Daniel turns over, releasing my neck from his arm.

I creep out of his bed, pull on my pants and leggings, and am in the process of balling up my bra and stuffing it in my jacket pocket when he startles me by saying, 'You goin' somewhere, Ris?'

'Yeah,' I say, my voice gruff, cringing at the thought of Daniel seeing me almost naked, even though he's just had his hands all over me.

I pull on my top, noticing that it's back to front, the scrawled profanities of the reverse slung across my chest, articulating to Daniel exactly what I'm really feeling.

'Weren't it . . . good for you? Is that why you stopped? Seemed like it was going all right, to me, like, but I don't . . .'

It had definitely been different to my experiences with Zeke, who was all energy and enthusiasm, but also with an overconfidence that sometimes bordered on arrogance. Daniel was likewise the reverse of his everyday self. Not aggressive, but gentle, touching me as if I was some exotic flower that would wilt with too much handling.

It was also different in a more obvious way: I'd always insisted on using condoms with Zeke, but with Daniel I'd just relied on my implant, a decision I was already freaking out about. The memory of Kelly telling me about Daniel being on Tinder came back to me with alarming force and I couldn't stop my brain from scrolling through my mental list of STIs.

'I didn't want to carry on,' I say. 'But it was fine.'

'Why do you have that look on your face then?'

'Think about Cass! You're engaged to her!'

'No, I'm not.' He holds up his phone to me so I can read a text exchange between him and Cass. An argument. It ends with Cass telling him he's dumped.

'Look at the time on it,' he says, 'she broke it off right before we . . .'

That's who he was texting when I was messaging my mum to tell her I wasn't coming home?

'Why?'

'Rae saw you coming in my house and Cass went mental.'

'Oh my God,' I say, feeling the full force of my own selfishness and hypocrisy. I have to get out of here. 'Dan, I'm knackered. I want to get back home for a proper sleep in my own bed.'

'I'll drive you,' he says, handing me the carrier bag containing the number plate.

'I'll walk. It's not far.'

'Iris, let me come with you, all right? It's not even six o'clock in the morning, for Christ's sake, and you're not doing the walk of shame.'

'The walk of shame is bull,' I say as I accept the bag, because I know refusing will escalate things into a huge row.

When I glance up, I see he's looking at me with such determination in his eyes that I know there's no point trying to argue with him, so I shrug. 'Fine.'

I pick up my gear and walk quietly past Daniel's mum's room.

I hear the bed creak as she turns over, mumbling something indecipherable in her sleep. She must know I've stayed the night. My shoes are still in the hall downstairs.

When I get down there, I see they aren't on their sides, where I'd kicked them off; she's put them neatly on the rack by the front door. Right next to Daniel's. It was probably the last thing she did before she went to bed, wondering what on earth was going on upstairs.

My face is on fire, my hands are shaking as I hold my shoes, and I don't bother to tie them. I just push my feet in and tuck the laces beneath the tongues. Another habit of Zeke's I've picked up.

As soon as we get outside, the dawn chorus of shrieking gulls descends on us and I put up my hood. Daniel finds my hand and threads his fingers through mine.

I don't want him to hold my hand, because that makes it feel as if he's my boyfriend, and I can't bear the thought. But I can't shake his hand off either because then I'll have to explain why I'm doing that. This isn't just any boy; this is

Daniel, who has so many feelings he can barely function under the weight of them.

'I feel like I should apologize or summat,' he says, 'but I don't know what I've done wrong. I stopped when I heard what you was saying, but I thought you wanted us to do it . . .'

I glance at the pavement.

'So did I,' I say.

The sting of my words registers across his whole face, and he says, 'You regret it, don't you? *Already?*'

'I don't know what I feel yet.'

'Was it that rubbish?'

'Don't be stupid. It was . . . different.'

'Is it cos of that other bloke you slept with, or Zeke?'

I don't answer. Caleb – another person I've messed about. Everyone's better off without me. I'm a mess.

Daniel exhales and says, 'Cos to me it just seemed, like, really natural, or something. As if we was always supposed to be together. Then you pushed me off.'

Jesus, every time he opens his mouth he makes it worse. Now he's going on as if we're soul mates destined to walk the afterlife together.

His face is so eager and needy, but I know I can't give him what he wants.

We don't speak to each other on the rest of the walk home. Daniel knows something is wrong and he obviously doesn't know what to say to make it better, so he keeps his collar up and his head down.

I know he's probably going through some emotional stuff of his own. He's been wanting us to sleep together for years and at last we've done it. Kind of.

At the end of my street, I look over at my van, and say, 'This is fine, you can go now. See you later.'

Daniel leans in for a mouth kiss, and I turn away from him. He doesn't kiss my cheek. Instead, he turns his head and spits in my neighbour's privet hedgerow.

'Iris,' he turns back to me and wipes his mouth on his sleeve, then takes a cigarette and lighter from his pocket, and sparks up.

'What?'

'Meet me later, will ya?'

'I've got training.'

'I'll come to the beach with you. Give you a lift. My board got dinged up last week and the epoxy's still drying out, but maybe I could borrow one of yours? You must have loads.'

'They haven't all arrived yet,' I say, freaking out at the idea of Daniel riding one of the boards that Zeke's shaper made for me. It feels like blasphemy.

'You don't want me with you.'

'I need to keep my mind on the ocean, is all,' I say, which is true but also has very little chance of being an accurate predictor of what will happen when I attempt to train. I'm going to obsess about all of this, no question.

'You know what, Iris? Listen to yourself. "*The ocean*."

Call it the sea. He's even changed your bloody words.'

'No, he hasn't.'

He rolls his eyes and says, 'Yeah, well, thanks again. I needed that. Blue balls.'

I cringe, even though I know he's putting on his lad act, trying to hurt me.

'You are disgusting,' I say.

I think of what Lily used to say to me when I was younger: 'Be careful who you go to bed with, little sis, because once it's done, it's undoable.'

'*You're* telling me this? You go to bed with everyone,' I'd pointed out to her at the time.

'Exactly, so I know. Sleep with the wrong person and they'll have something on you forever. Sleep with the right one and you'll have something on them.'

'You are so disturbed,' I'd said to her. 'Like completely messed up beyond all repair.'

'You make a good point,' she'd said, and started whistling a Nicky Minaj song.

I give Daniel a hard stare, and wait for him to apologize, but I can't stop thinking about Lily's words, because it feels very much as if Daniel now has something on me.

'Whatever,' he says. 'Ride on the town bike was just what the doc ordered.'

'Fuck off and die,' I say, barely suppressing the urge to punch him.

He crushes his cigarette underfoot.

'Maybe I'll do that,' he says.

It's the sixth day of the fifth month of this crappy year and I have made the biggest mistake of my life.

chapter thirty-nine

At the far end of Trenance boating lake there is a rain shelter where lonely people go to sit in the shadows and get through their waking hours.

I sit there now, hunched in silence, curls of blue paint and fragments of green glass at my feet. The sky is clear except for a few perfect white contrails streaking across it; I think about those unknown travellers, sipping beer thousands of feet above my head as they make their way to America.

On a day like this, I should be in the sea. Should have salt air in my lungs, instead of the whiff of urine and smoke. I have so much training to do, so much preparation, but I'm here, still.

There is something freeing about crying in front of strangers, of being so upset that I don't even care what they think of me. People go past, and turn their heads at the sound of my sobbing; some come over and ask if I am OK, but I'm too far gone to reply. An old lady sits with me for a while and pats my hand, but I can't answer her questions, can't give her a smile when she asks me for one. Eventually she looks at her watch, and says she has to go and pick up her prescription at the chemist before it closes. It's late, and I've been here all day.

I close my eyes and, when I open them, my dad is looking at me.

I haven't seen him in forever and suddenly here he is in front of me, salting all the raw wounds from my childhood.

'What's going on, kid?'

I stare at the fountain behind his head and manage, 'Nothing. What are you doing here?'

'Looking for you. I already know it's bloke trouble, so don't deny it. I reckon you're better off without him, from what your sister tells me.' He sits down next to me and puts his hand on my knee.

'Why are you talking to Lily about me?'

'Take it easy. She's only looking out for you. Protective big sister and all that. So tell me, what did the little sod do?'

'Nothing.'

He gets out his phone and sends a text message to someone. I catch the words, *I'll have to ring you later, darl*, and wonder if the person on the other end of that message knows he's with his daughter. Or even has a daughter.

'Has your mother taken you for a spin in your van yet?'

'No.'

'Well, there we are then. We'll go out tonight. Give you a lesson before I leave. Don't have much time, either. Got a new job in Beijing. Starting next month, but we'll have you through your test by then.'

I look into his eyes; try to work out if he's joking.

'Thanks for telling me about it before you left. Nice one.'

'Come on, Ris, let me take you for a sandwich. You can tell me all about what's been going on in your life, and what's made you break your heart like this.'

'No thanks. I'm not hungry.'

He grabs my hands and pulls me off the bench. 'Come for a coffee then.'

But the Lakeside Cafe is packed, and we can't hear each other above the din. 'Oh, I know where to go,' he says. 'Follow me.'

He drives me to the harbour.

Where Daniel could easily be. Busy unloading fish from his uncle's boat, or casting out from the harbour walls. Or maybe walking his neighbour's new pug, which I know he does because there are three pictures of it on his Instagram feed.

We sit on the terrace of The Catch, beside polythene sheeting windows, which blur the view like a dirty contact lens. None of the boats are in and, save for a couple of walkers on the beach, it's empty. The view makes me even more depressed. I don't have any good memories here.

My dad is looking at me, worry lining his face.

'What's up?'

'This place. Zeke hated it.'

'Hated it? Bit strong. What's not to like?'

It had started with the lack of vegetarian options on the beach menu board. Well, that wasn't strictly true: there was one veggie option. A cheese sandwich. Zeke got all tense when he saw line after line of meat and fish dishes. But that was nothing compared to what followed. As we walked up to the restaurant, we went past a pool with a low tarp roof. The sign said, *Viewing Area*. I was too busy stroking a passing kitten to notice that Zeke had wandered away.

There were hundreds of brown crabs and lobsters in there. A pick-your-own deal for customers, and restaurateurs could come and get them too, if they wanted the freshest local ingredients.

'Wow, that's . . . humane,' Zeke said. 'From life to plate in twenty minutes.'

'Don't look at them. Come and get a drink with me.'

'Look at that little guy at the back. His shell is broken.'

I'd looked at the broken crab and nodded. Yes, it wasn't great to see them there, knowing that they'd be eaten pretty soon, but loads of places we'd visited had crab on the menu; Zeke only hated this place because the link between animal and meat was so blatant.

'Do they even feed them in there?' he said, looking around, like he was going to launch into an interrogation of any staff member he found.

'Yeah, I suppose they must do. They don't want them to die, do they? Not before they're bought and paid for, I mean.'

It did seem sort of sad to keep them prisoner like that before selling them, but that applied to basically all of the meat industry, and I didn't know how to react to Zeke's distress at the sight of this. He could be tough as nails when it came to extreme sports and surfing giant waves. To look at him you'd see an ultra-successful surfer with the world at his feet, but he was sensitive. Too bloody sensitive. Everyday normal things could hurt him and ruin his whole day.

'Do you want to go somewhere else?' I asked.

'No, it's fine. I guess you like this place.'

He'd set his mouth in a firm line and I could tell he was going to do the martyr routine and suffer nobly, thanks to me and my cutthroat callousness.

The cat followed us over to our table. Its purring took the edge off Zeke's moodiness; he stroked it and seemed to relax a bit. But he kept looking over at the pool, his brow furrowing each time.

'They should be in the sea,' he said, finally.

'Everything dies, Zeke, sooner or later. Even us.'

'Lobsters can live like eighty years or something. Do you know that they *feel* it when they're boiled alive? Scientists proved it. I mean, yeah, how anybody thought

293

boiling a living creature to death wasn't cruel is . . .
just . . . insane. But, denial, right?'

'Come on. Let's go.'

'What's the problem? We're just talking.'

'Ten feet from a pen of doomed crustaceans. It's
obviously upsetting you, so let's leave.'

Zeke ran his hands through his hair. 'I'm not upset. A
little angry, sure.'

'At me?'

He shook his head. 'I'm sorry. Look, I don't know how
to deal with this stuff. Sometimes it's like I'm an alien and
everyone round me is local, you know?'

I thought of Zeke with all his friends and all his fans: he
was a social butterfly. No way was he any kind of outsider.

'I don't think so,' I said.

'I, like, don't understand people.'

'Nobody understands people. I don't even understand
myself. You don't like this because it's so visible. But it's
real. This is life, Zeke. This is what happens.'

'You know what? You're right. Let's get out of here.
I hate this place.'

He threw down a fiver for the coffees that we hadn't
even started to drink and left.

I was flabbergasted. I'd never known him to throw
such a wobbly before. It wasn't like there was a bunch of
bleating lambs tied up and about to be slaughtered in front
of us. They were crabs and lobsters.

I took a gulp of hot coffee, grabbed my bag and went after him.

When I caught up with him, he was sitting on the damp sand near the waterline, watching a group of holidaymakers pick their way around the boats on stand-up paddle boards.

Suddenly, he stood up, brushed sand off the wet patch on his arse, and walked back into The Catch.

'What are you doing?'

Zeke strode into the empty restaurant with me right behind him, and said, 'Ma'am, I'd like to talk to the manager.'

I put my hand over my eyes, cringing at the thought of Zeke starting some official complaints procedure on the grounds of animal cruelty.

'She's up in town on her tea break.'

'Does she have a cell phone?'

'What's this about, son?'

At that moment the manager walked in, a half-eaten pasty in one hand and a carrier bag in the other. She took one look at Zeke and coughed on her mouthful.

'Can I help you?' she said, clearing her throat.

'Yes, ma'am. How much for the animals outside?'

'The animals?'

'The crustaceans.'

'Five pounds a crab, ten pounds a lobster. How many would you like?'

'All of them,' he said. 'Every last one.'

'For what? You setting up an aquarium?'

'No, ma'am.'

I took Zeke's hand and dragged him over to the bar area.

'Zeke,' I said, looking up into his eyes. 'I can tell you right now that your mum is not going to have that lot in the house. Or the garden. And Garrett doesn't have room in the apartment. Where are you going to put them all?'

'Back in the ocean.'

'They'll just catch more!'

'But these ones, the ones here now, will be safe. The little guy with the broken shell, he'll go back out to sea, where he belongs. He doesn't belong in some tourist's sandwich.'

'Says you. Zeke, you can't just dump crabs out in the harbour! The minute you go, the fishermen will catch them again.'

'I'm not dumb, Iris.' He turned back to the woman.

'How much for all of them?'

'Wait a minute.'

She went and looked for something under the bar and brought out a calculator. After jabbing at the screen for a while she seemed to arrive at a number she felt happy with. She showed the screen to Zeke and I caught a glimpse.

1630.

One thousand, six hundred and thirty pounds. For crabs.

Why couldn't I have taken him to Subway Sandwich?

'I'll be back here in twenty minutes. Nobody buys any. I've bought every last one, you hear me? Iris, guard them.'

I exhaled through gritted teeth and he walked off towards town, presumably to make a large cash withdrawal from the counter at HSBC.

'Starting your own crab pond, are you, love?' the manager said to me. 'You seem a bit young, but in this economy you have to create your own job, I suppose.'

'Hmm,' I said, not wanting to get into a conversation about crab welfare.

Zeke took forty minutes, not twenty, but when he got back, he looked pretty pleased with himself.

'We're all set. One of the eco wildlife tour boats is going to take us out to release them.'

'They'll just crawl into another pot sooner or later.'

'Nope. He knows a no-fish zone.'

'You mean off Lundy Island?'

'That's the place.'

'That's MILES away.'

'So they'll be safe there. He's not gonna be cheap, but he'll get the job done.'

'Zeke, I don't understand any of this. What is going through your head right now?'

'*Hope.* Come on, we need to get these into crates.'

'You want me to touch them? Er, no thanks.'

'Whatever. I'll do it, but it'll take a lot longer.'

'I have to go to work in an hour.'

'Can't you blow it off?'

'Not really. Not unless I want to get fired. I'm covering for Stacey; she has to go to her sister's ballet thing.'

'You're out of there in a week or two. It's not like getting fired would be such a big deal.'

'It would be to me.'

I watched him hand over the thickest wad of notes I had ever seen to the manager of The Catch and his face when he turned back to me was triumphant.

My phone beeps and finally Kelly responds to my message telling her that I've slept with Daniel. I scan it and see something's capitalized – a bad sign. I prepare myself for raging anger and disappointment.

Been trying to figure out what to say. All I got is this: NO JUDGEMENT. However, WTAF??

A huge weight lifts. Getting naked with Daniel is bad enough, but Kelly hating me for it would be completely unbearable. The thought of her turning her back on me made me want to fall asleep and never wake up.

I know. Massive strategic error. Won't be doing that again. xxx

*THANK GOD!*xxx

I look over at my dad, who's flicking through the menu. He jabs his finger at a line of text and says, 'Right, I know what I'm having. Nice crab sandwich. Want one?'

chapter forty

The wind has died. The evening air is heavy with roses and flowering gorse and I've been cycling for an hour, sparks of sweat flying off me as I blur up and down Newquay's hills with no clear idea of where I'm headed.

I know what you did, Cass had texted me earlier that afternoon.

I'm sorry. I wish I could go back and change it.

So do I. Reckon we're even now.

I know exactly what she means: she went behind my back with Daniel and now I've done the same and gone behind hers.

So, so sorry. It'll never happen again, Cass.

You sure?

Yes. I promise. Never ever again.

She was so understanding. I think about the way me and Kelly behaved after it all kicked off with Cass and Daniel last year and feel utterly ashamed.

Pedalling hard, my quads and hamstrings burn, and I

stop only because I see a grass verge covered in black and yellow caterpillars. Bike leaning against a tree, I settle on my heels to look at them, and I think about Zeke, and wonder if it would've been better all round if I'd never met him, because I'm not sure I can take this.

Kelly had dragged me into that yoga class in Hotel Serenity and there he was, this tall, blue-eyed boy with the experiences of a man. We'd gone surfing straight after the class, stayed late at a beach party, and I'd rested my head on his shoulder and smelt the sea on his neck.

From the pocket of my rucksack I retrieve a small net bag full of bright yellow spheres and I rub my thumb across the label.

Historic Wahiawa Town, Hawaii. Dole Plantation Brand Pineapple Flavored Bubble Gum.

He'd thrown these to me on our first day in Oahu.

'Enjoy,' he said. 'Best gumballs you'll ever taste.'

I snatched them from the air with one hand, without even looking.

'Nah, I'm keeping 'em forever,' I said, holding them aloft like a trophy, and I'd carried them in my rucksack all over the world.

I pop the first one in my mouth, roll it with my tongue and I'm hit by an intense burst of flavour. The pineapple coating is too strong but doesn't last more than thirty seconds, as I suck off the yellow and turn the gumball white. A piece of Hawaii in my cheek, I feel the saliva pool and run.

For a few more minutes, I allow myself to remember how it felt to be with him, to kiss him, to fall asleep beside him and to wake up in the dark with him.

Five minutes of remembering, I promise myself, and then I'll stop. I ration out these memories carefully, because like the gumballs, they are too strong, too much, but even as I do this, I know that one day they will also fade to white and there'll be no more to replace them.

I flick the pages. The long flight to South Africa: watching far-off lightning storms in the dark, as he slept beside me, twitching as he dreamed; so many nights under bright silver skies that whispered in our ears that we would be together forever.

I flick forwards to our boat trip to the Mentawais: surfing hollow turquoise waves on shallow reefs where I'd worried about smashing my head on coral; picking up a bug from the sea that would see me camping out in our boat toilet; making a fool of myself in front of the other surfers by backing off a wave that scared me; failing to get any impressive rides; disappointing everyone who'd ever had faith in me.

When I'm done staring at caterpillars, I reach for my iPhone, encased in the black Velcro band strapped to my bicep, and I swipe, just to check.

But I already know there's nothing from him. No texts, no emails, no missed calls. I'd have heard a beep, felt a vibration. I kid myself I'd have sensed him reaching out to me.

I snap a few pictures of the caterpillars and turn up the volume on The Staves' 'In The Long Run', which I am listening to, on repeat, as I have been for days. I'm about to put my phone back when it buzzes and lights up in my hand. I don't answer the call, and instead listen to the voicemail she leaves.

'Zeke called. I'm so sorry, honey. I can't imagine what you've been through. Zeke told me about the pills. We're all here for you, Iris, and you know I still want you to be my maid of honour, right? You're a daughter to me, irrespective of your relationship with my son. I want you with me when I get married to Dave, if you want to be there. There's a wedding fair at the Headland Hotel in a couple days. The aunts want to go. I'd love you and Kelly to come along. Maybe we can get you girls a dress? Anyways, think about it and let me know. Sending you so much love, baby.'

302

chapter forty-one

When I get back home, my mum accosts me within seconds of going into my bedroom.

'You've been weeping,' she says. 'Your face is all blotchy.'

'I'm fine. Just tired. Didn't get much sleep.'

'You weren't with Kelly last night. You were with Daniel.' My mum's clairvoyant powers are evidently still functioning.

'How'd you know?'

'Because you always weep when that bloody boy is in your life.'

During my relationship with Daniel I had cried most days. The magazines tell you to watch for that, the crying. When you're crying all the time, it probably isn't the right relationship. It sounds so obvious, but even with all the crying, it never felt wrong with Daniel. Right up until the point where he dug into my chest, ripped out my heart and fed it to Cass.

I'd thought that crying was a sign of how strongly we felt about each other; that it meant what we had was real.

'Also,' she says, 'guess who I bumped into at the Gannel Texaco petrol station this morning? Pam Penhaligon.'

'Oh.'

'And she mentioned that my daughter, for reasons I still can't fathom, spent the night in her son's bedroom.'

This was the problem with Newquay being so small. News travelled like wildfire and could scorch its way through the whole town before the tide came back in.

I see the GoPro on the shelf behind her, and figure it's the perfect time to put those pictures on Facebook.

'I, uh, just need to do something,' I say, stalling, and then slowly type out a status update on both my personal and athlete pages, with a few pictures of the happy couple. When I finish this, my mum is still looking at me.

'Mum, just because I was in his room, that doesn't mean something happened.'

'Didn't it?'

'Well, yeah, but—'

'Don't you think it's significant that you've only been in Newquay a matter of days and you've ended up in the bed of the most problematic boy in Newquay?'

'Daniel's not "problematic". He's just . . . Daniel.'

My phone beeps with people commenting on my posts and sharing them, everyone wanting to help track down the owners of the camera.

'And who's that? The boy who cheated on you and destroyed one of your closest friendships. The boy who was almost responsible for Zeke dying. Twice.'

'I can't just, you know, stop caring for people. It's not like switching off a light,' I say, feeling suddenly angry. Once I let myself love people, I love them forever, no matter what they do.

'So you still care for Cass, or does this policy only apply to romantic relationships?'

My athlete Facebook page is still open and I look down at it and see the likes racking up. Most people have commented to say they'll try to help and then there's Daniel's contribution, *Who gives a shit about some knackered old Go Pro?*

Apparently I do, I write back to him. My mum takes the phone from my hand, turns it off and places it on my desk.

'Yeah, Mum, I still care about Cass, but I'm never going to trust her again.'

'But you'll trust *Daniel*?'

'I don't trust Daniel! I never said I trusted him, did I?'

'For the love of all that is pure, Iris, you have got to stop doing this to yourself.'

I sniff back watery snot and wait for the rest of the lecture.

'It's as if you are deliberately chasing unhappiness.'

'I'm not doing that. That's the opposite of what I'm doing.'

305

She gives me this particular look of dismay, as if she can see a funnel cloud and I'm walking towards it with closed eyes and outstretched hands.

'Oh, Iris. This is not what I wanted for you,' she says, exasperated. 'You know, you were never named after that blasted flower. I named you for the goddess of the rainbow. The sky's the limit – that's what I wanted you to feel when you were growing up. I did not – I *do* not – want you to make it all about some boy. There is so much more to living than one other person.'

I move my hand, brush her words aside.

'Zeke will be here for the wedding. I'm gonna have to see him,' I say, then begin to cry into my forearm, face slipping on the wetness of my skin, because whatever happens, it can never be the same again. I've seen to that.

'Shhhh, now, don't cry. Everything's going to work out. All it needs is time,' my mum says.

'It's not even just about Zeke. What am I gonna do about surfing? What happens after the contest?'

'Well, that's up to you, but I expect you'll sign with some new corporate sponsors, won't you? Be off travelling the world again, leaving your mother to worry herself into an early grave.'

I say the thing I have been dreading saying since I came home, dreading even more than telling her about Zeke: 'I don't think I want to compete any more. Once the Billabong competition is through, I think I'm done.'

306

My mum is aghast and she transitions into teacher mode. 'Oh, no, you're not, young lady. You have a gift and you will not squander it.'

'It's too hard. The other girls are tougher and they want it more. You know what I wanted? To come home.'

Despite all the highs, a big part of me had craved my normal life, with no training or contests to worry about, no cameras and no pressure.

'You really think your opponents never got homesick? Come on, Iris, of course it was hard. It was never supposed to be a holiday. You were there to work.'

'Yeah, and now I don't even enjoy surfing any more. It used to be the thing I loved most in the world, but the competition sucked all the fun out of it. I can't even look at a picture of a wave now without feeling stressed.'

I glance at the tatty surf posters on my bedroom walls, crazy shots of Stephanie Gilmore, John John Florence, Gabriel Medina and Jordy Smith punting airs, images which had made me so happy when I was twelve, but which now make me feel inadequate every time I catch a glimpse of them.

'Look, this is all new, but you've done marvellously well and everyone thinks you have a bright future ahead of you. You've only just turned seventeen and look how well you've coped with the pressure and all that change.'

I go and retrieve my phone from my desk. I don't risk switching it on and annoying my mum, but just having it next to me is a comfort.

'I haven't though, Mum. I'm a massive fraud. Everyone thinks I'm all cool and confident, what with the travelling and contests, but some days, loads of them, I panic over everything. Stupid things, like I'm standing outside a door I've never seen before and I panic that I won't be able to open it. I'll be stuck on the outside, everyone laughing at me for not knowing how to get in. Or I'll have my hand on some public toilet faucet and worry like mad, in case I can't make the water come out. And don't even get me started on my contest heats. The "fake me" has it all together but the real me is afraid of everything.'

My mum smiles. 'Ha! You said "faucet". I knew you would eventually!'

'Tap. I meant tap.'

She sighs, swings up her legs and lies next to me on the bed. We both look at the ceiling and the stars I'd placed there when I was light enough to sit on my dad's shoulders.

'Look, Iris, you don't seem to have understood something quite fundamental about yourself. You assume your more negative emotions are the real you, which you're desperately hiding from the world, but that's nonsense.'

'I'm just pretending to be confident but inside I can't stop worrying,' I say, trying to explain, to make her understand.

'I know, and when you're anxious, that's you, of course it is. But the confident part, the part that fights the

308

anxiety, is also you. You're not a person in disguise. There is no *real* you or *fake* you. The more positive elements are just as valid as the more negative ones. All of it is you and all of it is real, even the happy part.'

I stare at her, taking this in. I can almost feel the circuit boards in my brain rearranging themselves.

'Why couldn't we have had this conversation when I was thirteen?' I say, and she cuddles me and makes soothing shushing noises. Eventually, I rest my head against her arm and sleep.

When I wake up the next morning, my post has been shared over four thousand times and the owners have been found. They're Londoners, still together, and living in Germany now with their first kid on the way. They're completely over the moon that their camera survived being lost at the bottom of the sea and that they'll now always have a record of their romantic trip to Cornwall. I write them a message to say that if they give me their address, I'll post it to them, and I go downstairs and find Caleb chatting to Lily in the front room.

'Come to Fistral,' he says. 'It's basically a lake.'

chapter forty-two

The sea is freakishly flat, the water is getting warmer and me and Caleb are splashing around in the shallows, acting like kids on the first day of the school holidays.

At one point Caleb insists on swimming through my legs, but he mistimes it and accidentally kicks me in the crotch, at which point I decide I've had enough, and go to towel off.

I'm on the sand, getting changed into a jumper and shorts under my Robie, when I hear a shout from Caleb. A hundred yards out to sea, something is sticking out of the water. A fin.

Instead of swimming back, Caleb swims after it.

I run down to the water to call to him, but he's out of range. Whatever he's following, it's moving slowly. It's not a dolphin, the fin is all wrong, and it doesn't look like a shark either. It might be a whale, but whatever it is, Caleb's on its tail.

Caleb suddenly turns back to shore, scans the people

on the beach, finds me and gives me the thumbs up.

An old man in a straw trilby and a Hawaiian shirt walks to stand next to me.

'You see something?' he asks.

'Yeah, there's definitely a fin out there,' I say.

Whipping a miniature pair of binoculars out of a satchel with crossed golf clubs on it, he trains the lenses on the fin, which has now moved a little further offshore, and says, 'Girlie, that's a sunfish! My grandmother always told me they were a good omen. I reckon you got some real good luck coming your way.'

Caleb stays out there until the sunfish finally swims around the headland towards Crantock, and when he comes out of the water, the old man turns to me and says, 'That there's a fine-looking young man. Reminds me of a sailor I once knew, although the hair is different.'

For a moment, he looks so wistful as he remembers his past glory days that I feel bad for him.

As if reading my mind, he says, 'Do whatever you want, dear, except get old. Getting old is worse than getting fat, getting heartbroken, and getting poor, put together. Take it from me. Grenville Ford. Nice to meet you.'

'Iris,' I reply. 'Nice to meet you too.'

The next moment, Caleb is with us, all 'Did you see it? So cool! I can't believe it! Hello, mate.'

The old guy shakes his hand and Caleb looks down at the satchel.

311

'Nice bag,' he says. 'You play golf?'

And then they start going on about handicaps, irons and birdies, and eventually I'm being asked if I mind Caleb taking a couple of hours to play a round of golf at the Newquay course with his new senior citizen best friend.

'I'm hanging out with my girlfriend today,' Caleb says, and there it is. *Girlfriend*. I know I have to tell him.

Grenville walks away, disappointed, and I turn to Caleb. 'I'm not your girlfriend, Caleb.'

'I know, but I didn't know what else I should call you. I don't think he'd have got "friend with benefits".'

'Caleb,' I begin, 'I slept with Daniel. Sort of.'

Caleb looks at me coolly and says, 'When was this?'

'Two nights ago.'

'You seeing him again?'

'No. God, no.'

'Do you still wanna see me?'

'Yeah, if you're cool with that.'

'Course I am. It's not like we ever said we were exclusive. It's all good.'

We walk to the new Stable pizza place, which used to be my old Billabong shop, and eat the most delicious pizza I have ever had in my life. There are long wooden tables like a medieval banquet hall and spectacular views of Fistral through floor to ceiling windows. They're playing chill-out music over the sound system and I recognize Wolf Larsen's 'If I Be Wrong', which is one of Zeke's favourite songs. Next week, the waiting period starts for Zeke's contest in Brazil; if he even bothers to turn up, that is.

Caleb doesn't say much, but ploughs through an avocado and pineapple pizza, which Zeke would love, and I think about how weird it is that I have no idea what country Zeke is even in when I'd once known his itinerary down to the minute.

When I get home, Sephy is in the front room with my mum, waiting for me.

'Time's gone real slow since you got home, every hour dragging, am I right?' she says.

'Pretty much,' I say, nodding.

'So let's speed it up. We got work to do.'

chapter forty-three

Two days later, I sit with Sephy and the aunts but no Kelly, because she's working again, and I take in the grand surroundings. My eyes skim over glazed arches, a brass gong, golden chandeliers, nooks and crannies stuffed with armchairs, glass-topped coffee tables, floral displays so lavish they look as if they belong in a cathedral during a royal wedding, a silver salver of red apples – Caleb would know the type, I think – curtains heavily embroidered in terracotta and gold, as if the interior should match the exterior of this red-bricked hotel, yellow walls, ornate white plaster period details, mirrors reflecting sea light. So much light, coming at me from all directions, making my head ache.

Elevenses arrive served on porcelain. Scones. Cakes. Sandwiches with the crusts cut off. Ritz-style.

One of the aunts, Verity, touches my knee. 'What *are* you thinking about, dear? You look quite peaky.'

'Nothing,' I reply.

'Leave the child alone,' her sister Elaine says. 'She's pining.'

Elaine goes back to her knitting. I can't make out what she's working on, but probably a tea cosy or something for the Women's Institute.

Sephy comes back from the posh lavatories, and I say, 'Are you totally sure you still want me to be a bridesmaid, now I'm not with Zeke?'

'Sure I do! I'd be honoured.'

We eat our sandwiches and Sephy goes to have a look at the stalls of the bridal fair.

She comes back with, 'Dang, there's nothing here for me.'

'Nothing at all, dear?' asks Verity.

'It's all so fancy. Too many white dresses.'

'Why don't you let us make the frocks? You pick the fabric and the patterns, and we'll put them together for you.'

'That's so kind, but it's too much work. I couldn't ask you to do that,' Sephy says.

'Well, you'd pay us, naturally, so it wouldn't be charity.'

'Yeah, I mean, sure, I would love that, and of course I'll pay, of course!'

'No pretty accessories on sale?' Verity asks.

'Nothing I liked. I thought there might be beach crafts or something.'

'Well, I can knit you a few herring gulls if you like,' Elaine offers. I look down at her current piece of knitting and get the sense that maybe it isn't a tea cosy after all. She looks at me.

'It's a scrotum, dear. I've made a fortune on my blog with specialist pieces for hen nights. "Erotic Knits". Look me up. I do vulvas too. I don't discriminate. Sephy, for the hen night perhaps I could knit some tiny miniature penises, to clip onto handbags?'

'Sounds awesome!' Sephy says, looking genuinely excited at the prospect.

'Well, Elaine,' Verity says, 'I'm still miffed that you won't employ me on that web thingy of yours.'

'You've never been a good knitter, Verity, and we both know it.'

'I'm sure I could do something. Embroider handkerchiefs with quotes from the Kamasutra?'

'Nobody uses handkerchiefs any more, dear. They've gone quite out of fashion. Sephy, why don't you have another look. Start with a few bits and pieces for the rehearsal lunch.'

'The rehearsal lunch . . .' I say. Where I'll see Zeke for the first time since we split.

chapter forty-four

I wake up at 4 a.m. and I can't get back to sleep. It's been weeks since my mistake with Daniel and everyone who cares knows I'm no longer with Zeke. The only person who gave me attitude about it was Garrett, and I suspect that was mostly because I'd stopped Kelly from telling him, but at least he's over it now.

I've kept myself busy, not letting myself obsess about the past. I've been at the Waterworld gym every day, and my dad has taken me for countless driving lessons, which thankfully improved after the first one in which I accidentally mounted the kerb and got laughed at by some school kids. I've been seeing Caleb most days too and word has started to spread that there's something between us, but I've been clear that it's not serious.

Now I'm awake before dawn in a silent house and my body has been taken over by apprehension. In just a few hours, Zeke is going to be in Newquay. I don't know how I'm going to be in a room with him, what I'm going to say to him. I have to steady myself. I need to go surfing.

The sun isn't up yet, but I don't care. I'd once been so cautious about nightsurfing, as if some sea monster would rear up and spirit me away in its mouth. I'm not afraid of the darkness. I want it, because under my arm I have my first LED board, which is covered in purple lights and has been sent to me by Zeke's awesome shaper as a good-luck-in-the-final-contest gift.

I reach Fistral on foot, and there's not another soul in sight. Fistral is still only technically safely surfable at low tide, because of the freshly exposed rocks higher on the sands, but it isn't as if the lifeguards will be around this early to stop me.

Surfing here feels different now, I'm not the same surfer as last summer. I paddle out, stronger and heavier than before, under bright moonlight, and I catch the first throaty wave that comes through. It's going to be a long one and I feel the adrenaline kick in as it opens up in front of me. I shift my weight from one rail to the next, building speed until I spot a perfect ramp section. I feel the fins release, and take off.

This moment when I'm completely disconnected from the wave is unlike anything else I do in surfing. Getting barrelled is one kind of awesome, as are big powerful carving turns, but airs are next level and for this one moment I'm completely at peace. I ready myself for landing, pray I'll find a flat part to slide my board onto and hope my knees will be able to absorb the impact without buckling.

I crash into a section of whitewater, the neon purple glow of my board's LEDs lighting up the froth, and I wipe out painfully.

But I surf until I'm exhausted. The break now is dotted with other surfers who look at my board with envy. Back on the beach, I tear off my wetsuit, change into my jeans and T-shirt and bump into Carina, who's been running on the beach before school.

'How's it going?' I say, and we fall into stride together.

'Good. Loving the board. Reckon I could borrow it one day?'

'Sure, whenever you like. Is Cass OK?'

'She's fine. She's pretty tough, you know.'

Carina knows what happened with Daniel. She told me as much one day when we were both out in a quiet South Fistral line-up. She hasn't held it against me. 'People make mistakes,' she said. 'Cass's made enough of 'em. Don't sweat it.' I'd been dreading her freezing me out or giving me stink-eye, but she'd been as friendly as ever and I'd felt overwhelmed with gratitude, as well as quite a lot of guilt for swerving her after I'd fallen out with her sister.

'So Zeke's back today?' she asks me and I nod.

'Later this afternoon. I don't know how long he'll stay but yeah he's coming back for the wedding.'

'So you're just killing time until then?'

'No, I'm gonna train for my contest. Gym, swimming, maybe a bit of kayaking later.'

'How'd you feel about seeing Zeke?' she asks, looking at me with a worried expression on her face. 'Do you think it'll be upsetting seeing him again?'

I ponder this for the millionth time. 'I don't know. Probably. But we need to get it over and done with,' I say.

'So you can move on?'

'I have moved on,' I say, and she gives me another one of her worried looks.

chapter forty-five

We are milling around the garden. The spring day is warm; the forecast tells us we're gearing up for a heatwave. The marquee is up and long tables are set extravagantly with white linen and yellow roses, and we're about to take our places.

Garrett, standing to the left of me, nudges Kelly. 'What time you think Zeke'll show?'

'I don't know. He should be here already. Maybe his connecting flight from Gatwick was delayed,' Kelly says.

'How long do these rehearsal lunches go for?' he asks her next.

'Why're you asking me? This is the first one I've ever been to. I didn't even know this was a thing.'

'So, like, six thirty? I give my Best Man speech and we can bounce, right?'

'Garrett, I have no idea!' Kelly says, exasperated. 'Ask your mum and stepdad. It's their party.'

'Mom will be here till the sun goes down. She's

always last to leave.'

'Given she's pregnant, I seriously doubt it,' Kelly says.

I look at Sephy. She is standing at the other end of the garden, the point nearest the sea, resplendent in a filmy orange dress that flutters in the breeze.

She's staring out over the horizon, where the sun is hours from setting; strips of golden light darting through the clouds down to the water. She turns and beckons me over.

'Jesus rays, my mom used to call them,' she says, with a sad smile.

I look at the horizon. 'Yeah, I can see why.'

'How are you doing, Iris?'

'I'm OK.'

'I heard from Wes that you'd gotten a new boyfriend,' she says. 'Is it love?'

What kind of question is that? Not the kind you want your ex's mother asking.

'He's not my boyfriend,' I say, frustrated that I'm being made to answer.

'It was love with Zeke, right?'

This takes my breath away.

'Yes, it was love with Zeke,' I say, more snark in my voice than I'd intended. Sephy is lovely and I don't want to be rude to her.

'I thought so,' she says, simply.

Her bump has come out more in the past two weeks

and my eyes keep flicking down to it. Zeke's little brother or sister is in there.

Of course I loved Zeke, I think. There'd been so much love there that I don't think I'll ever recover from the void it's left in me.

'You know he has PTSD, right? He told me on the phone a couple days ago,' she says.

I rub my forehead with the heel of my hand.

'I was making it worse, Sephy. I was making him miserable.'

That's what I'd told myself. Leaving Zeke was for the best. Best for everyone: best for me, best for Anders, best for his family, best for the sport of professional surfing and best for its most promising son.

'He's not coming,' Sephy says, her voice full of fear. 'Is he?'

'He'll be here,' I say, looking to the sea, as if Zeke could appear at any moment, strolling over the waters of South Fistral.

'He wouldn't miss today,' she says. 'Not if he was OK. Something's wrong.'

Dave appears behind us. 'Try not to worry, Seph. He'll have just got delayed. He'll turn up. He wouldn't miss this for the world, would he?'

He might, I think, especially if he's methed out of his head or would rather get drunk than face a big family drama. He'd missed his Brazil contest, citing an old knee

323

injury he'd apparently aggravated at Mavericks.

'I'm not celebrating this without my son,' Sephy says to us. 'You must know that, right?'

'I know, and you won't need to,' Dave says.

They embrace and Sephy breaks down; her sobs shaking me to my core. Half of the party guests, including my mum, are looking over, wondering what's wrong, wondering if earth-shatteringly awful news has arrived on our shore.

I see Wes and Elijah rushing over, and Kelly and Garrett aren't far behind. I stand there in the middle of their sorrow, and I am to blame.

The lunch is a disaster. Everyone is so tense that the party has the atmosphere of a wake. The only people who manage to eat a decent amount of food are Nanna's sisters and Dave, who wouldn't lose his appetite in a nuclear war, a fact Sephy has always put down to his work as a paramedic not letting him sweat the small stuff.

Kelly is seated at the other end of the table from Garrett and they keep catching each other's eye and talking in miniature semaphore.

Finally, it gets to six o'clock, which seems like the earliest I can legitimately bail. I gulp down half of my main course but don't wait for dessert. I can't bear it any more. Kelly follows me to the gate.

'You're not leaving, are you?'

'I have to get out of here.'

She sees me shivering and puts her arm around my shoulder, drawing me close.

'I'll come with you.'

'I sort of want to be on my own.'

'I get it,' she says, hugging me gently. 'I'll see you in the morning.'

'OK.'

I turn over the waistband of my silvery chiffon skirt, get on my penny board and weave through the town's narrow streets, and ride along Headland Road, turning my head so I don't have to look at Zeke's apartment, which still sits empty, a Sold sign in the window.

Sephy's questions have made me realize something.

I open a message window to Caleb. In this rampage I've been on, this spiral of misery and self-indulgence, I have hardly thought about his feelings.

I really need to talk. You home?

No, I'm out. Everything OK?

Where are you? I'll come find you.

Cemetery. I'll look out for you.

Caleb is sitting on the grass, his back against a very old-looking headstone.

'I got the job at Newquay Orchard,' he says. 'I'm their new Communications Assistant.'

'Congratulations. That's brilliant news. How come

325

you're here? Weird way to celebrate.'

'My grandparents and great-grandmother are buried underneath us,' he says, shining a pen-torch on the weathered stone so I can see their names. 'All of 'em's stacked up in the same grave. Family plot. Least they have company.'

I notice a smaller, rectangular black stone, which looks brand new and is set in front of the main gravestone.

'My Uncle Nigel died. We tipped his ashes on here. He was the one who told me to go for a job there when he first heard about the project. Thought it'd be a cool place to work.'

'Shit, I'm so sorry, Caleb. I didn't know.'

'Don't worry.'

'When did it happen? Why didn't you tell me?'

'A while back. It was on Facebook. You must've missed it. He had cancer.'

'I'm so sorry, Caleb,' I say. 'I kept off there for ages. Zeke's fangirls were doing my head in. I'd have come home for the funeral if I'd known.'

'It was in the middle of your Santa Cruz contest. He wouldn't have wanted you to miss that. He thought it was brilliant you were competing on the world stage.'

I'd known Nigel since I was a child. He was the relative Caleb was closest to. A tall, bearded Welshman with a big laugh, the best stories, and the soul of a poet.

I can feel tears prickle in my eyes and I reach forward

for Caleb and hug him, feeling the warmth of his chest against mine.

I have to put a stop to this. I'm starting to have feelings for him, and I don't like the way he's looking at me, either. Our sketchy little thing is turning into something solid and I'm in no fit state to start anything else. If I hadn't been so totally self-absorbed, I'd have realized that earlier.

'Did Zeke show at the rehearsal thing?'

'No. Everyone's really worried. I don't think he's coming back here.'

'Doesn't seem like him to bail on his family,' he says.

'He's going through some stuff,' I answer, then take a deep breath. 'I'm really sorry, Caleb, and this is a horrible time to say this, but . . .'

'You've had enough?' he says, his voice devoid of emotion.

'I think I have, yeah. Is that all right?'

'Yeah, course. It was cool and I'm glad we, er, hung out, but I never thought it was going anywhere. Did you? Deep down, like?'

'I don't know. Maybe.'

'Nah. It was a nice few weeks, though. Wanna grab a burger? Gusto's still open. I'm starving.'

And that's it. We're broken up, if you could say that about two people who had never really been together.

We walk together to Gusto and chat about everything from the week's surf report, to a coming close encounter

327

with an asteroid that's due to swing by the earth at midnight, and his feelings on gherkins in veggie burgers.

That's it for me, I decide. I'm done with boys. I have a contest to train for and a career to build.

We scoff our burgers in ten minutes and say goodbye. Since there's still a couple of hours of light left, I jog down onto the beach, drop my gaze to the scatter of wet shingle strewn across the sand like a path of jewels, and follow it to the person waiting for me with a six-pack of beer in a two-man tent in the dunes.

chapter forty-six

I find Beth outside the tent doing press-ups.

'Hi Ivy,' she says.

'Seriously? Aren't we past this by now?'

'Huh, what?'

'It's IRIS.'

'That's what I said.'

We've done this name dance a lot over the past six months. It's become our ritual. How she still finds it amusing, I don't know.

'Over there,' she says, motioning to a six-pack of Carling.

'Not Fosters?' I ask, trying to wind her up. 'Thought you Aussies loved a bit of the old amber nectar.'

'As if,' she says, jumping up and pulling two cans out of the pack. She hands me one, snaps the ring pull and says, 'Cheers, big ears.'

'Same goes, big nose,' I reply in a terrible Australian accent and I down a third of the can. She belches and thus begins a game of burp tennis that almost results in me vomiting when I try too hard to squeeze out the winner.

'How you doing?' she asks. 'I've been worried about you since Perranporth.'

'I've been better,' I say.

'Heard from your bloke yet?'

'Zeke? Not my bloke, but nope.'

'Where do you think he is?'

'Well, he's been in Hawaii, Angola and California, but I don't know where he is now.'

'Don't worry, mate. He's a tough bloke. He'll be fine. Kelly about?'

'She was with Garrett at the party. Has she, uh, been to see you today?' I ask.

'I couldn't possibly say.' She grins. 'So what you been up to lately? Kelly says she hasn't seen much of you.'

'Yeah, I've been going through a weird time. I slept with my ex, who Kelly hates. Well, I sort of slept with him, and I've been concentrating on my training ever since. That and learning to drive. My dad's teaching me.'

'Your ex? The meathead lifeguard with the crazy-long eyelashes?' Beth says, picking at an old ball of scraped-off wax.

'Daniel, yeah. I don't know what I was thinking.'

'How did you "sort of" shag him?'

'It started, and then I stopped it.'

'Don't beat yourself up. We've all been there. Sex

with an ex. Not always a bad thing. Can give you some closure if that's what you're after.'

I drink the rest of my lager, burp again, and say, 'I'd better get on home.'

'Nighty night,' she says.

'You think you might want to quit free-camping and get some actual digs in Newquay? You've been here ages and don't seem too keen on leaving.'

'I'm waiting to move in with Kelly,' she says, winking. 'Nah, I like living out here. Can't bear all the squares.'

'Thanks very much.'

'No, I mean like the houses, the TVs, the iPads, the rooms. Nature is all flowing lines and curves. You don't get squares in nature.'

I nod and then remember something from my old chemistry class. 'Salt crystals can be square. Cubes, I mean.'

'Apart from bloody salt crystals.'

'Thanks for cheering me up, Beth.'

'Hey, don't get too carried away,' she says. 'Remember, at our next contest I am going to demolish you.'

She grins, and fist-bumps me, and I leave feeling much happier than when I arrived.

I walk down to the south end of the beach, clamber over the rocks and climb the stone steps to the esplanade, which is jam-packed with vans.

Most of the surfers who sleep over in their vans are up to no good in the usual ways, with spliffs and girls they haven't even known a day. Some of them have gone to the trouble of purchasing retro stickers to put on their vans that brag, *Don't come knocking when the shagwag's rocking.*

A few kids are larking about on the grass, out past their bedtimes by the looks of them, drinking cider and dancing to their own music through headphones. I sit on one of the wooden benches and try to get my head together.

My phone beeps and it's a text from my mum.

I forgot to tell you! Aunt Zoe is having a boy! Just found out this morning. She had something called a 4D scan. And he's already on the 100th centile. He's going to be so tall! Is that good for surfing?

It's good for paddling, I text back, and then add, *Awesome news, Mum.*

I want to tell Zeke this news, because I know he'll be happy for my aunt, but I can't because he's off the grid. I wonder if Sephy is carrying another boy too. Her fourth son. Or maybe she's having her first daughter. Either way, I know Zeke will be stoked. He won't be the youngest any more. He'll have someone little to look out for.

Somewhere out there, Zeke will be trying to make himself feel all right about bailing on his family. He's fine. Whatever my worst fears whisper, I know he's OK. He has to be.

I watch as a surfer comes up the steps from South Fistral, a shortboard under his arm. I can't help checking. I look at every board to see if it's Zeke's; look at every surfer to see if it's him.

This guy is a similar height to Zeke, but thinner, and I feel my gut wrenched by an acute pang of longing for him.

I look down, get out my phone and check for messages, so I don't have to make eye contact or small-talk with the guy as he walks by.

For the millionth time in the past weeks, there are no texts, no communication from him at all. He'll probably never voluntarily get in touch with me again.

I think about my first real kiss with him, here by this road. He was warm in the cold night air, and we had laid back, the cosmic art of a billion stars splashed above us.

He had this way of scrutinizing me, like he was holding up a gem to the light and marvelling at the loveliness of it. No one had ever looked at me like that before.

This is real love, I remember thinking, because I could see it there in his face and I could feel it in every part of me.

I look up from my reverie, and there he is.

chapter forty-seven

He's walking towards me. I stare at him, trying to find words that are appropriate for seeing the person I used to believe I'd be with forever.

I never imagined it would be like this; I thought when I saw him it would be in some dramatic reunion with his whole family present or at a surf contest. I'm not ready for crossing paths with him on a patch of dog-poo-dotted grass by the esplanade.

Zeke catches sight of me. He doesn't say anything, but swallows, his face drawn, as if he's facing his executioner. My head reels with the idea that he might be afraid of me. Me. The person incinerated by the love he breathed.

I don't know what to do, so I get up and hug him, like polite people are supposed to do, but he isn't hugging me back.

I release him, find my voice and go with, 'You're here.'

'Yeah.'

'Congratulations on winning Mavericks!'

'Thanks.'

He turns to leave.

'Hey! Zeke, talk to me.'

'You know what, Iris? I really don't want to do that,' he says.

'You didn't come to the rehearsal lunch,' I say in a wounded voice.

'I went. I took one look at you, and left. Then I came here and surfed.'

'Oh, well, that's OK then. Hope you got some good ones.'

I can't believe this. He has no idea what he's put everybody through; what they're still going through up there at that terrible party.

'Yeah, I did.'

'Where are you staying? Garrett said the new people already have the keys to the apartment.'

'I'm in a motel.'

'Which one?'

'Why do you care? It's not like you're gonna be coming over.'

I flinch. 'Zeke, don't be like that, OK? This is hard for me as well.'

'Sure it is.'

'Is that why you didn't answer the messages I left this week?' I say. 'Because you're still angry?'

'Ditched my iPhone. Tossed it off a cliff. I have an

Android now.'

'Seems like a bit of a waste,' I remark. 'And not very environmentally friendly.'

'It was defective, so I ditched it. I apologized to it first, so that makes it OK.'

I hear the insult. This is what he thinks I've done to him. Decided he's broken and thrown him away.

I thought he'd got over the worst of the anger, but he's still furious. I can see the hurt in his eyes. But he told me to move on. *He* made out that he was fine.

'It's good that you've been surfing,' I say, in a pathetic attempt to change the subject. Zeke had barely surfed the last few weeks we were together, and when he'd talked about Newquay he made it sound as if he never wanted to ride a wave here again. Too many bad memories.

'I'm always gonna surf. Even here. I just took a break from surfing waves of consequence for a little while. Around the time you left. Shocker. I guess you preferred your boyfriend riding big waves.'

He thinks I left him because he said he no longer wanted to surf bombs? He really believes that?

'Zeke, no. That had nothing to do with it. We were hiding things from each other, lying, and we were tearing each other to shreds. You were taking pills and smoking weed in secret and punching people, for God's sake!'

His hair has grown out a bit and is darker than before, not yet damaged by saltwater and sunshine. He rakes his

336

hand through it, and I see how he still takes comfort in this old habit.

'Yeah, you go with whatever makes you feel better,' he says.

'It's the truth, Zeke, and there's no need to be so bloody horrible.'

I can hear the shake in my voice, and his face softens.

'I'm sorry. It's been a real long day and I'm pissed at the whole world right now.'

'We have to talk properly. I'm a bridesmaid at your folks' wedding.'

'Do we? Do we have to talk? Because the last time we "talked properly" I told you I had PTSD and then you got on a plane to England with your sister. So, yeah, I don't think I'll be doing that again.'

'Fine,' I say, and then add, like a stroppy kid, 'Whatever makes you happy. Have a nice life, dude.'

'Yeah, I'll do that,' he says. 'You be happy too, Iris. If that's even possible for you.'

And then he walks away.

I sit down on the bench, shell-shocked. I can't move for twenty minutes.

Zeke hates me. Can't stand to talk to me. He is cold with fury.

But it doesn't make sense. When we last spoke on the phone, he seemed like he'd made peace with it. Something's changed.

I watch him walk towards the surf lodge next to Hotel Serenity and he doesn't look back at me once. I can't go after him. Can't make him talk to me. I was the one to cut the filaments that bound us together. I did it in one sweeping motion. Told everyone it was for the best.

He's free to do whatever he wants. He owes me nothing.

chapter forty-eight

Kelly sees me walking through the open gate into Dave's garden, which is lit with hanging lanterns. The party's wound down and most of the remaining guests look half-cut. She clocks my expression and says, 'What's wrong? You look like you just ran into the zombie horde.'

'I just saw Zeke.'

'What? NO WAY. So he *is* in Newquay? Why didn't he show today?'

'Because he fucking hates me. I have to go and tell Sephy he's here.'

But Sephy already knows because she is holding up a message on her phone and I see in her face sheer delight and relief.

'He's coming!' she shrieks.

Dave is next to her, smiling and smug at being right.

'Just perfect. I'm leaving, Kel.'

'He doesn't hate you, Iris.'

'Uh, yeah, he really does.'

'What did he say?'

'That he blames me for everything.'

Kelly laughs. 'Bit dramatic. Sounds like he's just angry and lashing out. It's not like you're planning to get back together with him, anyway. Get through the wedding and you won't have to see him again. Sod Zeke bloody Francis and the wave he rode in on.'

Someone coughs. 'Thanks a bunch. I guess I shouldn't have bothered with dress pants.'

He's changed out of his wetsuit and is wearing a fancy black jacket, white shirt and evening trousers. I didn't even know he owned clothes like this.

Kelly nods at him, not bothered that he's heard her slagging him off, and says, 'You'd better watch out for Wes and Garrett. They're pretty annoyed with the Prodigal Brother.'

Zeke flinches, like she's prodded a wound, and he opens his mouth to say something, when Garrett comes barrelling towards him and gets him in a headlock. Wes is just behind, and he attempts to prise them apart.

Sephy lands third with a shrieked, 'Baby, you are *not* too old to get spanked. Get over here.'

Dave comes to stand near me as all this play-fighting rolls on, and says, 'Told you he was all right, didn't I? You spoken to him yet?'

'It didn't go well.'

'Cold shoulder?'

'Yes, and it's absolute zero.'

Dave chuckles. 'Don't worry about Zeke. He's an emotional little bugger.'

'I'm out of here.'

'Stay,' Zeke says, suddenly in front of me. 'Please.'

We're all sweating in tight dresses and suits, and the dining area is stuffy with breath and body odour. I turn away from Zeke.

'Let's get out of the marquee,' I say to Kelly. 'I'm suffocating in here.'

Kelly nods and we pick our way through messy tables.

'Wait up.' I turn and see that Garrett has followed. Behind him are Wes, Elijah and Zeke.

We walk across the garden and I listen to them talk about their plan for a north–south surfari of Portugal in the autumn, or the 'fall' as Garrett keeps insisting on calling it, much to Kelly's annoyance.

Behind me, Zeke walks alone and he looks completely morose. He lifts his chin, widens his eyes and motions his head towards the gate.

'I'll meet you later,' I say to Kelly and Garrett.

They look at me and then at Zeke.

'Okaaay,' they say in unison.

I wait for Zeke to catch me up and we walk past the golf course and around to Towan Head.

Zeke takes off his jacket and offers it to me. I take it, but don't put it on.

341

'I won't wear it, but OK if we sit on it? The grass is freezing and the chiffon in this skirt is two atoms thick,' I add, noting as I say this that the label on his dinner jacket says Armani.

'Sure,' he says, and we sit together on this expensive piece of tailoring and look out at the wave that nearly killed him.

The last of the sky's gold is fading and the melancholy's setting in, cool purple and blues spinning out from the epicentre, taking over.

I started on the edge, I think. I moved with Zeke to the heat and light of the inferno, but couldn't take it, so I fled to the cool safety of the outskirts.

'Why were you so angry earlier?'

'I don't know, Iris. It could be because you totally abandoned me.'

'You were going to break up with me! You started talking about it first. And then you told me to move on! I thought you'd be happier without me.'

'Bull. Tell me the truth.'

'Fine,' I say, and I lay out all my reasons.

It was too intense.

I don't want to be eaten up with jealousy.

I don't want my sense of self to be defined by my love for you.

I want a love that gives me room to grow and change.

I want a love that will not transform me into you.

When I'm done, he looks at me.

'OK,' he says. 'I hear you.'

'Zeke, I have to tell you something,' I say, and brace myself. 'While you were gone, I slept with . . .'

'Daniel. Yeah, I know.'

'What? How do you know? Who told you?'

'Who'd ya think?' he says. 'I landed in Newquay, stopped at Morrisons to get some champagne for my folks and bumped into him at the beer section. It was pretty much the first thing out of his mouth. I thought I'd at least try to be polite and opened with, "How are you, bro?" and he said, "Good thanks. Especially since I started shagging Iris." Yeah, I totally see why you like that guy.'

'Firstly, uggh, GROSS, and secondly he hasn't *started* anything. That was the one and only time and it lasted about thirty seconds.'

'That long, huh? Good times.'

'Sorry you had to hear it like that.'

'Forget it. You can do what you want. You sure don't have to explain anything to me.'

'Did he at least look awkward about it?' I ask.

'Are you kidding? He couldn't wipe the stupid-assed grin off his face.'

'I can't believe he told you. He is such a massive dick.'

'Uhh, I really don't want to hear about that,' Zeke says, fake grimacing.

'I obviously didn't mean it that way.'

'No?'

'Absolutely no. *No, no, no.* So, um, were you with anyone else?'

'Iris, I went to a desert in Angola.'

'You also won a contest in California.'

I think of all the girls who slipped pro-surfers bits of paper with their details on. Thanks to Zeke, I knew that over the course of a major contest, surfers could end up amassing dozens of phone numbers from up-for-it fans. Sometimes over a hundred. He would definitely have had options.

'I didn't wanna be around people,' he says. 'So no.'

'Oh,' I say, feeling both pleased and guilty. 'Um, since we're on the subject,' I say, 'not of massive . . . y'know, but, er, I also slept with Caleb. It wasn't a one-night stand. It was more than once. Quite a lot more.'

Zeke sighs. 'Nice guy.'

'You seem to be taking this quite well.'

'I don't care that you slept with other people. I mean, I care, but I don't think you did something wrong and even if I did, that wouldn't be your problem. Maybe I wish one of the guys hadn't been that fuckin' douchebag, but it's not like I'm in any position to criticize someone for having sex.'

'So we can be friends?' I say.

He looks at his polished shoes. 'Sure we can.'

I try to stifle a sudden yawn, but I can't hide the fact that I'm exhausted.

'Can I walk you home?' he says, turning to me with
that dazzling blue gaze of his.

'Yeah, that'd be awesome.'

chapter forty-nine

This is the first official day of me being Just Friends with Zeke. I've been stressing all morning that it'll be weird and I'm nervous of saying something that'll make him or his family feel uncomfortable. I know Zeke must be feeling awkward too. But it's only a day until the wedding, and our lives are always going to be intertwined. We have to try.

The day is abnormally sweltering and Zeke's entire extended family has converged on Fistral.

Zeke and his cousin Colton – who is three, but as tall as a five-year-old – are playing in the waves, and it's hard to say who's having more fun. Colton is on Zeke's back and clinging onto his neck as they dive with the onshore waves, body surfing like dolphins – no boards necessary.

Colton is only a little bit older than my cousin Cara, but twice as fast and about eight times as hyper. Cara pays attention when an adult speaks to her, but Colton is activity all the time and words don't seem to reach him, unless they're bawled by Lianna, his very serious mother.

I make this remark to Sephy and she sighs and says, 'Yup, Zeke was the same way. Too busy exploring his world to listen up.'

I watch Zeke sweep Colton out of the water, haul him onto his shoulders and wade to shore.

'Hey,' Zeke says, setting down Colton and kicking back next to me, long legs stretched out, surf scars shining in the sun.

Zeke's great-uncle John, a sixty-year-old man with a grey ponytail and floral shorts, is hot on his heels, paddling in with a bunch of other male relatives.

'Kinda nice you don't gotta worry about the men in grey suits checking in here,' he says.

'Oh, we have sharks,' I say, 'but little ones that stick to sushi.'

'Lunch?' John says, turning to Sephy.

'You're looking at me?' she replies. 'You think I have a picnic under this dress? Get your own damn lunch!'

'No one puts together a better sandwich than you, Seraphina.'

'If I wanted to play servant to a man, I'd have stayed with my first husband,' is her only reply, and she glances at Zeke as she says it.

I wait for Zeke's reaction to this, but he displays zero emotion.

'Hey,' Uncle John says, breaking the tension, 'can't blame a guy for trying.'

'How about you try the Pasty Shack?' Sephy says.

Dave is walking towards us and Sephy goes to meet him, which leaves me, Zeke and a three-year-old.

Lianna and her husband Kalif walk slowly along the Fistral waterline, hand in hand, their eyes on each other instead of their kids. Strapped to Lianna in a harness is Elisia; a chubby outline of pink flesh, bright eyes and black hair, with a wail that could trigger a thousand migraines. Apparently, the flights from Oahu were not easy.

Zeke chugs down a bottle of water. Colton does the same and then begins to yawn, a thing that looks strange on that little whirlwind. I watch as Zeke rearranges the beach umbrella and some towels into a den for the little boy. When it's ready, Colton crawls into the metre-wide shade and promptly falls asleep.

Zeke starts yawning too.

'Taking it out of you, is he?'

'It's all good. Damn, I love these kids.'

'I see that.'

'Their parents are so lucky,' he says. 'Must feel so awesome to be able to raise whole new people. Hope I get to do that some day.'

'Only you would be looking forward to that,' I comment, thinking how funny Zeke is for getting broody around his cousins.

'Not any day soon. You know, when I'm like twenty-four or twenty-five.'

'That's only six years away!'

'A whole lot of adventure can happen in six years.'

'Yeah . . . and even more can happen in twenty.'

'Sure, sure, but, sooner or later the time would come to stay home.'

'Stay home and do what?'

'Raise a family.'

'And how many kids would be in this family?' I ask.

'At least three, I guess. Maybe four.'

'Oh, just *four* kids, because that's not mental at all.'

He tilts his head at me, eyes serious. 'You don't want kids?'

'I don't know. I mean, children are cute and funny and everything, but they also seem like a lot of . . . hassle.'

Zeke looks at me, surprised, like the hassle part of parenthood hasn't even occurred to him. I can see him turning it over in his head and trying to see it from my point of view.

'What's with the face?' I ask.

'Nothing.'

'How could you not consider the hassle factor of having loads of kids?'

'I don't know,' he says, frowning. 'I never really thought about it that way. I can't imagine not having my brothers. They were the best part of growing up.'

I look at Zeke's aunt and uncle by the shoreline, and I have to admit that they do look happy. Exhausted, possibly anaemic, but happy.

Then Zeke takes off the wet T-shirt he'd worn in the water to protect his sunburnt shoulders and I see it.

I can't help it. I touch his chest, trace my fingers around the petals of the iris.

'Nice tattoo,' I say, looking up into his eyes.

'Oh, uhh, yeah – it felt like time for some new ink,' he says, sounding embarrassed. 'Are you OK to stay here and watch Colton for a minute? The little dude'll be out for a while.'

'Where are you going?'

'I have an idea.'

Zeke gets to his feet, and I notice his knee seems to be troubling him a little, but he says nothing about it and walks down to the waterline where his aunt is dancing and trying to soothe her baby, whose cries I can hear from two hundred yards away. All afternoon the talk has been about how badly the baby is teething, and there's a lot of worrying about if she'll feed with sore gums, and if she doesn't feed properly, whether she'll get dehydrated in the heatwave we're having and if they should just stay indoors and ride it out without inflicting earache on everyone in a one-mile radius.

Colton stirs in his sleep and I rearrange the beach umbrella, which has moved in the sea breeze, so that his face is in the shade again. When I look up, Zeke has reached his aunt and uncle and is being strapped into the harness and the baby slotted into it. Lianna hands him Sephy's white parasol, which he angles so that the baby is completely out of the fierce sunlight.

He doesn't seem embarrassed to be carrying an accessory mostly defined by the creative use of broderie anglaise and he wades up to his knees with the swash swirling in around him. Gulls bob on the water a few metres out to sea and as Zeke turns, I can see the baby looking at them, fascinated as each one takes flight.

Zeke's aunt and uncle, in Newquay for the first time ever for the wedding, walk back to their beach blanket and take the opportunity to close their eyes and lie in the sunshine, sharing one set of earphones and listening to their iPod music in mono. They've been on the move all day, looking after one or other of their kids, so it's no surprise they're keen to take a break.

Zeke doesn't come out of the shallows for ages and I feel restless. I want to go and talk to him, but Sephy and Dave have gone for a walk and I can't leave Colton unsupervised in case he wakes up. Thirty seconds of freedom and he'd be scaling a cliff or trying to ride a Rottweiler.

Eventually the heat gets to me and I curl myself around Colton to try to steal some shade.

I wake up to Zeke's hand on my bare arm.

'Where's Colton?' I say, when brain-fog gives way to panic, looking under the giant beach umbrella and seeing thin air where his little sleeping form has been.

'I sent him to take the trash to the beach cans. He's literally twenty feet behind you.'

'I was supposed to be watching him. Anything could have happened. Jesus, I'd make the worst parent ever.'

'Hey, don't sweat it. His folks are right over there. It's all in hand. Relax.'

'Where's the baby?'

'My aunt's feeding her again. Heat's making her thirsty.'

I sit up and see Zeke's aunt reclining against his uncle, who is acting as her own personal chair, supporting her back as she breastfeeds their daughter. There's no blanket, no shame, just skin and calm. Zeke doesn't seem at all fazed by this and I figure it's something he's seen many times before.

Colton runs down to his parents and they look like this perfect little unit, each one of them wanted and needed.

'You're a pretty good nephew, you know that?'

'Stoked to help out. I can surf whenever. But there aren't so many days I get to see Colton and Elisia. I already don't wanna leave them. Sometimes I wish I could just stay home, you know? It's like I wanna see the world, but I also wanna stay in my own backyard.'

'Yeah.' My thoughts round on my impending contest and what will happen if I lose. What will happen if I win.

Zeke cracks open a store-bought can of espresso and

352

says, 'Seven hours of surfing is not as tiring as one hour looking after Colton. I'm on my fourth coffee of the day – poor man's cocaine, right – and I'm still beat.'

He leaps to his feet and stops a football that Colton has sent hurtling towards his head. 'Iris, you wanna be in goal?'

I groan. 'All right.'

Maybe us being friends won't be so bad after all, I think.

chapter fifty

It's the morning of the wedding, but there's still five or six hours until the ceremony and Zeke is in my living room. He's helping me edit a surf clip of Fistral for my YouTube channel, when someone starts aggressively ringing the doorbell. I balance my laptop on my forearm, like a waitress with stacked plates, and swing open the door.

Standing there with an ultra-serious look on her face is Kelly. Wes is next to her.

'Hey, what ya doin'?' he asks me.

'Nothing much,' I say.

Zeke hears their voices and comes to the door too.

'Hey guys,' he says. 'What's happening?'

'Get your flip-flops on,' Kelly says. 'You don't need a jacket. It's boiling out.'

'Where are we going?' I ask.

'Bay of dreams.'

'There's no swell. It's completely flat,' Zeke says.

'Never mind that, just get moving.'

'But what are we doing?' he asks again, but Kelly is relentless.

'You'll see.'

We walk through town and towards the steps that lead down to Tolcarne. Periwinkle and thrift are scattered in the verges, the hedgerows are shot through with yellow swirls of honeysuckle. Moored in the bay is the most enormous ship I've ever seen. Around it is a flotilla of smaller vessels; locals who've come out to inspect the warship.

'What is that?' Zeke says, shading his eyes from the fierce sun. 'A battleship?'

'Some kind of frigate,' I say.

'HMS *Tyne*,' Wes says. 'We just Googled it on my cell phone. It's a river class ship, which is why it can come in so close to shore. If you look real hard you'll see the guys on board jumping off. It's some kind of training exercise, I guess.'

I look but can't see any people at all. Wes must have sharper eyes than me.

'Look,' Kelly says, 'the gigs are rowing out to have a nose as well. Probably racing to see who can get there first.'

This I can see. Five long, brightly-coloured rowboats are moving swiftly towards the ship, behind them a few sailboats, plus various people on stand-up paddleboards and a few jet skis causing giant wakes and annoying everybody else.

Wes and Kelly are both looking at me, as if they're waiting for something to break the moment, for something to happen. Maybe I'm supposed to glean some insight from such a huge ship in the bay, but I have no clue what that is.

As we walk onto the sands, I watch a young couple messing around at the waterline. The lad, Zeke's age maybe, strips down to his boxers and piles his clothes on the sand. The girl doesn't get undressed, but she goes into the sea wearing her clothes and they wade out deeper together, shrieking as the water creeps higher up their bodies. When she's up to her chest and he's just past his waist, they stop and kiss.

I feel deep sadness in the face of their happiness, because last summer that had been me and Zeke. I had watched him ride round my town on a skateboard, his shortboard balanced on his hip, laughing at the stupid jokes I'd made. I'd watched him shred the waves of my beaches. The waves of my beaches and all my defences. I'd seen him in his private moments and he'd trusted his love with me.

I look up again at the young couple. What they haven't seen is that the tide is coming in. One long wave curls around the neat little pile of clothes and moves it a few inches seawards. The next wave will soak the lot and send it swimming up and down the tideline.

Zeke and I leave the others and run over to grab the clothes. As I lift the guy's folded trousers, I can feel a phone vibrating in his back pocket. We're moving the bundle higher up the beach, by the rocks, where the tide won't reach it for at least forty minutes, when I turn to see them looking at me in alarm.

'The water,' I shout, gesturing at the sea. 'Your stuff was gonna wash away. We're saving it.'

The lad comes tearing out of the sea, shouting something at us in French. His boxers, which were once white, have gone pretty much see-through, and my eyes flick from his crotch to his face. When I point at his damp clothes and the dark print of the waves on the sand, I see understanding break over his face. 'Thank you,' he says to Zeke and me, and shakes our hands. 'For being good citizens.'

'You're welcome, buddy,' Zeke says, smiling.

'Come on,' Kelly says, joining us, 'we don't have all day.'

The four of us walk across the beach and Kelly talks the whole time, almost as if she's deliberately not letting us get a word in, not letting us even hear our own thoughts.

At the water's edge, I see a familiar figure. Garrett. Bobbing slightly in the water behind him is a jet ski. I nod at it. 'Yours?'

'Today it is. I rented it from Lusty Glaze. Been out to see the ship. You want a spin?'

'OK.'

'I'll drive and you can sit behind.'

'I can drive a jet ski, Garrett,' I say.

It's one of the things my dad taught me. We'd fly a mile out to sea and then, secretly, without my mum ever knowing, he'd let me take the controls. Those were the best afternoons we ever had together.

Garrett looks uncertain. 'You know what?' I say. 'Forget it. You and Zeke take the ski. I'll paddle out.'

'I'll come with you,' Wes says.

We rent three longboards from the beach shop and by the time we return, Garrett and Zeke are already on the jet ski and making their way towards the ship. There is hardly any surf and the sea looks shallow and turquoise, so clear we can see the fish just a few feet beneath our fingertips. We skim over the water towards the ship, Kelly suddenly silent.

She turns and gestures for me to paddle around the ship. I take it slow, focusing on the sensation of water slipping past my fingers. Splashes from the men and women jumping from the ship into the water send tiny waves my way. I turn onto my back and face the sun. It's so still, so hot, so quiet, and my board holds me fast.

I feel a surfboard bump mine; a hand on my hair.

Kelly has reached across and is looking down at me.

'What's wrong?' I say, sitting up and throwing my legs astride my board.

'Iris,' she says, 'we're going on the boat over there.'

I look past her outstretched hand to a sailboat with a

blue and white sail.

'Whose is it?'

'You know that thing I wasn't supposed to be doing? Well, um . . .'

My brain is playing catch-up, and I can tell from Kelly's expression that I'm not getting whatever message she wants me to receive.

'Kel, what is this?'

'Oh hell, just follow me and you'll see.'

We do the awkward dance of getting ourselves and our surfboards onto the sailboat, which isn't tiny by any means and must have cost a small fortune.

Sephy and Dave are there, evidently ignoring the tradition of not seeing each other until the ceremony. Zeke is slouching at the prow and there next to him is Erik Matthiesen, the man I last saw with blood gushing from his nose, thanks to Zeke losing his shit and punching him in the face.

'We gotta get things cleared up before the ceremony,' Sephy says. 'I don't want to go into our wedding with the shadow of this hanging over us. Thanks, Kelly,' she says, looking genuinely grateful.

'You did this?' I say to Kelly.

'I wasn't sure it was going to work, but yeah, I've been chatting to Erik on Facebook.'

'She convinced me I must come to Cornwall. I have always wanted to see this coastline, so I have chartered this boat for a week. I hope you will all do a little sailing with me?'

Zeke nods, as if he is actually considering this offer, which seems bizarre, given his massive hostility towards Erik in Florida. There is a long silence, which Zeke breaks with, 'So, I guess we have some things to tell you guys.'

Erik takes off his jacket, unbuttons a cuff, rolls up his white shirtsleeve and shows me what's there.

Three words. Three dates.

LUCAS   10.24.88
MARIA   12.12.92
EZEKIEL 05.02.96

'What?' I say. That's Zeke's name. Zeke's birthday. But why would his uncle have that tattooed on his arm, and . . . and then it clicks. 'Do you mean . . . ?'

'These are all my children. Sephy and I were in love,' Erik says, 'but she was married to my brother. Kurt did not stray – we did. Zeke is my son.'

My brain struggles to process this. A huge part of Zeke's identity is based around some notion of perfect brotherhood. He's told me often enough that his adventures with Garrett and Wes were the best part of his childhood. They are the clearest points of reference on his mental landscape.

'You knew this?' I ask Zeke.

360

'Yes, he told me just before you left.'

'That's why you hit him?' I say, and he nods.

'He said he slept with my mom. That he'd gotten her pregnant and that's why she had to get a divorce. Cos of me, I guess.'

'My husband couldn't accept Zeke,' Sephy says. 'We were trying again, trying to work through it, but he barely touched Zeke. Never held him. Never smiled at him. He was so cold. I told him to go.'

Erik tells us everything, with Sephy filling in the gaps. At last, when everyone is finally in the know, Zeke says, 'So much bad shit had already happened. I couldn't handle this. It felt like everything had changed. Like all the good things were gone.'

Wes turns to Zeke, puts his hand on his shoulder. 'Wait. You thought this would change something?'

'Sure it does. I'm not who you thought I was. I'm only your half-brother. You and Garrett are . . .' he pauses, 'like, real brothers.'

'Are you kidding me? You're our brother,' Garrett says. 'Hundred freakin' per cent. For all time.'

I watch them embrace, Zeke and Garrett in tears, and Wes just about holding it together. Sephy joins the hug, while Dave and Erik stand next to each other and look on.

Kelly turns to me and says, 'If these boys communicated on a regular basis, life would be a lot simpler.'

Yeah, I think, *maybe I should try that too.*

361

chapter fifty-one

Dave and Sephy have a simple ceremony on Lusty Glaze Beach, say the words that mean the most to them, and vow to be true to each other forever. At the very last minute Sephy managed to get her father, Pop, on a plane from the Big Island. He sits grinning and holding on tight to a bottle of Cornish Knocker and another of Betty Stoggs, which my Aunt Zoe thought would be an appropriate gift for an eighty-year-old Hawaiian guy visiting Cornwall for the first time.

I look at Zeke a lot throughout the service, and almost cry when he reads Brainard's 'The Deep' in honour of Nanna. When he finishes, he comes to sit with me and it's not awkward. We're friends and I'm glad of that, but I can't stop thinking about that punch. What it had changed. I'd thought it was round ten of Zeke going off the rails, the final straw after months of erratic behaviour. But it was more than that. He'd just heard news that had turned his world upside down. If he'd been real with me, trusted

362

me enough to confide in me, maybe I'd have stayed.

At the end of the ceremony, the happy couple turn to their guests and Sephy says, 'So . . . we got the second sonogram this week and guess what? IT'S A GIRL!'

Zeke, Wes and Garrett mob their folks and Zeke steps away to punch the air and says, 'I'm getting a *sister*.'

'Congratulations,' I say, laughing at the face he's pulling, which is total wonderment mixed with extreme anxiety.

'I gotta find her a board!' Garrett says, and Wes muscles in to say, 'Hey, maybe you get to choose the board, but I'm teaching her to surf.'

'Ha. Yeah, you're not,' Garrett says. 'I taught my brothers and I'm teaching my sister.'

Sephy puts them all in their place with, 'Hey. I believe it was actually me who taught all my children how to ride waves and I'll be keeping on with that with my daughter, you hear? But you boys can help.'

We walk inside to the reception rooms, Zeke still looking stunned. Before long, Wes is spinning Elijah around the dance floor while Garrett, Kelly and Beth – who Sephy insisted was invited – take turns embracing Sephy and Dave. Then Saskia, Anders and Zeke's friend Chase arrive, barefoot, sweating and carrying gifts that include a huge rectangular cake covered in a hundred miniature surfboards, as well as a dozen helium balloons, which Zeke immediately makes them promise they won't release, pointing out that they almost always end up twisted in the guts of marine mammals.

Saskia, my once-rival, who'd let me take her spot on the Billabong tour after another girl sabotaged my board, comes over to me, smiles and says, 'Iris! I'm so glad to see you survived the winnowing.'

'Hey, Sas,' I reply, hugging her and catching the scent of some exotic perfume. 'Um, the *what*?' I'm pretty sure I've never before heard the word *winnowing*.

'You know, ancient process of sorting the wheat from the chaff. Think farmer chucking the lot in the air and the light bits blowing away. The good stuff, the heavier grain stays put. The tour's almost over and you haven't drifted off. You're still here. Good for you!'

I'm still here.

'Yeah, just about,' I say. Because she's right. I haven't floated away with the chaff, no matter how fierce the winds have blown against me. The outer husk may have gone, but I'm heavier now, and my centre has held.

'Good luck in the final contest,' she says, looking serious. 'Whatever the outcome, you should be proud of yourself for working so hard and sticking with it, even when things were awful.'

I look at her red hair curled into some glam Forties style, and her long gold dress embroidered with tiny pearls. I'd once been envious of her. More than that: I'd wanted to *be* her. Until it became terrifyingly clear I could only ever be me.

'Thanks, I appreciate that,' I say, feeling the sea breeze glide through an open door, 'and for everything else you've done for me. Let's get together after the competition, OK?'

'I'd love that,' she says, and hugs me, before striding off to the champagne table, where Anders stands, a glass in each hand. When he meets my gaze, he grins, downs the contents of both glasses and gives me a thumbs up.

Everyone is invited to the reception. Even Erik comes along, and gets on surprisingly well with the aunts, who apparently have a deep and abiding love for his home country Denmark, where they once took a winter steam train voyage and skated on frozen lakes. Everyone is smiling, Dave and Sephy are walking on air and the day shoots by in a blur of their happiness.

When things begin to wind down, Zeke and I kick back under the star-spangled sky, bottles of Budweiser at our feet.

We've dragged plastic chairs to the middle of the beach and around us there's the usual symphony of ocean sounds, plus faint music from his parents' wedding reception – a jam with a mechanical bull out front, an emo band on stage and a free bar. A reception attended by the whole of Newquay's surf community.

The air smells faintly of seaweed and I look up at the

sky and feel like I'm finally home.

'Shocker to think I almost died out there,' Zeke says, glancing across the bay to Towan Head, where the Cribbar breaks.

'I used to have these nightmares about that morning,' I say, touching the buttons on my chest. Sephy was OK with me and Kelly choosing vintage-style silk tea dresses for the wedding. The aunts put them together and based them on a style they'd worn as young women.

'Same. Garrett and Wes were underwater with me. Then my mom was there. And you, Iris. You guys all drowned right in front of me. Then there were the flashbacks I had during the days. Like, I'd just be walking and something would be in front of my eyes. Not the whole scene, even. Little parts of it. My hand trying to release the leash strap on my ankle. The surface of the water far above me. The sound of the ocean in my head. The pain of no air in my chest. The blue stars.'

I knew that one of the final symptoms of oxygen deprivation was blue stars.

'I should've talked to you more. Asked what you were thinking about.'

'It was breathing, mostly.'

I nod. 'You must have been so scared.'

'Uh-huh, but also on a physical level afterwards my breathing was all screwed up. It took weeks for my lungs to feel better. I couldn't inhale deep and it hurt a little literally every time I took a breath, so I couldn't even forget about what happened for a second.'

I had curled up with him night after night, fallen asleep on his chest, and I had completely failed to notice there was a problem with his breathing.

'I kept it from you. From everyone,' he says.

'So we wouldn't worry.'

'Yeah, that was part of it, but mostly I think I didn't want to acknowledge it, because then I'd have to do something about it. I couldn't believe it got to me the way it did. I thought I was tough. I thought I would always be OK in the ocean, which is not just my office: it's the place I feel most like me.'

'So,' I say, 'it was like losing your home?'

'Yeah, nowhere made me happier than the ocean and, like, don't mistake me here, I hurt every part of my body surfing, beat up on reefs, snapped bones clean in two, busted my knees, got held down on so many waves, but it was always cool because I could hold my breath longer than anyone else I ever met.'

I smile, thinking that Zeke is not exactly selling this lifestyle to me.

'Sure, I said to myself. I'd take those odds, accept the risks, but in my heart I thought I could make any wave, survive any hold-down, ride out any danger,' he goes on, his voice becoming quiet. 'At the Cribbar, I was just destroyed by this, like, *terror*. An old guru guy I knew used to talk about this "enlightenment experience" he had in the woods one day. He said for a few minutes he left his body, understood the nature of the universe and knew that nothing mattered cos everything was just as it was supposed to be. Well, I guess the Cribbar was the opposite of that. It was the worst thing I ever went through and it poisoned everything that went down after.'

'Oh God, Zeke, I don't know what to say.'

'Man, I was in a dark place. It was like the bad vibes just closed in on me and took over. I lost my confidence. It started to feel like I was losing everything. You, surfing, the tour, my sponsors, even my mind. When Erik came to me and told me he'd cheated with my mom and I was actually his kid, I couldn't take it. Stuff going down with my family felt like the end and I lost it so bad. I still can't believe I hit the guy.'

'He doesn't seem to have held it against you,' I say, thinking about Erik back at the party, Zeke's family already taking him under their wing.

'He's actually pretty cool. He said this winter he wants to take me skiing in Sierra Nevada, and I'm gonna teach him to surf. He's never even tried — can you believe that? The dude who gave me half my genes has literally never been on a surfboard. Yesterday he asked me which side of the board you have to wax. Seriously!'

I smile at him, imagining Erik lying on a foamie and Zeke waiting patiently behind and pushing him onto gentle waves. Clapping and hollering the first time Erik catches one and stands.

'That sounds really nice, Zeke.'

I look towards the reception again, and wonder if we should go back. 'And everything's OK with your mum now?'

'Yeah. I mean, she said not to sweat it, but I'm so ashamed of how I acted. The things I said to her, and about her, were totally out of line. I knew it was fucked up, even at the time, but it was like my brain was firing off in all the wrong directions. I think maybe I had some kinda breakdown, and I'm only just starting to come through whatever that thing was. But I have a therapist now, and he's helping me out so much. I also have a legit script for head-meds, so no more street pills.'

'I'm glad to hear it,' I say, feeling immense relief.

'Hey, Iris,' he says, taking my hand. 'I acted like such an asshat, but you know I'm super-sorry, right?'

'Please don't apologize,' I say, gently withdrawing my hand, because I can feel the chemistry kicking in, and it shouldn't, because we're just friends now. 'I get it. I'm sorry too.'

We watch some oystercatchers swoop across the sky in front of us.

'I'll never forget you saved my life,' he says.

'Yeah, you owe me one, Francis.'

He catches my eye and winks.

'What was that?' I say, laughing. 'Did you genuinely

just wink at me? Like in a serious way?'

'Hey,' he says, fronting. 'Folks wink in Cornwall.'

I look at him here with me, and for the first time maybe ever, I see him: flawed, hopeful, trying, and I make a decision. 'You wanna get out of here, Zeke?'

'Hit it.'

He stands up and yanks me out of my chair, sending a bottle that had been jammed between my knees to the ground with a thud and a fizz.

'Where do you wanna go?'

'Follow me,' I say.

The tide is out and I lead him down to the water's edge and around the headland towards Tolcarne. This stretch of the coast takes ten minutes to walk across and is only accessible for a few hours a day. It's peppered with saltwater pools and rock stacks. A person could get lost here, cut off by the tide and trapped against the cliff. Never seen again.

He's right behind me and I stop so suddenly that the toe of his shoe bumps my sandal. I kick off my shoes, and he does the same. He picks one up and throws it hard, then the other. They land what looks like a hundred feet away. I do the same and mine go just as far. I leave them there, reach up and interlace my fingers at the back of his neck. I pull his head towards me and kiss him, a beery kiss on unsteady feet.

My brain is calm. I'm not stressing, not worrying, not mentally listing all the things that could go wrong from

370

here on out. I don't know what this means or what will happen in the future. I am kissing the boy I love and he is kissing me.

Suddenly, I have a sensation of being watched, but when I open my eyes the night is quiet and still, the only movement gulls drifting along the coastline above us.

Then, he takes off his shirt, I kiss the tattooed flower on his chest, and he spreads the shirt on the ground for me. I lay back and he sits beside me on the cold ground and leans over me. He has stubble on his cheeks, and moves close to me and grazes his face over the side of my neck and ear. I feel his mouth, dry and rough, and my nerve-endings light up. The muscles of my legs stiffen. My shoulder blades wing together and a deep ache starts up between them. He doesn't kiss me again, but the friction of his face against mine, the feel of his breath on my throat, the cool skin of his lips is enough.

I open my eyes for a moment, and whack him on the shoulder.

'Damn!'

'Bloodsucker.'

But we're grateful to that mosquito because walking towards us from behind one of the stacks is a man. The dregs of the sunset have burned out and I can't make out his face.

'We have company,' I say.

The man raises his hand in greeting and, as he gets closer, I realize it's not a man at all, it's Daniel.

chapter fifty-two

'Beat it,' Zeke says. 'We're kinda busy here.'

'You heard him,' I say, as Groover appears from around one of the stacks, stopping every few paces to sniff the sand. If Daniel's walking Cass's dog, maybe he's patched things up with her.

'You're back with Cass?' I say and he nods.

'Engaged. For real this time.'

'Good.'

He's still standing there, looking at us, and Groover comes over to me and starts licking my toes.

'What do you want?' Zeke says.

Daniel takes a deep breath, his fist tightening around the dog lead wound in his hand. 'I just wanted to say I'm sorry, mate.'

I'm caught off guard by this, and so is Zeke, judging by his expression of extreme incredulity.

'Who are you even apologizing to? Like, me or Iris?'

'Both of you. I'm not taking the piss. I should've come

and seen you last year, after it all kicked off. I've been such a twat. I don't expect us all to be friends or nothin', but I just felt like I needed to say it. Anyway, that's it.'

He turns to leave, and me and Zeke look at each other.

Zeke shakes his head, bites his lip.

'OK, bro,' he says, 'apology accepted. We leave it in the past, right?'

Daniel holds out his hand and I watch as they shake on it.

'Yeah,' Daniel says. 'Appreciate that, mate.'

They both look at me.

'Fine, whatever, it's all in the past,' I say.

'Let me buy you a drink,' Daniel says. 'I'm off the beer at the minute, but I'll have a Coke while you hit the hard stuff. When you've, er, finished here, I mean.'

We return to the reception, and for the next few hours, me and Zeke chat to Daniel at the Lusty Glaze bar and it is the strangest thing to see. They actually get on. Daniel asks us loads of questions about the breaks we've surfed and he grills Zeke about what it was like growing up in Hawaii.

Zeke drags me onto the dance floor for a long slow dance to Sebastien Tellier's 'La Ritournelle' and when I catch Daniel's eye from across the room, he nods at me and his mouth softens into something like a smile. Then it's the chorus of the song and Zeke is looking into my eyes and saying all his love is for me.

Later, Kelly and Garrett come over and chat while we watch an arm-wrestling tournament kick off, with Daniel and Beth up first. Daniel loses.

'Hey,' Kelly says to me, taking me to one side. 'So I've made a decision. I'm gonna take a year out before uni. Go travelling.'

'Wow, really? Good for you, Kel.'

'Thanks, and, um, after your contest, I'm going to take a trip to Australia this summer with Beth. She wants to show me Maroubra and go for a surf. Seriously, I know it's sharky as hell but it looks like paradise. And . . . I'm gonna meet her folks.'

'Wow,' I say. 'Sounds like it's getting serious.'

'It sort of is, really.'

'What about Garrett?'

'Oh yeah, I'm also going to Oahu later in the year. Same deal.'

'You're not choosing?'

'Nope. Everyone says they're cool with it, so I'm gonna see where it goes.'

I grin at Kelly. 'Beth and Garrett. Australia and Hawaii. You are the jammiest girl in the world, you know that?'

'Life is pretty great, not gonna lie,' she says, before kissing me lightly on the lips.

We watch as Dave, Sephy and Erik have an embarrassing freestyle to some Seventies jam, and Sephy comes up, a look of surprise on her face as she sees we're still deep in conversation with Daniel. She tells us that she and Dave are leaving for their hotel, a fancy boutique place overlooking Watergate Bay.

Sephy kisses me and Zeke, and nods at Daniel. He wishes her congratulations, holds out his hand and she shakes it. The last thing Sephy does before she leaves is turn her back to us and launch her small bouquet of irises into the guests. Zeke, still talking to Daniel, catches it on reflex with one hand and without even looking, which everyone finds deeply hilarious, and then passes it absentmindedly to Wes, who passes it on, same as everyone else, until it circles back to Zeke.

Then my mum, Aunt Zoe, Uncle Oli and a still-very-much-awake Cara – who has been playing with Groover and Maverick for two straight hours – come over for a chat. Not even this feels awkward.

'Right, we're leaving now,' my mum says to me, 'and since it's two a.m., you're coming with us. Zeke, I'm afraid there's no room for you in the car. Will you be able to find your own way home?'

I look around at Zeke's family members and every one of them is clearly inebriated, even the aunts.

'Sure. No problem. I can walk.'

'Don't worry, mate,' Daniel says. 'I have to drop Cass and her sister back from some house party, so you can jump in with us.'

I raise an eyebrow at Zeke.

'That'd be great,' he says.

We walk up the 133 steps from Lusty Glaze Beach to the car park, our thighs burning, and Zeke kisses me on the cheek, before climbing into Daniel's Beetle and settling Groover on his lap.

We watch them drive off towards town to collect Cass and Carina, and then my mum turns to me.

'I'm so glad you've all made it up. You know how much I like Zeke. Naturally, I'm not Daniel's greatest fan, but I do understand life hasn't been easy for him.'

We go home, drink cocoa, and listen to the rotor blades of a helicopter flying low over the town. St Mawgan airbase is close by and when they're on military exercises the noise can go on all night.

I let myself daydream about what will happen if I win my competition. It will set me on a course that could give me the life I've dreamed of. My brain gets carried away and I think about getting sponsored by a big non-endemic brand like Samsung or Red Bull and earning enough money to buy my mum a new car, or a new house, or my dad his own workshop in Newquay, where he could work on his art without having to travel all the time for his day job.

I think about shredding the waves of a dozen more countries and styling so hard that no sexist jerk would even consider dropping in on me.

Then I think about Zeke and the path he's on. One day

he will be too old for the trials of contest life. His body will begin to wear out under the pressure of decades and decades of relentless, reckless surfing. I will stand in a hospital, with him green-capped and gowned, and watch as he's wheeled into a theatre to receive new knees, and later new hips, and we'll both know that despite all his injuries, the minute he's fit enough to get back in the water, he'll be frothing to surf, even if his competing days are long over.

Before that, though, he is going to be World Champion. I know he is. Everyone knows he is. He will hold that trophy above his head, shaking with excitement and euphoria in the flashes of the world's press. Despite his inner battles, he will achieve the thing he's dreamed about and worked towards his whole life.

I'm just getting out of the shower and my mum is already in bed, when the home phone rings.

It's Sephy.

My chest seizes up the moment I hear her voice.

She is calling at 3 a.m. She's calling in the middle of her wedding night. Something is very, very wrong.

She's talking so quickly and her voice is so warped with sobs that I can't make out what she's saying.

'I can't hear you,' I say. 'Slow down.'

'There's been an accident . . . They had to call in the Medevac. Dave's there with the emergency services. I don't . . .'

The rotor blades we heard. Not an Air Force exercise. An air ambulance.

The truth begins to dawn on me.

'Daniel's car,' I say, my voice hollow.

'Honey, you gotta prepare yourself,' she says, breaking down again.

Everything slows down, and I sink to the hall floor, the sound of my mum's footsteps hammering down the stairs.

chapter fifty-three

We don't know where to look, don't know what to say. This is not one of those funerals where the rain comes down in sheets against tear-stained faces. The sun is shining and a mackerel sky is spread above us. The sort of day they'd both have greeted with a damp wetsuit and a jog to the sea. They'd have beamed with happiness as they paddled for a wave, laughed with pure joy as they caught ride after ride.

I lock eyes with Garrett and he looks completely lost. Wes is standing grim-faced beside them, hand in hand with Elijah. Sephy is already inside the chapel, along with Daniel's mum, and a hundred other mourners who are in complete disbelief. Kelly is standing at Garrett's side, grim-faced and using everything she has to hold back tears.

Daniel was driving just above the speed limit, when a fox ran into the centre of the carriageway, near Trenance Stables, three cubs behind it. Daniel swerved. Lost control. Hit the kerb almost dead-on, so hard it launched the car over the low crash barrier.

The car flipped and hit the riverbank. Zeke and Cass were on the passenger side. It landed on the driver's side and rolled into the knee-deep water of the river. Groover slipped out of Zeke's arms, flew through the wound-down window and survived.

I look at Cass, whose eyes are different now. She has seen things no one should ever have to see.

She got everyone out, strong as a fireman when it came to it, and Zeke helped as much as he could. Daniel and Carina took the worst of the impact.

'I'm so sorry, honey,' Sephy said in the hospital waiting room that night, sobbing. 'Cass's little sister is gone.'

'Gone where?' I asked, unable to fathom what I was being told.

I saw Kelly running through the double doors, Garrett behind her, their faces blanched with shock.

'She's died, Iris.'

'How can she be dead? She's fourteen.'

'I'm so sorry. I can't even imagine what this will do to her family. To this whole community. Cass is OK. Zeke is hurt but he'll live.'

Zeke will live.

'What about Daniel?' I said, Kelly now at my side, tears escaping the hand over her eyes.

'He's in intensive care and, baby, he hasn't woken up yet. He has a head injury. They think it's serious.'

Carina is dead. Daniel might die.

Cass's whole world has changed.

Cass and her parents look as if they can barely stand. They lean on each other, walking with slow, frail steps towards the place of their worst nightmares. When they pass, Cass looks at me with wide, confused eyes. I pull her towards me in an embrace and feel the pressure of her bones.

The cemetery car park is overflowing and Zeke has gone to park his van in the back streets. I look towards the entrance of the churchyard and see him push open the gate. His arm is in a sling but apart from a chipped collarbone, he's physically OK.

Hundreds of people from the town have come out for Carina's funeral. Zeke strides towards me and reaches for my hand. Together we walk into the chapel, where we will say goodbye to fearless, amazing Carina, and in two days' time I will paddle out in front of my entire town and try to win a surf contest that means nothing now.

chapter fifty-four

That night a deep low moves in. Heavy grey clouds race high across the sky but there's no rain. The wind is onshore and higher than I've ever known it; the gusts are so strong that sand and small pieces of shingle from Little Fistral are being whipped up and blasted against our faces. We shield our eyes, taste salt on our lips, and battle our way to the top of Towan Head. I hold Zeke steady, I don't want him to fall, not when he's hurt already, but he's determined. He was the one who wanted to come up here, even in eighty-mile-an-hour winds.

'To feel it,' he said.

The wind is gusting so ferociously, swinging around us like a tornado, that halfway up we both stagger sideways. I link my arm into his good arm, try to keep us from flying apart, and push on towards the coastguard lookout at the top, a whitewashed octagonal shelter with two open windows; one facing the bay and one looking out to a wild Atlantic ocean.

At the foot of this headland the Cribbar breaks, the place where Zeke almost drew his last breath, but on this day we can hardly even see where the swell catches the reef, because the storm has changed everything and it's white horses as far as the eye can see.

When we reach the top, someone is sheltering in there already. The last person I imagined would be here.

Cass.

'Hey Cass, how's Daniel doing?' Zeke says, immediately.

'No change. I stayed at the hospital last night. His mum's frantic. She can't bear to see him like that, but she won't go home either, so she just walks around the hospital corridors, praying. I had to get out of there. Couldn't take it any more. I needed to see the sea.'

I think of Daniel's lovely mum with her mad cooking skills and big generous heart. Going out of her mind with worry, when she had already been through so much.

'How are your folks holding up, Cass?' Zeke asks.

'I don't think it's properly hit them yet. It's like they still think she's coming home. They keep listening out for the front door to go, and they jump every time they hear her phone's crazy message tone. She forgot to take it that night, left it on charge, and it's still there charging by the kettle. Her friends keep on texting her phone to say how much they love her and miss her. Mum and Dad can't bring themselves to turn it off, but whenever they hear that noise

383

it's like they think she's still in the house somewhere.'

'Cass,' I say, the word barely leaving my throat. 'I'm so sorry. About Daniel and about Carina.'

I can't believe I am having this conversation. The world is no longer spinning around the sun. It's left orbit and is racing towards some new realm that I can't even imagine.

'She hardly had a mark on her,' Cass murmurs. 'At first I didn't even realize.'

I know this already. Zeke has told me that apart from a small trickle of blood on Carina's face, there was nothing. She looked as if she was sleeping, but she was killed instantly on impact.

Cass starts crying and Zeke steps forward to hug her. She looks so small against him. Like a child, almost. She weeps quietly against his chest, and I stand there, unable to help. They have been through this thing together. They were the two who walked away. They survived the worst car crash our town has ever seen and this terrible bond will endure. Zeke reaches for me and pulls me into the embrace and the three of us stand there, the gusts lambasting us through the windows of the old building. Up there, hit on all sides by the worst of the elements, I stop fighting it, and feel it. I let it all go. Cry tears of crystal clear sorrow. No bitterness colouring them, no anxiety, no anger, just grief.

Eventually, Cass turns to me. She stands tall and takes both my hands.

'You can win it tomorrow, Iris,' she says.

'I don't know.'

'Why don't you know? Tell me.'

'The other girls are hungry for it. I don't even care any more.'

'Carina would want you to care,' she says. 'She'd want you to win. So would Daniel.'

'I don't know if I can, Cass.'

Not only do I not care about winning, I don't even want to compete. I don't want to go on as normal. Everything has changed, and it will never, ever change back.

'This is your beach. You know Fistral better than any of those other girls. You can take this whole thing. Do it for Daniel and Carina, Iris. And do it for me.'

chapter fifty-five

Fistral is a mass of angry whitewater and the unbroken waves beyond are charcoal grey. The tide is coming in, meaning we'll be surfing over the reef, which is most exposed at the north end of the beach. Thanks to that and a fierce rip-current sucking surfers around the rocks to Little Fistral, the organizers have moved the contest area down onto the sandbanks at the south end of the beach, where in theory we'll have more chance of getting a few good rides and less chance of smashing our faces in.

I have to win this, but I can't even make my way through the impact zone. The tide is coming in and the conditions are hideous. Too much swell, ugly, blown-out waves slamming into me every time I duck-dive and sending me too far back to shore again. I don't feel like I'm making any progress and all my family and friends are on the beach watching. They want me to win because, after all that's happened, our town needs some joy, one moment to celebrate.

I'm through to the final round and Zeke is spotting for me from the headland outcrop, where the long-lens photographers stand. The conditions are making the surf really hard to read, with so much backwash coming off the rocks.

It's a big wave but not clean. The lumps and bumps meant that in my earlier heats it was difficult to drive a clean flowing line. The surfers finding it easiest are the shortest girls, as they have a lower centre of gravity and aren't so affected by the bumpy surface of the wave. Height-wise, I'm somewhere in the middle, and have been finding it almost impossible to keep control after sharp turns.

I know wave selection will be everything so the plan is that Zeke will whistle when a good-looking wave rolls through and I'll paddle like hell for it.

The problem is that sometimes waves that look good turn out to be short or close-outs, which means battling through the impact zone again, something that's both time-consuming and absolutely knackering with the conditions like this.

I look up at Zeke and he gives me the hand signal that I know means to wait for the third of the set waves.

Beth's sitting over another sandbank at the other edge of the contest area and is not in position for this beast. When I go for it, I instantly feel that it's good and I manage a snap off the lip into a big carving turn and then I wait for

387

the reform at the end section. The heats of this contest are being won on the end section manoeuvres so I have to get something good out of it. I manage to punt a little bunny hop 180, but it hardly got any air and I have to complete it in the whitewash.

The clock is ticking down; Beth is sitting out back with priority and I'm getting beaten up in the impact zone and can't get back out.

Getting beached will be the ultimate humiliation. Not being able to paddle out to the line-up of my own home break will make me a laughing stock on the surf scene. Clips of this will get shared around the internet forever.

And then it happens – I get washed in.

chapter fifty-six

Out of breath, totally humiliated, I figure my only option is the run-around.

There's no shame in this, I tell myself, I've done this before. Not at Fistral, never at Fistral, but once at Steamer Lane in Santa Cruz, where the impact zone was so fierce it was often easier to get out of the water after riding a wave, scramble over the boulders while trying not to ding your surfboard, dash up the steps and run across the cliffs, before jumping down into the water from the headland rocks, out past the breaking waves, which was how we paddled in at the start of a heat. The run-around was obviously really tricky in its own right because it meant climbing and jogging and it took a few minutes out of precious heat time, but it was still less exhausting than paddling out through that violent impact zone. My feet got dirty and embedded with tiny stones and I had to run the gauntlet of the road, which was filled with spectators, some of whom were cheering for me as I ran past, which was nice, but most of whom weren't. I didn't have time to take off my leash so I had to hold it really tight in my hand so that I didn't trip and go arse over tit, which would be mortifying, especially as about a hundred smart phone cameras were being pointed at me.

Some of the girls on my tour won't do it on principle, they pride themselves on their extraordinary fitness and being able to battle any zone. But I know when I have reached my limit and in Santa Cruz I was panting so hard from the effort of paddling that I wasn't sure I'd be able to hold my breath under any more waves.

And here I am making the same decision at Fistral.

I climb up onto the rocks, clamber past a few photographers, and am then confronted with Zeke, who is on his mobile phone, his face bright with amazement.

'Daniel's awake,' he says. 'And talking!'

I look back to the beach and see Cass at the water's edge, waving. She turns and runs towards the South Fistral steps, Groover at her heels. She's going to her fiancé.

The relief almost floors me. 'Thank God,' I say. I don't have enough breath to say more; I jump into the water with my board to one side of me and begin to paddle furiously for the line-up.

I have to win this. I switch my brain into work mode and sweep my emotions to one side.

Another set is rolling through and Beth is up, riding a bomb. It even has a small barrel section. She's riding tight in the pocket and is able to fly out of it and finish with a really big, fast turn which throws up a huge rooster-tail of spray. The whole ride looks sickeningly good and I know it's going to get a good score. There's no doubt it's within the excellent range, and will lock in something between eight and ten points.

I kick myself. If I'd been able to punch through the zone, I'd have been in position to catch that wave. Still, at least I have priority now which means that whatever wave comes next, I'll be able to claim it, even if she wants it.

Zeke signals to me again, manically this time, and I go for it. I catch a wave, build speed, find a ramp and take off for what is literally the highest aerial 360 I have ever managed.

I have to complete it. If I stick it down for the re-entry without spinning out, my score will rival Beth's. I pray for Neptune's mercy, land with bent knees, and wobble.

My knees are my shock absorbers and the pressure on them from the landing feels like they've both been shot with a crossbow. But I am still on my board. I haven't fallen.

The beach erupts in applause and cheering, but I'm not done yet. The wave still has a fairly steep wall on it so I finish with a huge carve that has loads of power, and then I'm through.

There's two minutes left on the clock but there's no way I can paddle out again. Those last waves of ours will be the decider. The judges will have to discuss it and figure out which ride was better, either mine or Beth's. And whoever gets the best overall score, even if it's just by 0.1 points, will win the whole competition. My future rests on the decision of some judges I don't even know.

The buzzer sounds but the numbers still haven't dropped.

The judges are pondering the replay, arguing. Whatever the result, it's going to be close.

Beth comes over to me to shake my hand, and she looks as exhausted as I feel.

'Good luck, Iris,' she says, getting my name right for once.

'Cheers, big ears,' I say in my awful Australian accent. She grins at me and I know exactly what Kelly sees in her, because I see it too.

'Same goes, big nose,' she replies, with a wink.

Kelly comes racing down the beach and hugs both of us. 'You were incredible,' she says. 'No matter who wins you are total legends and I love you both.'

Then Zeke is with me. Sephy. Dave. Lily. My mum, Mick, Aunt Zoe, Cara, Garrett, Elijah, Wes, Caleb. My dad. They are showering me and Beth with compliments, telling us that whatever the result, we're both superstars who've done so well and come so far.

Then the scores drop.

'Oh my God,' my mother says.

chapter fifty-seven

A month later. The sky is blue, the air crystal clear and we look out to A-grade Fistral. There's plenty of swell around, the sea sparkles in the morning sun, the wind is offshore and only three surfers are out, one of them Daniel. As soon as we finish this class, we'll be out there with him. We're not inside a hotel, we and the other eight people in this sunrise yoga session have lined up our mats on the grass across the road from Hotel Serenity, overlooking the south end of Fistral, and we move through round after round of sun salutations, reaching up and bowing forward, to still our minds and feel the light.

Our teacher, Natasha, who'd taken the lesson in which I'd met Zeke one year ago, has asked us each to dedicate our practice to someone important, to move through the postures whilst holding them in our heart. I am holding Carina in mine when Natasha looks over and says, 'Iris, will you demonstrate a handstand for us?'

Once upon a time, Zeke had helped me to kick up into

a handstand against a wall. Today, I flatten my palms on the ground, centre myself and take my weight into my hands.

I finally let Kelly cut my hair and it hangs loose in a shaggy bob, not touching the ground. Gently, I lift myself into the stand, inch by inch, using every muscle to hold myself steady. I think of the time I surfed with Carina and it feels as if she's here with me. My eyes are open and I focus my gaze on the water's reflected sunrise.

Natasha counts me in for ten deep breaths and applause erupts from the others in the group.

'Way to go,' Natasha says. 'You're strong, Iris.'

I bend my knees and bring my feet to the ground slowly, maintaining control.

'Thanks,' I say to her casually, as if I haven't understood that she is saying something important to me.

'You're no longer living your life braced for impact. Look how certain of yourself you are. When you were in the posture, with no support, did you even once believe you would fall?'

'No, I don't think I did.'

The others get into pairs to practise and I look at Zeke, so capable, so defenceless, his strength shot through with weakness, fault lines hidden in the bedrock.

He is my best friend, and I am his. Despite the hassle, the tension, the crashing highs and lows, we go to bed together, wake up in each other's sweat, and head for the beach, where we paddle through waves to the calm of the line-up. And then we do it all over again.

'So what now?' he asks, sitting out the handstand, as the others in our group hold each other upright, hands around the ankles and thighs of strangers.

'How d'ya mean?'

'Like, where? I've been fighting it out in surf contests since I was seven years old.'

'Are you saying . . . ?'

'I'm gonna take a year off the tour. Take some real time out to heal. I'll follow you anyplace you wanna go.'

'Really?' I smile, endless possibilities opening up in front of me.

'Yeah. You cool with that?' he asks.

'Totally,' I say, buzzing with excitement. 'But wherever we go, I always need to come back here for a little while. Like, at least two months. Ideally in summer.'

'Sure, and we go to Oahu for some of the winter, right? Because that's home for me and winter's when the big waves hit.'

'Deal,' I say.

'So, what about the rest of the year?' he asks.

I look at my van, proudly displaying its FI57RAL number plate, tucked neatly on Esplanade Road where I've parked it myself, and I wonder how many countries it'll see and how many surfers along the way will grin and understand what those seven numbers and letters represent.

'We'll see.'

'Oh, we'll *see*,' he says, grinning and jumping to his feet. 'You got this all figured out.'

'Yeah, *we'll see* where the road takes us.' And there are so many roads to travel down now.

I won at Fistral because of the run-around. I didn't take the direct route, it was not what I'd planned and it didn't look pretty. It involved sweat and humiliation, but it got me where I needed to be. I'd taken off in the exact right spot at the exact right moment. For three heartbeats I spun in the air and when I landed I defied all my doubts and fears and somehow I held on.

The sponsorship deals I signed to make my own videos and travel on my own terms as a freesurfer will change my world. If it goes well, I may even have enough platform to start my own projects and change things for a new group of surfer girls.

'So, champ,' Zeke says, as I chalk my hands and feet again so that I won't slip, 'after this, you gonna show me how it's done?'

'Up for a paddle battle?'

'Always,' he says, grinning at me.

I know that whatever we do, wherever we go, he will mess up and so will I. But we will learn. We will grow into surer, grander versions of ourselves and come what may we will never turn away from the sea, because surfing is not just what we do on a quiet Sunday afternoon. It is who we are and who we want to be. And when we're feeling brave and the waves are fast and clean, we will release the fins beneath our feet and take to the spinning skies for that dazzling, fleeting, blue air ride.

'Thinkin'?' he asks, grazing his palms along mine, so that some of my bright yoga chalk transfers to his hands.

'About the future.'

'It's gonna be really something, you know that, right?'

'Yeah,' I say, turning my face from the morning shadows, towards the light. 'It is.'

I kiss him, and we move to the front of our yoga mats and ready ourselves for this last round of sun salutations, ending the class right where we started, reaching for the sky.

acknowledgements

At the start of the Blue books I have always written: *For Amelie, Alyssa, Laura and Eve.*

Eve is Eve Harvey, my dear friend and colleague, who offered me so much support and encouragement during the pre-publication years, and who was the first person to suggest I try writing YA fiction. Eve, I am privileged to know you and call you my friend.

Laura is Laura Ellen Ward, the girl I met at a Surfers for Cetaceans fundraiser at Cafe Irie. She had just arrived in Newquay and was spending the summer here alone before going back to university. Laura changed my life: she took me surfing. We went to that event knowing no one, but found each other and had an amazing few months playing in the waves of Fistral Beach. *There's definitely a book here*, I remember thinking. It turned out there were three.

That first evening with Laura, I also met a pro-surfer who seemed an extraordinary mix of laidback charisma and fearless determination, and I had the germ of an idea for a character like Zeke.

Amelie and Alyssa are my girls, who light up my life with their wit, humour and love. They have already begun to ride their own waves and I am more proud of them than I can say.

I would also like to thank my wonderful parents Alicia and Geoff, for everything, including but not limited to: emotional support, delicious food, sleep, childcare and dog walks. My debt to you can never be repaid. But I'll try!

Huge thanks to my editors Rachel Faulkner, Roisin Heycock and Jane Burnard, who have spent so much time thinking and talking about surfers with me. Your ideas are brilliant, as are you.

Likewise, thanks to my agent Ben Illis. You are a rock star and I salute you, sir.

I am grateful to Arts Council England for kindly awarding me a grant, which helped to support me during the writing of this novel.

Thanks to my friends. Lots of the things I've written about in these books happened to me, usually while I was up to no good with you lot. Possibly the most mortifying one is the 'bodyboard incident', which happened on a trip to Newquay when I was fifteen. I walked the full length of a very busy Towan Beach before I noticed. It's taken me this long to think about it without blushing.

Thanks to the indomitable Rosy Barnes, who is just the

right combination of wildly encouraging and gently critical. Thanks also to Emma and Oli Adams, plus Tom Butler and his mother Sue, who first mentioned to me the Never Never Land kids. Likewise, my wonderful colleagues at Vulpes Libris: Hilary Ely, Moira Briggs, Leena Heino, Jackie Hixon, Kate Macdonald and Kirsty McCluskey. Thanks also to John Duigan, Leighton Lloyd, Tassy Swallow, Aimee Stapleford, Jaide Lowe, Katherine Neal, Claire Beney, Beki Jenkins, Lindsey Campbell, Tina Beresford, Paul and Laura Glass, Sarah and Francesco Rigolli, Sarah Clarke, Rhys John, Max Hepworth-Povey, Christopher Hunter, Jessica May and Karl Michaelides, who have all given me so much encouragement and support.

Rachel Lamb. Only you will know which parts of this book were inspired by our adventures, but that wild afternoon at the coastguard look-out during the worst of Storm Imogen, I will never forget. Thanks also for introducing me to the joys of Jägermeister and goon.

Jon, you're last, and I know you find it slightly embarrassing to be thanked in books. Well, too bad. Thank you. For the optimism, the love, the shoulder rubs, those crucial cups of tea, and more patience than could be reasonably expected of any human being. It's been a cool fifteen years.

And for all of the people who ask me about the name Zeke: a surfer boy called Zeke used to cut my hair.

get to know lisa glass

Did you always know how things would end for Iris and Zeke?
I knew what kind of future they could have together if they were able to overcome their problems, but I didn't know if they could do that until I'd written the books . . . There was a point in *Air* where they were both really getting on my nerves and I considered killing the pair of them off!

What about the unfinished stories: do you know what happens to Garrett and Kelly, for example?
I do know what happens to Garrett and Kelly, but I won't say, as I'm thinking of writing a book about the Kelly/Garrett/Beth triangle. We'll see.

What did you do before you became a writer?
As a teenager, my first job was as a cleaner in a local sports centre, which I did at 6 a.m. on a Sunday morning. Nothing quite like turning up with a mop, bucket and hangover to an outdoor changing room, only to discover that members

of the rugby squad had seen fit to use the showers as a toilet (and I'm not just referring to urine here). I worked in an independent bookshop and as a sales assistant for Young Fashion at House of Fraser. My highest paid job was as a promo girl, which involved handing out free samples of fragrance or toothpaste to mostly inebriated people in pubs and clubs, some of whom would try to consume these things (with interesting results). I also worked in a call centre for a while but hated it. After my BA in English, I studied for an MA in Creative Writing and was signed by a literary agent shortly after graduating.

What inspired you to write Iris's story?

I spend much of my free time at Fistral Beach, and I'm friends with lots of local surfers and pro-surfers. I wanted to write a story that talked about the pressures they face, as well as their extraordinary adventures.

Having journeyed with them for so many years, do you have a favourite character in the books?

No, I don't have a favourite character. I know lots of readers hate Daniel, but I'm actually quite fond of him. Zeke is always fun to write and I share some of his interests (Sea Shepherd, surfing, yoga . . . not crystal meth), and I love writing scenes between Kelly and Iris. Their friendship parallels my closest female friendship at secondary school, although I think I was probably more of a Kelly than an Iris.

In the books, amid the glamour of Iris's surfing life, you write about some of the not-so-glamorous experiences young adults have – particularly when it comes to relationships and drinking. What inspired you to write so honestly about these aspects of growing up?

There's a lot of drama and humour to be found in the not-so-glamorous experiences. Also, I can't bear the idea of writing about relationships and drinking and filtering out the less pretty parts. I want to write as frankly as possible, even if it means I blush at the thought of my parents reading the books.

What made you want to write for young adults?

I wanted to write *about* young adults and this meant the books were marketed as YA. I'm pleased when anyone reads the books, whatever their age. Although, having said that, it's always a joy to meet teen readers at book events.

What was the hardest thing about writing *Ride*?

The lack of sleep. As well as writing *Ride*, I was working on the film adaptation of *Blue* and I was also the primary carer for my children. In order to meet my book deadlines, I wrote in the evenings from 10 p.m. till 2.30 a.m., which was not too bad as I'm naturally a night owl and it meant I had a blissfully quiet house with no interruptions, but I felt completely knackered when the children woke me up at 7 a.m.

Which writers inspire you?

I'm fortunate to be friends with several authors who have written brilliant contemporary young adult books. Luisa Plaja, Liz Kessler, Hilary Freeman, Keren David, Keris Stainton, CJ Daugherty, Anna McKerrow and Lu Hersey, to name just a few of the authors who continue to inspire and amaze me.

Can you describe your writing process to us?

Massive highs and lows. Feelings of panic and doom, replaced by feelings of bliss and euphoria. Rewriting, headaches and sore eyes. Worrying about deadlines, plotlines and making ends meet. Hope. Disappointment. Repetitive strain injury. Putting on headphones and firing up a playlist of the same old songs (if I mention a song in a book, it's usually because I've been listening to it on repeat while I write, for at least a month). Air-punching and dancing the minute I press send. Weeping two days later. Vowing to never write another book. Opening a fresh Word document and typing Chapter One.

Tweet Lisa @TheSeaSection
and follow her on Instagram @LisaGlassAuthor

Lisa Glass lives in Newquay, Cornwall, with her husband, daughters and dog. Lisa is part of the team behind Vulpes Libris, which was selected by the *Observer* as one of the best literary blogs in the UK. She is also working as a producer of *Bluer Than The Sky*, the forthcoming film adaptation of her young adult beach novel *Blue*.

Photo © Sarah Clarke, Checkered Photography

discover where it all started . . .

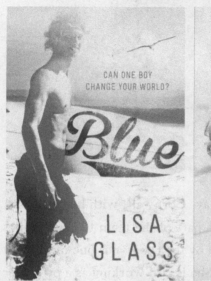

Can one summer
change your world?